RIVERBEND

Gap

Center Point
Large Print

Also by Denise Hunter and available from
Center Point Large Print:

Autumn Skies
Blue Ridge Sunrise
Bookshop by the Sea
Carolina Breeze
Honeysuckle Dreams
Just a Kiss
Lake Season
On Magnolia Lane
Summer by the Tides
Sweetbriar Cottage

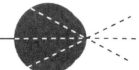

RIVERBEND

Gap

A RIVERBEND ROMANCE

Denise Hunter

CENTER POINT LARGE PRINT
THORNDIKE, MAINE

This Center Point Large Print edition
is published in the year 2021 by arrangement with
Thomas Nelson.

The text of this Large Print edition is unabridged.
In other aspects, this book may vary
from the original edition.
Printed in the United States of America
on permanent paper.
Set in 16-point Times New Roman type.

ISBN: 978-1-63808-141-8

The Library of Congress has cataloged this record
under Library of Congress Control Number: 2021944078

AUTHOR NOTE

Dear friend,

I'm always so excited to start writing a new series! This one is centered around a North Carolina town on the Appalachian Trail and a particular family who lives there, the Robinsons.

I first envisioned this series when I was in Georgia, researching the Blue Ridge series. Quite by accident I found out that the Appalachian Trail started in a nearby town, so I decided to check it out. From there I became more curious about the trail. I learned that the AT is over two thousand miles long, and each year three million people hike some portion of it. More than four thousand of those are thru-hikers (walking from Georgia to Maine), but only one in four complete the journey due to injury, illness, weather, or lack of perseverance. Some are seeking an adventurous challenge or looking to escape the stress of city life. Others want to go off the grid or are simply looking to heal a broken heart.

Along the trail there are towns that cater to and encourage these thru-hikers in their formidable quest. One such town is Hot Springs, North

Carolina, the inspiration for my fictional town, Riverbend Gap.

I hope you enjoy learning about the AT, and I hope you come to love this trail town and the characters who live there as much as I do.

Blessings!
Denise

1

This is going to leave a bruise.

Katelyn Loveland stomped on the brakes of her Honda Civic. Upon impact her air bag would deploy, collide with her face, and she'd look like a monster when she met her boyfriend's family.

She jerked the wheel to the left. "No, no, no!" The squeal of tires merged with her shriek.

She missed the deer by inches.

Thank You, Jesus!

Her tires slipped off the shoulder. She turned the wheel but overcorrected. Her breath caught on an exhale.

Then she was spinning, spinning. The world swirled: green, brown, blue. Dread sank in bone-deep. Katie braced for certain impact with a guardrail, a tree, the mountain. Braced for the air bag, the pain, the aforementioned bruising.

Instead branches clawed the car like a bear, scratching, scraping. The car jilted forward. A scream.

Then a jarring halt.

She looked up, breaths ragged. Unpeeled her fingers from the wheel. Leaned back in her seat, head spinning. Throbbing. She touched her temple, and her fingertips came away red and sticky. She must've hit the steering wheel. Her air bag hadn't deployed after all.

Okay. I'm okay.

She drew in a full breath and assessed. The engine hissed. Smoke curled heavenward. The engine wasn't running. She reached trembling fingers for the key and turned it.

Nothing.

So she wouldn't pull up to the house in a wrecked car—she touched her forehead again—with a head injury. But she would be bruised *and* late. So much for a good first impression. She needed to call her boyfriend; he'd have to come get her.

Her phone was in her purse—which was where? There, on the passenger-side floor, contents scattered. She unbuckled her seat belt and reached for the phone.

The car shifted farther forward.

She froze, heart stuttering. *Forget the phone.* What was happening? Why was the car unbalanced? Dare she move?

Slowly, not so much as breathing, she straightened in her seat. Dear God, what was going on?

She peered through the front windshield. The murky blue of the late-afternoon sky seemed to go on forever. She dared to lean forward an inch, two, breath held, eyes seeking the ground in front of her.

But it wasn't there.

• • •

Cooper Robinson leaned into the curve, the motor of his Triumph Street Twin humming beneath him. The hot August wind ripped past, the smell of pine permeated the air. Riding brought him a sense of calm and ease, a feeling of freedom. The sound of the motor and vibration of the bike were like oxygen to his soul. Riding was his therapy. His thoughts were full of family today, though, and that didn't exactly jive with the whole calm and ease vibe he sought.

His brother, Gavin, in particular weighed heavily on his mind, as he had often since Gavin's divorce last year. Earlier than that really—since the death of Gavin's young son. The two tragic events were like links in a chain, one leading right to the next.

When Gavin had moved home the Robinsons circled the wagons to comfort and support him. Not that it did much good. He'd only lately begun to come around—but not because of his family's efforts.

Cooper accelerated through another turn, trying to regain the calm and ease thing. Normally nothing cleared his mind like a ride through the mountains surrounding Riverbend Gap, a town tucked deeply into the Appalachian Mountains.

Coming out of the turn, he straightened the bike, his gaze locking on skid marks on the road just ahead. Saw them all the time on these winding roads—tourists misjudged the hairpin turns despite the traffic signs.

But these skid marks were on a straightaway, and they were new; no accidents had been reported here. Probably a deer or other wildlife, judging by the deceleration marks on the pavement. Despite the lack of a carcass, he slowed his bike and kept his eyes peeled for the car.

Something had disturbed the gravel on the shoulder. Intermittent skid marks marred the pavement just beyond. Someone had lost control.

And there, just ahead to the left—flattened brush about the width of a car.

He slowed further and rolled up to the scene. Tire tracks led through the foliage. Small car, he guessed, based on the size of the tracks in the mud. A sinking feeling weighted his gut—just beyond the scrub lay a formidable cliff.

He pulled well off the road to avoid causing another accident, dismounted, and removed his helmet. The emergency was probably over, only an investigation—and likely a funeral—remaining. But he withdrew his phone anyway as he scrambled through the brush.

No cell signal. And being off duty he had no radio.

A flash of silver caught his eye. He pocketed his phone and scuttled through the dense thicket. Branches poked him in the neck and scraped his arms, but he forged on, homing in on the car.

Honda Civic, not running. North Carolina plate. Rear wheels—oh jeez—several inches off the ground.

"Hello?" He pushed through the low-growing brush alongside the vehicle. "Can you hear me?"

"I—I hear you," a woman replied.

"Don't move. I'm coming." He shoved aside a branch and inched forward until he was beside the car. Then he knelt and assessed the situation.

The front tires had cleared the edge of the cliff. The nose of the sedan pointed downward, the car balancing on its frame. The vehicle and its occupant would've plunged to the bottom of the ravine—some fifty feet—if not for a lone tree growing from the cliffside. The tree had broken off at some point and now stood about five feet tall. It hardly seemed sturdy enough to support the weight of the car.

One little movement could send the thing crashing to the ravine below.

"Don't move." Cooper stood and approached the driver's side. He appraised her through the partly open window. Midtwenties, blonde, petite. Small cut on forehead. She stared, stricken, out the windshield.

"It's going to be okay. My name's Cooper. What's yours?"

"Katelyn. Can—can you get me out?" Her voice trembled. "I can't open the door."

"I'm a sheriff's deputy, Katelyn. I'm going to get you out of here, but I might need your help." His gaze fell to the door where the car had wedged against a large rock, leaving a dent. "This door's jammed. Do you have a phone?"

"I—yes. It's down there, on the floor."

"Sit tight, okay? I'll go around the other side and grab it." Hopefully it had a signal—though it was unlikely since his didn't.

He made his way around the vehicle as quickly as possible. When he reached the other side, he found the door accessible.

"I'm going to open the door and fetch your phone." Cautiously, he reached for the handle and slowly pulled until it was open. So far, so good. He reached for the phone, careful not to put any weight on the car. Once he retrieved it he checked for a signal.

He looked back at Katelyn who stared at him as if he was her last hope. "No signal."

He wasn't sure the car was stable enough for a safe evacuation, but he didn't have a chain or even a rope to secure it. He had to extract her before that tree gave way.

"Okay, here's what we're going to do. You're going to very slowly climb over the console."

Fear blazed in her wide blue eyes. "I'm afraid to move. When I reached for my phone, the car tipped forward."

"You're going to keep your weight against the

seat back this time. Once you're over the console, I'll snatch you right out of there. You can do this, Katelyn."

Her expression shifted, her eyes growing determined, her jaw setting. She gave a nod, then slowly lifted her leg. She swung it over the emergency brake, over the gearshift. On a steady exhale she lowered her foot until it dangled on the other side. Her pulse leaped in her throat.

"Good job, Katelyn. You're doing great. Now I need you to lift yourself up on the console. Keep your weight back."

"O—okay." She put a hand on the console, paused for a beat. Then she began lifting her weight, back pressed to the seat.

"That's it. You've got this." A few inches more and he could reach her. He'd be quick about it, and even if the car—

The vehicle groaned, shifting forward.

Katelyn screamed.

Cooper flung his body onto the trunk. The back of the car sank a couple inches and stabilized. He expelled a breath. Sweat trickled down the back of his neck.

"Hello?" Her voice quivered. "Are you still there?"

"I'm here. It's okay. Everything's going to be fine."

He could have her evacuate while he weighted the rear. But even now the back wheels were suspended above the ground. He could feel the car wavering beneath him.

The car was in too precarious a position for her to move around. He needed a rescue wench. Which meant he needed a fire truck. Which meant he'd have to go for help.

"I'm going to ease off the car, okay, Katelyn? It might move a little, but you're not going anywhere." *Please, God.*

"Okay." Her whispered prayers carried on the wind.

Cooper lowered his body until his feet touched the ground. Slowly, he removed his weight from the car. It bobbed beneath him like a fishing float.

Katelyn gasped.

Please God, he begged again as he carefully withdrew the last of his weight. The vehicle tottered slightly, then settled like an equally balanced scale.

He made his way back to the driver's side. "Katelyn, you still with me?"

"Yes." She was back in the driver's seat, pressed back as far as she could go, staring through the windshield.

"Are your windows automatic?"

"Yes. Is now a good time to tell you I'm afraid of heights?"

"You're not going to fall, Katelyn."

"How—how big a drop is it? Are we talking your basic ravine or Half Dome?"

"Now see, you gotta have more faith in me than that. You're hurting my feelings."

She glanced at him, a flicker of humor in her eyes.

"We're going to fasten your seat belt, okay? Let me do it." He reached inside the window and grabbed the buckle. Then he stretched it across her, leaning in. The scent of her enveloped him—oranges and sunshine. He focused on the task when what he really wanted to do was study her face. The buckle slid into place with a click.

He leaned back, locking his gaze on hers. "All right, there we go. Listen, Katelyn . . . I'm going to need you to sit tight while I go for help."

"*No.* Don't go, please."

"We have no phone," he continued calmly. "And I have no way of securing the car."

The look she turned on him melted him into a puddle. "Please don't leave me."

"I'll just go as far as the road. Flag someone down and send them for help. I won't be far away, and I won't be gone long." The road got a decent amount of traffic. But the day was wearing on, and he hadn't heard a car pass yet.

Her eyes closed, her dark lashes fanning the tops of her cheeks. Her chest rose and fell fast, and her hands clutched the sides of the seat, knuckles blanched.

"Katelyn." He leaned down until his face was inches from hers. "I need you to listen to me."

15

Her eyes opened, vulnerable and afraid, and clung to his.

"Let me do my job, okay? I happen to be pretty good at it. As soon as I flag someone down I'll be right back. You'll keep me company, right?"

"I'm—I'm not exactly going anywhere." Her lips wobbled in an attempted smile.

"That's the spirit. I'll be back soon." He gave her a confident nod and started back through the thicket. "Think of all the things you're going to tell me. I want to know everything about you— grisly details, skeletons in the closet, all the good stuff, okay?"

"Okay," she called.

But he could barely hear her now. He was past the car and moving as quickly as he could, all the while thinking that the car—and its sweet little occupant—could plunge to the valley floor at any second.

2

"All right, God, it's like this . . ." Katie whispered, unclenched her fists, careful to remain perfectly still otherwise. "I'm at Your complete and total mercy. I know, I know. That's always been true but . . . I'm quite literally hanging on the edge of a cliff here, God."

The late-afternoon heat had infiltrated the car, and sweat beaded on the back of her neck. There was no breeze, but she should probably be thankful for that. A stiff wind might just blow her right off the overhang. Her stomach turned at the thought. This was so, *so* much worse than the scary roller coasters her brother used to drag her on.

She was going to be fine. The deputy would come back with help. How long had he been gone anyway? Seemed like an hour, but it was probably only minutes. She closed her eyes, conscious of every breath—it might be her last after all.

No, no, she couldn't think like that. Happy thoughts. Positive thoughts. The deputy's steady eyes. Confident demeanor. Capable hands. Yes, that was better. He'd be back soon. This was his job, right?

Her head began to spin. She gasped for air.

This was not a good time to hyperventilate.

Get a grip, Katelyn Elizabeth Wallace.

Of course, it was Loveland now—she'd changed her last name when she turned eighteen. But it was her foster mom's voice in her head, the familiar full-name warning. The remembrance nearly brought a smile to her face as she worked to slow her breathing.

In through the nose, out through the mouth. Once. Twice. Three times.

Beyond the windshield a hawk swooped into her line of vision, its red tail translucent in the sunlight. It soared, wings spread wide, lofted by the air, then swooped down, headed somewhere below. Possibly far, far below.

Why was this happening now, when she was finally making a fresh start? When she'd found a new town, a new home, a job she loved, and a good man?

Something trickled down her temple—blood. But she was too afraid to wipe it away. Best she sat tight and hoped for a lifeline. Where was Superman when you needed him?

A bird tweeted from a nearby branch. She would focus on sounds. She closed her eyes again, gladly blocking out the great abyss stretching out in front of her. The leaves overhead swished. A squirrel nattered nearby. A tree trunk creaked.

Branches snapped and underbrush rustled. The sounds grew louder.

"Deputy? Is that you?"

"It's me. Thanks for waiting."

Relief coursed through her veins. "I almost ditched you, but I'm not that kind of woman."

"Knew I was right about you." He appeared outside her window, eyes twinkling.

"Is help on the way? Please say yes. That's really the only acceptable answer."

"Lucky for me that I flagged a guy down then. He's headed toward the valley, and he'll call for help as soon as he gets a signal."

The valley was twenty minutes away. Her stomach plunged.

"What's wrong? Afraid I'll bore you with childhood stories?" He sat on a rock just outside her door, elbows on his knees as if he were perched on a porch instead of the cliff's edge. "The Riverbend Fire Department will be here before you know it. They're always ready to show off. We might not even have time to become properly acquainted."

He was really handsome with that crooked grin. Dark-brown hair, just long enough on top to be unruly (and littered with debris at the moment). Brown eyes set deeply beneath prominent brows. A square jawline, the amount of stubble riding the line between five o'clock shadow and beard.

Well, she'd wanted a distraction.

She thought of her boyfriend and winced. She was supposed to be there by now—she'd updated him on her progress only fifteen minutes before the accident. He'd be worried, and she had no way to notify him.

She'd just had to get her hair done, hadn't she?

"So, what do you have for me?" Cooper asked.

"What?"

"You were going to give me all the dirt, remember?"

"I recall the conversation but, sad to say, I'm fresh out of dirt."

"What do you do for a living, Katelyn?"

"I'm a nurse. If I had the tools handy I could stitch up my own forehead."

He leaned in, studying her wound. "I don't think it's going to need them. You'll have a heck of a bruise though. And probably a headache. Where were you coming from? Walnut? Marshall?"

"Asheville. My old hair salon—big mistake."

His gaze roved over her carefully curled beach waves. "Doesn't look like a mistake to me."

Something fluttered in her stomach. "Well, it ended with me on the edge of a cliff so . . ."

"Asheville . . . That where your family's from?"

"I don't have any family to speak of."

"No parents? Siblings?"

"I have foster parents and a lot of foster siblings." She paused before going on. "I had a brother—we were really close."

"Tell me about him."

She didn't normally talk about her brother.

20

Then again, she didn't normally hang on the edge of a cliff. "His name was Spencer. He was my best friend. He was a private person, kind of a loner. But once you got to know him . . . he was a softy on the inside. And so creative—he could just pick up an instrument and teach himself to play it."

"Sounds like someone I could call friend."

She smiled. That was just the right thing to say. "What about your family? Are they from around here?"

"They are. We're close, though my siblings are a pain in the butt sometimes."

"Where do you fall in the lineup?"

"Dead center."

"Ah . . . the middle child."

"We're not all jealous and needy. Was your brother older or younger?"

"Younger by two years."

"Which makes you the oldest child. Are you driven and compulsive, Katelyn? Always right?"

"I guess I bucked the trend too. My upbringing probably had something to do with that. Having a dozen or so foster siblings tends to disrupt the natural order of things. Aw, don't look at me like that. My brother and I were loved. The Clemsons were good people—we landed there when I was eight. They run a gas station in Asheville."

At the thought of Jill and James, her stomach twisted. She'd gone into town for a haircut and

21

hadn't even made time to see them. Had she ever told them how much their love and support meant to her? To Spencer?

"I'm a terrible person," she muttered.

"What?"

She lowered her lids in a slow blink. "Can you open Notes on my phone?"

"Is this where you tell me all your dirty secrets?" He pulled the phone from his pocket, touched the screen, then looked up at her, waiting.

"I want to leave my foster parents a note."

The humor fled his eyes. He scowled, lowering the phone. "You don't need to leave a note. You can tell them whatever you want the next time you see them."

She couldn't leave things unsaid. Not after all they'd done for her. "Please."

He gave her a long, searching look. Then his eyes softened to melted chocolate, and he let out a resigned sigh. "All right. But you're going to feel silly when you open your phone later and see this."

She collected her thoughts as he stared down at the phone, thumbs poised. Then she began, speaking slowly enough for him to keep up.

"Dear Jill and James, I don't have words to express how much you've meant to me. You took us in when we had nothing and no one. You loved us as your own."

Her eyes stung. She cleared her throat. "I'll

never forget helping you make peanut butter cookies in the kitchen on Saturdays, Jill. Even now it's my favorite cookie because of all the precious memories it represents." She paused. "Is that stupid?"

"No." His voice was rough. He returned his attention to the phone.

"Jim . . . You had the patience to teach me to drive and even change a flat. You're a legend for that and so many other reasons. Christmases in your living room, countless meals around your dining room table, prayers by my bed. You are the center of my best memories, and I love you more than words can say." She paused for a beat. "That's it. Just sign my name."

After she spelled it for him, he pocketed the phone. Then he held her gaze for a drawn-out moment. Something passed between them. She'd just bared her heart to a stranger, and he seemed to understand.

"Thank you," she said.

"You're welcome. Now, can we stop being so maudlin and get on with the fun stuff? I bet we can find people in common. I know some folks from Asheville: David Young, Evelyn Murdock, Richard Lewis—"

"Richard was my pastor. He's a good guy."

"I've never been to his church, but yeah. Good guy. So you're a believer."

"I am." She studied his face, something softening

inside. She'd known there was something special about him. "So if I, you know, fall off this cliff and die in a fiery crash, at least you'll know I'm headed to heaven."

"Now, now, no martyr's death for you. You'll more likely die in your sleep at the ripe, old age of ninety, having told your children and grandchildren all about your narrow escape from death and the handsome deputy who rescued you."

"You call this a rescue, Deputy? So far you've only flagged down a vehicle and asked a bunch of nosy questions. And let's not forget, I'm still hanging on the edge of said cliff."

His lips turned up, almost a smile. "So you do think I'm handsome?"

Laughter bubbled out of her. "If you're asking if I prefer to look at you instead of the sheer drop-off in front of me, then yes. And should you really be flirting while you're on the job?"

"Technically, I'm off duty."

"Yes, well, technically I have a—"

The car pitched forward and whatever she'd been about to say died abruptly in her throat.

3

Katelyn screamed.

Cooper pivoted, throwing his weight against the window frame, pushing back with all his might. It was futile—the car outweighed him by more than a ton. But he had to try. He grunted with the effort, his skin breaking out in a sweat.

Katelyn's scream echoed in his ears.

The car's frame groaned. Then it stilled.

He didn't move. Didn't lessen his efforts. Was afraid to remove his weight.

"Oh, dear God in heaven . . ." Katelyn's breath came in gasps. "Don't let me die. I'm too young to die."

"You're not going to die," he squeezed out. "Hear me, Katelyn? You're not going anywhere but home."

Her whimper ripped at his heart.

Pressed to the window frame and facing the trunk, he couldn't see her. But she'd grabbed his arm, was wrapped around it like a snake. Her nails bit into his bicep. Even so, it was nice. If only he could forget about the ton of metal. And, oh yeah, the cliff.

"You're right. I can't die—who'd keep Oreo in business?"

"That's the spirit. And I don't like Oreos, so clearly your work here isn't finished."

"That's not possible." Her breath whispered against his skin. "Everyone likes Oreos."

"I really don't care for sweets in general."

"And here I was starting to like you." Her words trembled. "You're very calm in a crisis, Deputy."

"Part of the job."

"Whoops." She removed her nails from his arm. "Sorry. Didn't mean to cut off your circulation."

"Yeah, I really hate it when pretty women hang on to me."

Once she was back in place, he eased his weight off the door frame, one pound at a time. When he'd completely removed himself, he backed away from the vehicle.

"If this car does go, you won't be able to save me, you know. I'd rather you didn't die trying."

"The car's not going anywhere. And I've already decreed this a rescue. I've even filled out the accident report in my head. Done deal." He sank back onto the rock. "Now, where were we?"

She let out a mirthless laugh. "I have no idea."

He did. Things had just been getting good. But the brush with death had sobered him right up. His damp T-shirt clung to his back. "What brings you to Riverbend, Katelyn? I assume that's where you were headed. Planning to hike the Appalachian Trail?"

"My idea of roughing it is sleeping on two-hundred-thread-count sheets, so no." She gave him a wry smile, but the corners of her eyes were tight.

"Not everyone's a thru-hiker. Lots of people just do day hikes. There are some good ones around here: Lover's Leap, Roundtop Ridge, Hickory Fork . . ."

"My brother always wanted to hike the whole AT. He talked about it all the time, starting in Georgia in the spring and working his way up to Maine."

"That's the way most people do it."

"Have you hiked the whole trail?" she asked.

"Only parts of it. Georgia and North Carolina. Takes a lot of time and I have to, you know, work."

"That work thing gets in the way, doesn't it? I'm not a complete slacker though. I do jog for exercise."

"Oh yeah? Like that runner's high, do you?"

"No, I just like to eat cookies. Do you work out?" Her gaze flickered over him. "Scratch that. *How* do you work out?"

"I have a home gym. And I hike a lot, of course."

"I guess you have to stay in shape for your job."

"I like working out. Great stress reliever."

"What do you get stressed about?"

"Did I mention my family?" He instantly regretted the words, given her lack of relatives.

But she laughed and set her head against the headrest, her chest still heaving. "I'm so hungry right now. How ridiculous that I'm thinking about food at a time like this."

"Why didn't you say so? I have protein bars in my bag." He started to get up.

Her eyes flashed with fear. "Oh no you don't. If I go down in flames, you're gonna be right here watching."

He sank back down, *tsking.* "There you go again, hurting my feelings."

"You're pretty soft for such a tough guy."

"Tough guy, huh? And handsome too . . . I'd better get your number quick."

"Isn't it already on that accident report? Besides, as I tried to tell you before—"

The sharp, piercing wail of a siren interrupted her. His gaze locked with hers. "Hear that?"

Her features eased as she released a soul-deep sigh. "Thank You, Jesus."

"What'd I tell you, huh? Done deal."

Her pretty lips turned up at the corners. "This isn't quite over yet, Deputy."

And then he smiled back. Because that was exactly what Cooper Robinson was hoping.

4

Cooper was late. But that happened all the time with his job. He still had to stop at his apartment for a quick shower. He was sweaty and grungy from the ordeal, and he had minor scratches on his arms and neck from the thicket.

When he arrived at his place, he found five texts on his phone. One from Gavin, one from his sister, Avery, and two from his mom—all asking where he was.

He texted Avery that he'd been delayed, knowing she'd spread the word. Amber Clarke, a hairstylist from the Beauty Barn whom he'd gone out with twice, had also texted him. She couldn't be further from his mind right now.

He could think only of wide blue eyes and a sprinkle of freckles across a pert little nose.

That and the letter she'd written to her foster parents. Man. Sometimes he forgot how blessed he was. Maybe his dad was a loser, but he had a great mom. And his stepdad, Jeff, had turned out to be a lot cooler than Cooper had thought at the age of ten when his mom married him. Plus, Cooper had gotten a decent stepsister out of the deal.

He whipped his belt from his jeans as he walked into his bedroom. That's when he realized he still had it—Katelyn's phone. He pulled it from his pocket, a dopey grin tugging his lips at the thought of her. He hadn't felt like this in . . .

Yeah. He'd never felt like this.

He went through the motions in the shower, reliving the rescue in detail. Rick Rodriguez, the deputy on duty, had arrived on scene first. The fire truck came next, followed by an ambulance and a tow truck. From there the scene had gotten hectic. He left Katelyn in the paramedics' capable hands while he helped Rodriguez with the accident report. Cooper stayed until the vehicle was secured and Katelyn was safely removed. She checked out fine. Pictures were taken, and at that point he realized he was over an hour late for dinner at his parents'. He couldn't hang around any longer, and Rodriguez had offered to give Katelyn a ride.

Cooper turned off the water and dried off. When he spied Katelyn's phone on the bathroom counter, he smiled again. In his rush to get to his folks' house, there'd barely been time for a quick good-bye. But Katelyn's address would be on the accident report, and now he had the perfect excuse to contact her.

Ten minutes later Cooper started his Silverado and pulled from the apartment lot. He hated being late for this, especially since they were waiting supper on him. And because this event seemed important to Gavin. His brother had just begun to climb out of his depression, and Cooper wanted him to feel supported. Wanted him to find some happiness. Maybe Gavin would quit pretending to be a campground manager and go back to being a highly sought-after contractor.

It appeared Cooper had come full circle—his thoughts were right back where they'd been when he found Katelyn on the cliff. Katelyn. There was that grin again.

He was off duty tomorrow. He'd drive to Asheville and return her phone—then he'd ask her to dinner. Normally he started with a coffee date, but they were way past lattes and Americanos. Maybe he'd take her on a picnic at Riverview Park. Picnics made a great second-date activity. Most women found them romantic, and there was ample opportunity for conversation— and enough privacy to make out if the occasion arose.

But no, not Riverview Park. He wanted to take Katelyn someplace new. Someplace he'd never taken anyone else. Maybe they could drive down to Max Patch, have a picnic on the summit, and catch the sunset. All of this was contingent upon her agreement, of course. But—not to be arrogant—he couldn't remember the last time a woman had turned him down. And he'd gotten certain vibes on that cliffside.

It took only five minutes to reach his folks'

place. He pulled up to the white clapboard farmhouse situated on three and a half acres—basically, Gavin's and his childhood playground. His mom and Jeff had bought the property shortly after they'd married. A fresh start, they said.

Cooper wasn't sure of anything at that point, much less his new stepfather and stepsister. Up till then it had been Cooper and Gavin against the world, united by their love for their mother and disdain for their father, Craig Burton—otherwise known as the town drunk.

Cooper pulled up to Avery's blue Jeep and shut off the ignition. Everyone was present and accounted for, car wise. He exited the truck, the familiar sounds of cooing doves and rippling river taking him right back to childhood.

Gravel crunched under his feet as he headed toward the front door. He tried to get into the right frame of mind. He would have to work at this tonight. He'd used an entire day's worth of words back on the cliff. Who was he kidding—an entire week's worth.

He mounted the porch and, as was his habit, walked right into the house. From the entryway he had an open view of the first floor. His mom, wearing jeans and a red shirt, stirred something on the stovetop. At the island Jeff poured a drink, the pendant lights glaring off his high forehead. Avery and Gavin were seated at the dining room table. Conversation hummed and a Luke

Bryan song played softly. The savory smells of homemade cooking made his bachelor's stomach rumble.

"Sorry I'm late," he called. "There was an accident on 70."

"Hi, honey." Mom's greeting mingled with the others. "Can you grab that extra chair from your bedroom closet?"

"Sure." He headed upstairs. His old room looked pretty much the same these days except cleaner and with the bed made. The Corvette Z06 poster was gone, as were his Braves memorabilia and basketball-hoop hamper.

He found a folding chair in the closet and carried it downstairs, the steps creaking in all the familiar places. Old framed photos stairstepped down the wall. His mom and Jeff on their wedding day, photos of the kids opening gifts at Christmas, Cooper in his baseball uniform, Avery graduating high school, Gavin and his son, Jesse, frozen in time on his third and final birthday.

"You hear what happened, Coop?" Jeff called as Cooper took the last step.

A knock sounded on the front door.

"I'll get it." Cooper turned and grabbed the knob, then pulled open the door and stilled at the sight of the familiar woman on the porch.

5

"You." Katie stared unblinking at the deputy. What was he doing here? At Gavin's house? Did she forget to fill out some form back at the accident site? But how did he find her here?

"Katelyn." His eyes softened and his lips lifted in a bemused smile. "What are you doing here?"

She blinked. "What are *you*—?"

"Katie." The voice came somewhere from the deputy's right. "Thank God you're all right. You are all right, aren't you?"

She pulled her gaze away from the deputy and saw Gavin striding toward her.

She glanced back to the deputy—*Gavin's brother.* It was all making sense now. But for some reason her stomach bottomed out at the realization.

Understanding also dawned in the familiar brown eyes that had offered her such comfort back on the cliff. The smile wilted from his lips.

Gavin nudged his brother aside and pulled her into the house. He surprised her with an embrace. Yes, they'd shared six dates, three kisses, and two tubs of popcorn. But Gavin wasn't a particularly affectionate man. Then again she *had* nearly died.

It was his lack of physical aggression that had gotten him a second date. Not that he hadn't been a perfectly good date. A little sad, a little cautious, but given his fairly recent divorce, who could blame him? She gave him a hug.

Gavin pulled back and gripped her arms. He stared at the bandage on her forehead. "Do you need to go to the hospital?"

For some reason her gaze slid automatically to his brother. Somehow she felt closer to him at that moment than Gavin. They'd just been through a catastrophe together. Of course it had . . . bonded them.

"I'm—I'm fine. Just a mild concussion."

Gavin glanced between his brother and Katie. "Do you and Cooper already know each other?"

Cooper cleared his throat. "I, uh, stumbled across her while I was out riding."

"He's the one who flagged down help for me. I had no idea until just now that he was your brother. He sat with me while we waited and basically kept me from losing my mind."

Her gaze met and held Cooper's, and her belly gave a low, tight squeeze.

"I didn't do much."

"Oh man." Gavin reached out a hand, and the brothers did that man handshake that ended in a shoulder bump. "Thanks, Bro. I owe you one."

"No problem."

"Katie." A blonde woman approached—had to be Gavin's mom, but she looked too young for that. She had a kind smile, blue eyes like Gavin, and a dimple in her left cheek. "Oh, you poor dear. Come and sit down. Avery, can you get her something to drink? I'm Lisa, by the way. This is my husband, Jeff."

"Nice to meet you both. I'm so sorry I'm late."

Lisa led her to the sofa. "Don't be silly. We're just glad you're okay."

Gavin settled beside her and took her hand. "Sure you're all right? You seem a little shaken."

"Of course she's shaken, poor thing," Lisa said. "What a terrible experience. Avery, come check her head."

Katie smiled at her friend and boss. "I'm fine. I promise. The paramedics checked me out thoroughly. Just a mild concussion."

Across the room Cooper stood, one hand cupping the back of his neck, staring at the floor.

How had she not realized who he was? She'd somehow missed his name. And the brothers looked nothing alike really. Gavin's hair was black, his eyes blue. But they were both tall and built similarly, and she'd known Gavin's brother was in law enforcement.

And of course Avery had mentioned Cooper before. Katie and Avery had been friends at undergrad school. They'd lost touch for a while afterward, but when Avery had reached out to her about a position at her clinic, Katie jumped on it. The rest was history.

It was all making sense now. Cooper was the

eligible, uniform-wearing brother who turned all the women's heads. She felt stupid for not putting two and two together. Then again, she had been a little, you know, distracted. Hanging between life and death.

Avery returned with a glass of lemonade, and Katie thanked her in a haze. The concussion must be messing with her mind.

"What happened out there?" Avery asked. "How'd you end up on the edge of a cliff?"

Gavin squeezed her hand. "You said on the phone it was a deer?"

Katie covered the basics of her accident, from the deer to the slide to the abrupt halt at the edge of a cliff, while the family listened intently.

"I had no idea what to do. I couldn't get my door open, and when I tried to move, the car dropped. I was so relieved when Cooper showed up."

His head snapped up at his name. She tried to think of something to say. Something about how grateful she was. Or how much his presence had meant to her. She grasped for the words, but they hovered out of reach.

Avery glanced between Katie and Cooper. "Good thing you were there, Brother."

"Yes, it was." Katie tore her attention from Cooper and turned a smile on Gavin.

"Well . . ." Lisa popped up from the recliner. "You must be hungry after your ordeal. Let's get some food in your belly."

• • •

It all made sense now. Katelyn was Katie—Gavin's Katie—the friend Avery had set Gavin up with. So the woman Cooper was more attracted to than any woman he'd ever met was the same woman who was bringing Gavin back to life.

Cooper's insides deflated like an old party balloon.

They settled in the dining room. In between bites of roast beef, he glanced across the table at Katelyn—Katie. But she seemed more like a Kate to him. Jeff had said grace, taking a moment to give thanks for her safety. After prayer the family quizzed her about her life. She kept her answers more general than she had on the cliff.

Cooper took some comfort in the level of intimacy that implied. Then he mentally smacked himself.

Gavin's girl.

Once the polite inquisition was over, the conversation shifted to the usual banal chatter that accompanied family dinners. His mind still spinning, he struggled to keep up.

Kate didn't live in Asheville as he'd assumed. She'd moved to Riverbend in May, hoping for a new start, following the death of her brother. She didn't state the last part, but he pieced it together from what he already knew. She'd bought a house on Maple Lane, liked to bake, and grew her own herbs.

Stop thinking about her.

"You've had an eventful day off, Cooper," his mom said.

Everyone turned his way, and Cooper's face heated at his thoughts. "Yeah. It's been a long day."

"That's my fault." Kate offered him a sweet smile. "After I got banged up, I took a peek over that cliff. Definitely closer to Half Dome. Thank you for keeping that to yourself."

"No problem."

Avery frowned. "That must've been a harrowing experience."

"I was on my way to a panic attack before Cooper arrived. He kept talking to keep my mind off of things."

All eyes turned his way.

Gavin snorted. "*Coop* kept a conversation going? Is this some deputy superpower we don't know about?"

"He's not exactly known for his conversational skills," Avery explained to Kate.

"He talks as much as he needs to," Jeff said.

Avery chuckled. "And not one more word than necessary."

"All that talking and you didn't figure out who she was?" Mom asked him.

Yeah, he felt a little stupid about that. "Nope."

Avery smirked. "There's the one-word answer we're accustomed to."

Cooper scowled at her. Was dinner almost over? He felt like he was on the hot seat now, and he wasn't a fan.

"Just goes to show," Jeff said, "he can rise to the occasion when he needs to."

"Well, he sure rose to this one." A smile glimmered behind those blue eyes. "You're gonna have to let me pay you back somehow."

"Not necessary." He definitely had to keep his distance. Which might be difficult if Gavin kept bringing her around.

The rest of the meal passed uneventfully, lots of talking and joking around. Cooper found it difficult to focus on anything other than the woman sitting across from him. The conversation went on long after the last fork hit the plate. Keeping up the pretense wore on him.

Finally, Mom tossed her napkin onto her plate and stood. "Who's ready for dessert?"

"I could really use a sugar rush." Avery joined her in the kitchen. "What did you make?"

"Cookies, and lots of them."

Cooper and Katie exchanged knowing smiles. They already had inside jokes. And that's when Cooper knew for certain—he was a goner.

"Good night, everyone," Cooper said on his way out the door. He was the first to leave, but man. It really had been a long day. A long evening. Darkness had fallen like a shroud over the valley, and night sounds had begun in earnest.

"Finally." Avery slipped out the door behind him and followed him down the porch steps. "I had to wait for you to leave—you blocked me in. I'm going to the early service tomorrow, and I still have to run home and grab a few things. I'm spending the night with Katie so I can check on her every few hours."

"Nice of you." They walked in silence, the gravel crunching under their feet and the oscillating buzz of cicadas swelling around them. Now that he'd escaped he was a little desperate to be alone with his thoughts, but he refrained from quickening his pace.

He was almost to his own car when she called out. "Hey, Coop? You okay?"

He stopped and turned. "Sure. Why wouldn't I be?"

"I don't know." She approached, studying him under the moonlight. "You seemed a little . . . starstruck, I guess. With Katie?"

"What? No. She's Gavin's girlfriend."

Avery had a way of looking at you that made you feel like she could see all the way down to your inner core. She was doing it now. "Yeah, that's true. But you didn't know that out there, did you?"

"I need to be getting home. I have an early morning too." And plans to return Kate's phone. He'd forgotten all about that. The mission no

41

longer brought a sense of anticipation. It seemed ridiculous that he could've gotten attached so quickly. That never happened to him. But somehow he'd come to care for her on that cliff. Why couldn't he have met her first?

"Well, good night, then."

Cooper said good night and got into his truck. His emotions had run the gamut today. But he couldn't deny that they'd just reached the lowest point. Kate was out of his reach—because he would never do anything to hurt his big brother.

6

A wave of dizziness rolled over Katie as she set the last mum into its hole. These poor flowers had been waiting a week to go in the ground, and she finally had a free day. She'd attended church this morning and made a quick lunch afterward. She might even catch a nap this afternoon—she had a bit of headache from the injury.

A breeze blew, stirring the wind chimes she'd hung from the eaves. Her earliest memory was of playing on a porch. It was before her mom had gotten really bad off. Before she and Spencer were taken away. She still remembered that small home, the scent of mown grass, and the tinkling of those wind chimes.

Katie tamped down the dirt around the mums, then surveyed her work. Pretty pink and purple blooms now bordered the walk in front of her house. Her tiny lawn needed mowing, but she was already pushing concussion protocol. Avery had stayed overnight and checked on her every three hours. She was a gem of a boss—and a friend.

The thought of Avery led her not to the clinic but to the Robinson family meal last night. Katie had been so nervous about meeting Gavin's parents, but they'd been warm and welcoming.

And Cooper—what an unexpected way to meet

Gavin's brother. He'd flirted with her on the cliff and was probably embarrassed about that now. But no, he hadn't meant anything by it. It was just his way of taking her mind off the situation—and it had.

Still, last night as she'd been trying to sleep, their conversation filtered back in pieces. Guilt nipped at her. She shouldn't be thinking about her time with Gavin's brother. On the other hand, wasn't it normal to relive a harrowing event? It was the mind's way of processing it.

It had probably been a little early in the relationship to meet Gavin's parents—she and Gavin had only just become exclusive. Still six dates weren't nothing. He was her first real boyfriend since college. Now that Spencer was gone, she had to make more of an effort. She craved attachment and let's face it, she and Spencer had been a little codependent. That sure hadn't done much for her love life.

Sweat trickled down her back. It was already a humid ninety-five degrees.

She gave the soil one final pat and stood, pausing a moment until the dizziness passed. Okay, she could take a hint. She'd take it easy the rest of the day—right after she watered her flowers.

As she entered the house the cool air brushed her skin, a welcome reprieve. She loved her new home, a little Craftsman-style bungalow. Loved having a house all to herself. Growing up at the Clemsons' she'd always shared a bedroom with two or three other children. When she'd gone to Duke on scholarship she shared a dorm with roommates. And after college she and Spencer had shared an apartment in Asheville.

But this house was all hers. She hadn't had to do much when she moved in. She covered the age-yellowed trim with a fresh coat of white and painted the walls cornflower blue. Now it was perfect. The entire house sported original wood floors, complete with the nicks and scars that gave it lovely character. Light poured into the kitchen from the back of the house, puddling on the newer granite countertops and gleaming off the white cabinets.

She reached into the hardware store bag and retrieved her new watering pail. The outdoor spigot wasn't working, so she put the pail under the faucet and turned it on.

Water spewed out, hitting her in the chest.

Quick in, quick out.

Cooper pulled into the vacant driveway, grabbed Kate's phone, and exited his truck. Empty flower flats and gardening tools lay next to the walk leading to the house. He hoped those had been there awhile. She should know better than to do yard work with a concussion.

A neighbor's dog barked from the backyard. It

was a nice street, only a few blocks from where the trail crossed through town. He rarely got a call from this neighborhood.

Kate's sunshine-yellow bungalow with white trim looked like her: bright and homey. He envisioned her doing the yard work, blonde hair pulled into a high ponytail, a smudge of dirt on her cheek.

He scowled at his thoughts. *Quick in, quick out.*

The porch was barely big enough for the one chair and tiny round table topped with a flowering plant. He lifted his hand and knocked, his foolish heart pounding at the thought of seeing her. *Stupid.*

Gavin's girl.

Maybe if he told himself that enough times his heart would buy in. He rolled his eyes at the thought. This was so unlike him. He'd never really been hung up on a girl. As Avery often reminded him it was usually the other way around.

He peeked through the window. It appeared that the light was on at the back of the house. Could just be the sunlight though.

If she wasn't home he'd leave the phone on her porch with a note. Probably what he should've done to start with. He also could've left it with Jackie, the sheriff's office's administrative assistant, and had Kate come in and pick it up. But she didn't have a car at the moment.

He knocked again, louder.

A muted squeal sounded. "Come in!"

He turned the handle and pushed open the door.

"Help!" Katelyn called over the sound of gushing water from somewhere beyond the living room. She let out another squeal.

He charged toward the sound. "Kate?"

"In the kitchen!" She mumbled something.

He made it through the living room in four quick strides.

Kate was on the floor, halfway inside the cabinet beneath the sink. Water spewed from the tap.

"Argh! This dumb, stupid—"

"Move aside."

"It's stuck." She backed out, her hair hanging in wet ropes around her shoulders. "I can't shut it off."

He fiddled with the faucet, then took her place beneath the sink. The water valve was good and stuck. A moment later it finally gave, squeaking as he turned it. The water stopped.

He inched out of the cabinet and hunched back on his knees in the pool of water.

Kate squatted beside him, cheeks flushed, hair askew, her wide blue eyes locked on his.

And then they were laughing.

"You look like a drowned rat." He ran a hand over his wet face.

"So much for my beauty shop hair." She pushed

47

the wet strands from her face, still laughing. "I don't know what happened. I was just trying to water my plants."

They grinned at each other, caught in the moment—at least he was. Drowned rat? The woman was beautiful, with the light streaming through the windows behind her giving her a golden halo.

Her gaze swept over his damp button-down and climbed back to his face. "You'll have to stop coming to my rescue, Deputy Cooper."

"Part of the job."

"I think plumbing falls way outside the line of duty."

She tilted her head. "You called me Kate."

"What?" He blinked at her. "Oh. Sorry. Do you prefer Katie? Or Katelyn?"

She seemed to weigh the question. "No. Kate's just fine."

He stood and offered her a hand, relishing how small and soft it felt in his. He was reluctant to let go. And there was that thumping heart again. He towered over her. He'd been too shell-shocked last night to notice much of anything.

"Jeez. How tall are you anyway?"

"Six two." He scanned her head to toe. "You must be all of five feet."

She lifted her chin. "Five two, thank you very much." She looked down at the puddles of water. "Ugh. What a mess."

While she took a towel from a drawer, he grabbed the one off the stove. "You get the counter; I'll get the floor. You should be taking it easy today."

So much for quick in, quick out.

"How can one little faucet make such a big mess?" she asked.

"Tell me you weren't out in this heat planting flowers."

"I wasn't out in this heat planting flowers."

He raised an eyebrow.

"Okay, I was, but I was just about to call it quits."

"I'll spare you the lecture since you're a nurse and all."

"I guess we don't make the best patients."

When the water was cleaned up, she took the sopping towel from him. "Thank you. This was really above and beyond. What brings you by anyway—official business? You're not going to give me a ticket for reckless driving, are you? I think I've probably suffered enough."

"We can probably pin this one on the deer." He reached for her phone and handed it to her.

"Oh! Thank you. I was going to call the sheriff's office tomorrow and track it down."

"No need." Obviously. Duh. His eyes drifted to the faucet and plumbing under the sink. He could probably fix it for her. But no. That wasn't his place.

"Guess I'd better call a plumber, huh? Know a good one around here?"

"Gavin's not a licensed plumber, but he can probably fix it for you."

"Oh yeah." Her smile lit up the room. "He handles those cabins. This kind of thing must come up from time to time."

"Right." He grabbed the pail. "Where's the bathroom? I'll water your plants before I go."

"It's that way." She pointed down the hall. "But I can do it."

He slid her a warning look, then went to fill up. She followed him out the front door.

Now that the emergency was past, he remembered the way she'd invited him in earlier. He tipped the pail over the flowers, and water sprinkled from the spout. "You know, you shouldn't invite random visitors into your home sight unseen."

"I thought you were Gavin. He's supposed to stop by."

"You should be more careful. And you should lock up at night, in case no one told you."

"Yes, sir." The impish light in her eyes gave her away. "I'll be more careful."

"This might be a small town, but thousands of strangers hike the AT every summer, and they all traipse right through town. Most of them are good folk, but you can't count on that."

"Point taken." She tilted her head, narrowing

her eyes. "Are you always trying to keep people safe?"

"That is my job."

"And you're running for sheriff . . . You didn't mention that little tidbit when we were having our chat out on the cliff."

"Slipped my mind."

"That's a big deal. You have to fundraise and campaign and all of that."

"It's small-town stuff."

"Are you running against the current sheriff?"

"He's retiring. I wouldn't try to unseat him— he's done a good job. I'm running against another deputy."

Sean Curtis was a competent fellow deputy, and he was a lot more sociable than Cooper. He hoped he wasn't wasting his time, but he'd always wanted to be sheriff, and with Roy Gilmore retiring, this was Cooper's chance.

"Well, you have my vote."

He glanced at the Robinson for Sheriff sign in the yard. "I see that."

"Avery asked me to put it up."

"Sounds about right." He emptied the pail and handed it to her. "I should get going now."

She beamed up at him. "I can't thank you enough for your help. I'd probably be swimming in my kitchen if not for you."

Her smile made his breath catch. He glanced at the bandage on her forehead, and he couldn't stop the words. "Take it easy today. No more gardening."

Humor lit her eyes as she gave him a little salute. "Yes, sir."

7

Tonight was the night Katie would see her biological mother. It seemed like it had taken forever for Friday night to roll around, and now that it had, she was all nerves. Her hands shook as she took a patient's blood pressure. When she had it, she pulled off the cuff, the release of Velcro loud in the small examination room.

"It's 120 over 68," she told the thirtysomething woman. "Can I get you some water while you wait for the doctor?"

"No, thanks. Will he be long?"

"She. Dr. Avery Robinson. And no, she'll be right in to examine your knee. Good luck with the rest of your hike. I hope you're able to complete it."

"Thanks. This will make it a little challenging, but I'm determined."

Katie gave her a conciliatory smile, then slipped out the door. She slid the clipboard into the assigned slot, then made her way to the office she shared with Avery and Sharise, the new nurse practitioner. It was after six and that had been Katie's last patient of the evening.

The meeting started in twenty minutes. Katie pulled off the stethoscope and tucked it into her bag. The clinic was a converted brick house on the edge of town. But Avery had it gutted before she opened last year. It still smelled like raw timber and new flooring.

The clinic was comprised of four exam rooms, a front office, a small kitchen/break room, and this smaller office. The staff and patients shared the one bathroom.

Avery occupied the upstairs apartment, which pretty much meant she never escaped work. But she seemed to prefer it that way.

Katie was shrugging off her coat when the door opened.

"Done for the day?" Avery swept into the office and grabbed a water bottle from the mini-fridge. Her hair was up in its usual topknot, but a few mahogany tendrils had escaped, framing her face in a lovely way. Katie had always admired her wide-set green eyes and ivory complexion.

"Unless there's something I don't know about." Katie kind of hoped there was and hoped there wasn't, all at the same time.

"Nope." Avery took a swig from the water bottle. "There's a patient in three with Sharise, and the patient in four is my last. Patti already turned over the Closed sign."

"Great."

"If you have a minute, I can recheck your wound. How's that concussion?"

"No need. It's getting better by the day. No more headaches or dizziness."

54

"That's good."

Katie checked her watch. It would only take a few minutes to drive to the meeting. And her legs were shaking—not concussion related. She lowered herself onto her desk.

Avery quirked a brow. "Big plans tonight with my brother?"

"He's busy at the campground." She didn't want to mention the meeting, so she changed the topic. "What about you? Going anywhere fun?"

Avery capped her water bottle and put it back in the fridge. "I have pretty much the perfect night planned—a quiet night at home with Boots and a good book."

Katie released a wry grin. "If you consider that the perfect Friday night, you need a boyfriend."

"A boyfriend is the last thing I need."

"Said the woman who set me up with her brother."

"How's that going anyway? We haven't had a chance to catch up since the family dinner. We didn't scare you away?"

"On the contrary. Your family seems pretty much perfect."

Avery laughed. "Oh boy, do we have you fooled."

"You'd never know you were a blended family. You squabble just like full-blooded siblings."

"Well, we've been together since we were young. And I have to give Lisa credit. She handled it all very well. I was pretty rotten in the beginning."

"How'd she handle it?"

"She waited me out. There's a very stubborn woman under that pretty veneer." Avery smiled fondly.

Did Avery know how blessed she was? Funny they were talking about moms on this of all nights. "She seems really great."

"She's always been there for me. For all of us."

Jealousy pricked Katie hard. Though Mama Jill had always been there for her, it was different. She'd been there for all her fosters—dozens of them over the years. And while that said worlds about the woman, it also made Katie feel just a little less special somehow. And the insecurity planted by a birth mother who'd basically abandoned her didn't help either.

"Well, I'd better go see my last patient so I can get home." Avery turned at the door and waggled her brows. "Mr. Darcy awaits."

"God, grant me the serenity to accept the things I cannot change, courage to change the things I can, and wisdom to know the difference." The group of about twenty chanted the prayer from a semicircle in a church basement that smelled of old books and coffee. Fluorescent lights flickered overhead, casting unflattering light on the attendees.

Katie had arrived just in time for the meeting and grabbed the closest open seat to the door. The fiftyish woman on her left, who was not chanting, had already snagged the closest one. Her hands were clutched, white-knuckled, around the purse in her lap, as though she might bolt any moment.

Katie let her gaze drift to the front row where her mother sat. She could only see the back of her head, but Katie knew it was her. She'd seen her photo on the website, and she was the only other blonde woman in the room.

An old man with a flannel shirt—despite the stuffy basement—was reading something. Katie couldn't focus on the words. Her heart was jack-hammering in her chest, and her palms were damp even though her fingers were like blocks of ice.

Someone opened up the floor, and a twenty-something man stepped to the front. He wore khakis and a button-down shirt and looked entirely like someone who shouldn't be here. Then again, the meeting was made up of a mix of people. All different ages, ethnicities. Some dressed up, others dressed down.

Katie wiped her palms down her pants, the man's words fluttering loosely in her mind but not landing anywhere. Would her mother speak to the group? Would she hang around afterward? Would she welcome Katie personally? And if she did, would she recognize her daughter?

Of course she wouldn't. Katie had only been five when she went into the foster care system.

When she'd been old enough to understand, she was told by her caseworker that her mother was an addict, and her father's identity was unknown.

Katie could only suppose that that made Spencer her half brother, but neither of them had ever acknowledged that or even cared really. They were all each other had.

And now he was gone.

They'd never searched for their mother. Why should they? If the woman wanted them, she would've tracked them down. It's what a loving mother would do.

But one lonely night three weeks after Spencer's death, Katie had searched for her mother on the internet. The woman wasn't on any social media sites. But someone with her name directed an Alcoholics Anonymous group in Riverbend Gap. There was a staff page with photos, and voilà. There was the mother she barely remembered. The mother who'd left Spencer and her in the dust. Since then, Beth Wallace had apparently fought her addiction and gotten her life together enough to help others.

But she hadn't sought out the kids she'd for-feited. Katie's chest tightened in that familiar way, squeezing the life out of her, or so she imagined. Even though her mother had failed her, there was still a little girl inside who dreamed of being wanted again.

In February when Avery had reached out to her

about the job in Riverbend, Katie decided it was a sign from God. She wanted to start over someplace else, why not here where she had actual family?

It seemed like such a foolish notion right now, with her mother sitting three rows up, completely unaware that her daughter was in the same town, much less the same room.

Another woman got up and spoke briefly about her life. Katie didn't hear a word. She fought the urge to flee. She'd waited months for this— she wanted to be settled, with a stable job and a home. Wanted her life to be sorted out before she came face-to-face with her mom. But hanging on the edge of that cliff had reminded her that life could change in an instant. So she decided to jump on her plan to get to know her mother from a distance.

But now that the moment was here, old insecurities rose to the surface. How foolish she'd been. Had she honestly thought she'd impress her mother so much that the woman would welcome her back into her life?

Her breath felt stuffed into her lungs. Heat prickled under her arms. This was pointless. This was another heartbreak, another rejection, waiting to happen.

She stood abruptly, skirted past the nervous woman, and darted out the door. Because Katie Loveland had already had enough heartache and rejection to last a lifetime.

8

Cooper needed an escape and he couldn't think of a better place than the Trailhead Bar and Grill. On the restaurant side of things, the brisket and ribs were pretty convincing. But the lively bar area with the chatty bartenders and friendly neighbors also held appeal. He pulled his truck into an open spot in the gravel parking lot in the heart of town.

At seven o'clock on a Friday night, Cooper had no illusions about getting a table in the dining room. He was shouldering his way through the crowded lobby when he recognized a familiar face. Cooper had worked a summer on Wayne Curtis's organic produce farm during high school, and they'd been friendly ever since. Wayne also happened to be the father of Cooper's campaign opponent.

"Hey, Mr. Curtis," Cooper said. "You're looking well."

The man's rugged face beamed. "Cooper. Good to see you, son. And please, you gotta stop calling me Mr. Curtis. You're making me feel old."

His wife nudged him. "We are old, dear. It's good to see you, Cooper."

"You too, Mrs. Curtis. How long's the wait for a table?"

Mrs. Curtis grinned. "Too long."

"Not too long for a slab of that brisket I smell," Wayne said. "You're welcome to join us. We could cut a good twenty minutes off your wait."

"That's awful nice of you," Cooper said. "But I'm pretty hungry and I think I see an empty spot at the bar."

"You'd better grab it then before someone else does," Mr. Curtis said. "Nice seeing you."

"You too." He gave them a nod, then headed straight to an empty barstool and ordered a drink.

Loud country music streamed through the speakers, mingling with the happy sounds of chatter. The tantalizing scent of smoked brisket settled his order—as if it hadn't already been decided. He placed the order with Bridgett, the brunette photographer who'd come to town a few years ago and stuck.

Even though it had been a long day, Cooper socialized with those around him. He was introverted by nature, but when you were in law enforcement, it was important to know your neighbors. Having a good rapport with people kept situations from escalating. Not to mention without community support his run for sheriff would be an epic fail.

He watched the Braves game on the big screen above the bar, applauding with the crowd when a runner scored and groaning when the Cubs caught a fly ball, ending the inning.

"Hey, Bro." Gavin settled on the stool beside him.

"Hey. Thought you'd be out with Katie tonight."

"Grass needed mowing. It's been raining all week, and the campground looked like a hay field."

"That's the beauty of living in an apartment— someone else does all the work. Get it done?"

"Yeah, after getting stuck in the muck twice. Stopped by Katie's place, but she wasn't there, so I thought I'd grab some dinner. What's the special?"

"Is there anything here besides barbeque?"

"The meatloaf's not bad and the burgers are—"

Bridgett set Cooper's platter in front of him. "Bon appétit."

Gavin reached for his plate. "Aw, thanks, man. You didn't have to."

Cooper swatted his hand. "Been waiting forty-five minutes for this."

Gavin flagged down Bridgett and ordered his own brisket. "So . . ." he said after they watched the Braves get another runner on base. "What'd you think of her?"

"Who?"

"Who do you think? Katie?"

Cooper chewed the bite. He thought she was beautiful and sweet and funny. He thought she made his heart jump and his palms sweat. He swallowed the bite. "Seems nice enough."

"She fit in with the family really well, didn't she?"

"Sure, guess so."

Gavin's gaze sharpened on him. "Why'd you say it like that?"

"Like what? She's great. Really. Everyone liked her."

Gavin returned his attention to the game. "I guess she was pretty scared out on that ridge. That could've gone really wrong."

"She was a real trooper."

"Yeah? She made it sound like she fell apart or something."

"Nah. She handled it well." Most people would've been freaking out, their life hanging in the balance like that. "She was real brave."

"Doesn't surprise me. She's been through a lot. She's strong."

Cooper didn't disagree. But he sensed Kate was kind of vulnerable too. Did Gavin see that? "So you really like her, huh?"

"Sure. It's been nice having something good in my life again. Something to look forward to."

It was about as close as Gavin ever came to mentioning Jesse. Or his ex-wife for that matter. "Can't blame you for that."

"How's it going with, uh, Morgan?"

Actually it had been Megan. She'd worked the front desk at the Shady Pine Motel but had since moved on. "That was weeks ago. We only went out a couple of times."

"That seems to be the case with every woman you talk to," Gavin said in a dry tone. "What was wrong with her?"

"I caught her in a lie and things went downhill from there."

"You called her on it?"

"I suspected it wasn't the first one."

"Yikes."

They hadn't clicked anyway. Actually, he hadn't clicked with anyone in a while—and never with anyone like he had with Kate. He pushed the thought from his mind. "She moved to Mars Hill shortly after that."

"Gotcha. Thought you were going to come over to the campground one night this week? You owe me a game of poker."

"Work got in the way."

A Braves player hit a fly ball that sailed over the outfield fence. The bar whooped and hollered as the team pulled ahead.

As soon as the noise died down Gavin said, "I'm thinking about getting back into the contractor business again."

Cooper's head snapped around. His family had waited more than a year for this. "You should. You totally should."

Gavin's gaze flickered his way. "Settle down, Sparky. I haven't made any decisions yet. Just mulling it over."

"So, you'd what? Move back to Asheville?"

"No." Gavin's tone implied he'd never go back there.

Cooper couldn't blame him. Laurel was still there, as well as a lot of memories Gavin would probably just as soon bury.

"I'm thinking about opening up shop here. I could do it on the side for a while, see how it goes."

"Sounds like a good plan. And there are always out-of-towners building up in the mountains. It'd be handy to have a contractor right here in town."

"That's what I was thinking. Might be nice to be my own boss this time, decide which projects I want to take on. Have some control over my hours."

"You built a good name for yourself. I'm sure you have great references. Let me know if I can help with anything."

"It's just a thought for now. Maybe you could keep it to yourself. I'm not ready for the family full-court press."

"Sure thing." That was enough for Cooper. Miles ahead of where his brother had been mentally only a few months ago. And Cooper had a feeling this complete about-face had been single-handedly brought about by one Katelyn Loveland.

9

Katie shifted in the camp chair planted outside Gavin's camper, the memory of last night's dream hovering in her mind like a vulture over a carcass. The recurring dream happened all too often—she was outside a house and desperate to get in. The reason was never quite clear, but the fear and panic were palpable. She banged on the doors and windows, begging whoever was inside to be let in. She always woke, heart pounding, breaths heaving, eyes wet.

The fire popped, startling her from her thoughts. She breathed in the smell of wood burning and resolved to enjoy her Saturday evening with Gavin. Muffled voices from nearby campsites joined the warbling trill of cicadas and the high-pitched chirp of crickets.

Gavin added another log to the fire and settled back into the chair beside her. He lived in the small camper, situated at the back of the campground on the loop. It was only temporary, he'd said. He used to work for a builder in Asheville and had moved back here after his divorce. He hadn't expounded much on his past and Katie hadn't pressed.

After all, she hadn't mentioned her mother living here in Riverbend. So they were taking things slow—nothing wrong with that. He no doubt had baggage from his divorce. And she'd had enough therapy to know her childhood had left her with trust issues and a fear of rejection.

"Dinner was delicious," Gavin said. "Best mac and cheese I've ever had."

"Thanks. The burgers were good too."

"We make a great team."

She smiled at him, though the words made her uneasy. She wasn't sure why and didn't really want to unpack it tonight. "Your mom stopped by the clinic this week. She brought peanut butter cookies for Avery and me."

"She loves to bake."

"She's so sweet." Katie loved how affectionate she was. Lisa had hugged her on first sight and touched her arm once while they were chatting in the front office.

"Don't let her fool you. She ran a tight ship when we were growing up. There was a chore chart and everything."

"Oh no, not a chore chart."

"You laugh, but it was brutal. To this day I hate washing dishes."

"Poor baby. But seriously, it must've been hard blending a family like that."

"No doubt. Coop and I weren't too happy about getting a new sister and a man who thought he was our dad. Especially since he was nine years older than Mom. But he eventually earned our respect."

"He looks a little like that actor, the one from Designated Survivor."

"Kiefer Sutherland? Mom says that, too, but I don't see it. Anyway, we eventually figured out he wasn't so bad. And Avery kind of grew on us too."

"Were you protective big brothers?"

"At first we just kind of ignored her. But then this punk started giving her trouble, and we set him straight. Seems like after that things kind of changed." He stirred the fire with a stick. "Jeff offered to adopt us when I was in seventh grade, and Coop and I took him up on it . . . You haven't said much about your childhood."

She'd only told him she had foster parents. Cooper actually knew more about her past than Gavin did. But then Cooper had been there for what she'd thought might be her last minutes. That had a way of making one divulge things one wouldn't ordinarily give up.

"My early childhood wasn't very stable, but I don't remember a lot of it. Then there were a few foster homes. Jill and James took Spencer and me in when I was eight and treated us like their own. They have a biological son, and they took in a lot of other foster kids over the years."

"Sound like terrific people. You haven't said much about your brother either. Just that he passed in December."

"He had a bad heart. He had to take it easy a

68

lot." Just thinking of Spencer made her heart twist painfully.

"You mentioned you were going to hike up to Max Patch and spread his ashes this summer?"

"That's what he wanted. I'm doing it on his birthday—hard to believe it's just a few weeks away now."

A log shifted and sparks shot into the night sky. A rowdy group from a nearby campsite heckled one another under the glow of their tiki torches. A group of girls giggled as they disappeared into the restroom.

"Would you like some company? It's a long overnight hike, and I'd feel better if you weren't doing it alone."

On the one hand, she might like some privacy. On the other, she didn't relish the idea of hiking in the wilderness alone. She wasn't particularly savvy about wildlife, and a woman hiking alone presented its own dangers.

She turned a smile on him, getting caught in his kind eyes for a long moment. "I think I'd like that. Thank you."

"Happy to do it."

Gavin was so handsome, especially when he smiled. He had straight white teeth that had surely seen braces once upon a time and eyes the color of worn denim. He really was a nice guy. He'd been a little melancholy at first, but he was coming around. Someone had drilled good manners into him. He came across as a tough guy, but he was ever the gentleman, pulling out her chair and kissing her on the cheek.

He hadn't kissed her properly until their third date. It was nice. Sweet and tender. Later he'd told her it had been his first kiss since the divorce.

An engine hummed closer, and headlights swept across the campsite as a vehicle made the loop of the cul-de-sac. The dark truck slowed directly in front of them, and in the driver's seat, elbow hooked out the window, sat Cooper Robinson.

Cooper bit back an expletive. He'd felt bad about putting off Gavin this week, so he decided to swing by for that poker game. Figured if Gavin had a date with Kate, he'd be out somewhere.

But nope. He was here. And sitting right there beside him, face glowing in the campfire's golden light, was Kate. No way out of this now. He had to at least stop and say hi.

Cooper gave a wave and pulled into the slot next to Gavin's Sierra Denali—literally the only thing the man had taken from his marriage. Probably would've handed that over to Laurel, too, if she'd wanted it. Guilt did terrible things to a person.

Cooper got out of his truck and joined them by the fire, putting on his best fake smile.

Gavin stood. "Hey, Brother."

"Hey." Cooper's gaze drifted to Kate. "Hi there."

"Hi. Just getting off duty?"

"A while ago."

Gavin pulled up a camp chair. "Have a seat. Join us."

"I don't want to interrupt. Just stopped to see if you were free for that game. Should probably head back to the office anyway, catch up on paperwork."

"Doesn't sound like much fun on a Saturday night. Sit down. We were just about to make s'mores, weren't we, Katie? You can give us the lowdown on the crimes and misdemeanors of Madison County this week."

"Well, just for a minute, I guess. Nothing out of the ordinary this week though. Everyone's still talking about the girl on the edge of the cliff." He smiled at Kate. "Clinic busy this week?"

"Oh yeah. Summer's in full swing, along with the accompanying hiking injuries. One poor girl had a compound fracture of the ulna. Pretty gruesome. Had to send her to the hospital."

"I guess that ended her hike," Cooper said.

"And then some."

"How's the new nurse working out?" Gavin asked.

"She's doing great. Getting her bearings. I think she'll take some pressure off Avery."

"That's good," Cooper said. "She's had her head buried in that clinic for a year. What about you, Bro? Things been pretty quiet around here?"

71

"I don't know if quiet is the right word." As if on cue the guys down the road let out some drunken whoops. "But everyone's behaving so far."

It was mostly a family campground. But over the years Cooper had come here a time or two to break up a fight, arrest someone for drunk and disorderly. Mostly on weekend nights when the campers sat around drinking.

"You get your plumbing taken care of?" Cooper asked Katelyn.

"Yeah, I ended up calling a local company. They had it fixed in no time."

"What happened?" Gavin's gaze toggled between them.

"My kitchen faucet sprung a leak. Cooper happened over to return my phone at just the right moment and helped me shut off the water."

"Why didn't you call me?" Gavin asked. "I do that kind of stuff around here all the time."

"I didn't want to bother you."

"It's no bother. Call me next time, okay?"

"Okay." Kate gave Gavin a slow smile.

Cooper felt like a third wheel. He started to say he was taking off, but Gavin's phone buzzed.

"It's Barbara Jean from the office."

"Go ahead," Kate said. "I'll run inside and get the marshmallows."

While Gavin took the call, Cooper watched her stroll toward the camper. She wore cutoffs and a white top that exposed her tanned shoulders and slender arms. He tore his gaze away.

Soon as Gavin got off the phone Cooper would make his excuses and go. He'd continue to cut a wide path around Kate. He was already having trouble keeping his mind off her. If he stopped seeing her, eventually he'd stop thinking about her. Wouldn't he? He never should've come tonight.

Gavin pocketed his phone as Kate emerged from the camper. "I hate to do this, Katie, but the commode in cabin five is stopped up. I need to go take care of it."

"Of course. Go ahead. I'll wait for you."

Cooper stood. "I'll go with you."

"No, I got it. Would you mind keeping Katie company though? The guys down the way are a little rowdy, and they've been drinking a lot."

No way out of this now. "Sure." Cooper sank back into his chair.

"Be back soon." Gavin kissed Kate on the cheek. "Save me a marshmallow."

"Will do." She sat down next to Cooper as Gavin got in his truck and drove away.

The cabins were on the far side of the campground, backing up to the French Broad River. The crackling sound of gravel under Gavin's tires faded into the night, the rippling of the river and muffled sounds of nearby campers taking its place.

Cooper's heart ticked off the minutes like a time bomb.

"You want to make s'mores?" She gave him that sweet smile. "It's not Oreos, but it's something. I know you don't have much of a sweet tooth, but you can't let a girl s'more alone."

His heartstrings gave a sharp tug at the reference to their conversation on the cliff. He ran a hand over the back of his neck.

He returned her smile. "Uh, sure. Hook me up."

She grabbed two skewers, handed one to him, then poked two marshmallows into place and passed over the bag.

"I keep thinking about that time up there on the cliff," she said.

Maybe he wasn't the only one caught in this sticky web. His stomach tightened at the thought. He stuck two marshmallows on his skewer. "Oh yeah?"

"It was a week ago today. I keep thinking how it can all end in an instant. How I haven't been thankful for the people I do have in my life. How we never know when our last day will be. I don't want to have regrets."

He put the stick over the fire beside hers. "I felt that way when my grandpa died—Jeff's dad. Technically he was my stepgrandpa, but we were close. Death—or near death—has a way of reminding you of the brevity of life."

"I told my foster parents about what happened

on the cliff. Sent them that note you helped me write."

"That's good. I'm sure they were touched by that."

"I could tell they were moved. And I put something in motion I've been wanting to do for a long time." She turned her blue eyes on him. "But I chickened out. I feel like such a coward."

He slowly rotated his stick over the fire. "What are you afraid of?"

"I don't know." She huffed. "Yes, I do. I'm afraid of getting hurt. Getting rejected."

"Everybody's afraid of that. Doesn't make you a coward."

"It does when you let it stop you from doing something you need to do. What are you afraid of, Deputy Cooper?"

"Me?" He chuckled. "I don't know."

"You're not afraid of dying. You would've gone down with my car if it had come to that. You're probably not afraid of anything. You carry a gun and protect people even when your life is on the line."

"There are scarier things than death."

"Like getting hurt and being rejected?"

He studied her for a long moment. Hated that she'd experienced those things and at such a young age.

"Maybe Gavin already told you, but our dad was a drunk. He and Mom divorced when we were little, but he still lived here for years. He was the screwup always getting locked up in the tank. The sloppy drunk our neighbors would find passed out in the alley on their way to church. If his mouth was moving he was lying. He was pitied and judged and scorned. I'd rather die than have people look at me the way they looked at my dad. So I guess I'm afraid of being like my dad."

Her face softened. "He doesn't sound anything like you. But that must've been hard in a small town like this."

"Everybody has stuff they have to deal with."

"And so you dealt with it by becoming a deputy—soon-to-be sheriff. After your father embarrassed you so badly, it makes sense you'd seek a position that offers esteem."

She was insightful, this one. It wasn't like this thought had never occurred to him. But no one had ever stated it out loud to him. Or made him realize that this was the primary driving factor in his run for sheriff.

"You've got me all figured out."

"You're pretty open." She slid him a fond look. "And you're easy to talk to, Cooper."

Their eyes connected for a long moment. Something passed between them. Something warm that grew hotter with each second. No woman had ever said that about him. But he had been open with Kate. Maybe because she'd been so vulnerable with him.

She forced herself to look away. A second later she jerked her stick from the fire. She blew on the flaming marshmallows, but it was too late. "Shoot."

He pulled his golden-brown marshmallows from the fire. "You can have mine. I like them burnt."

"You sure?"

"Positive." He switched sticks with her, then ate the marshmallows right off the stick. They were gooey and sweet with an ashen crust.

"Don't you want graham crackers and chocolate?"

"No, this is good."

She worked on her own creation like Hershey's was using it for a photo shoot. She made sounds of delight as she ate it, sucking the sticky bits off her fingers between bites.

Cooper scanned the campground, trying to block out the sight and sound of her. Where was his idiot brother?

When Kate finally finished the s'more, she pulled the second marshmallow off the stick and ate it plain. "Yum."

Cooper took her stick and set it in the fire beside his own to burn off the mess.

"That's an interesting place to live," she said.

He followed her gaze to Gavin's camper. "Yeah, it's got to be cramped. He won't be here forever though. He had a great place back in Asheville.

A modern monstrosity, all glass and angles. And white. Felt like I should shower before I sat on the sofa."

"I know the kind of place you mean. I guess his wife got the house in the divorce."

"Yep."

"At first I had second thoughts about getting involved with a divorced guy. But we all have baggage, right? He hasn't said much about his ex-wife, but he doesn't seem to harbor any resentment. I'm kind of surprised he moved back here though."

"With Laurel's folks living here, you mean?" That hadn't been easy for any of them. Made for some awkward run-ins.

"No, I just meant there's not much in the way of career opportunities for him here. Besides, Asheville's a big enough place to coexist with your ex-spouse."

"It's the memories mainly, I think—Jesse."

Her gaze sharpened on him. "Jesse?"

Oh man. Cooper gave a slow blink, cursing his own stupidity. "He hasn't told you."

"Told me what?" Her words sounded cautious.

He'd already stepped in it, but he shook his head. "It's not my place to say. He'll tell you when he's ready."

"Come on, Cooper. You can't mention another woman's name in relation to his divorce and not tell me. Did he cheat on his wife? Because I really don't want to get involved with a cheater."

"Gavin's not a cheater. And Jesse's not a woman—it's his son. Was his son."

Her lips parted. "Oh, my gosh."

"That's all I'm going to say. I've already said too much. He doesn't talk about Jesse, and he doesn't like us talking about him either." Gavin kept all that guilt he carried over his son's death locked up like Fort Knox. It couldn't be healthy.

"No, I understand. Thank you for telling me that much. I won't say anything to Gavin. You're right. He can tell me when he's ready."

Cooper should've kept his big mouth shut. That normally wasn't a problem for him. Time to lighten the conversation. "How's your head feeling? I see the bandage is gone."

She touched her forehead. "Oh, it's fine. And I got my car back. It's running great, and they were very reasonable. Thanks for suggesting them."

"No problem."

Headlights appeared down the drive, heading their way. A truck. Moments later Gavin pulled into the space beside them.

Time to go. Cooper pulled the sticks from the fire, leaned them against the cooler, and stood.

"Everything all right?" he asked as Gavin approached.

"Yeah, all taken care of. Nice people." He held out his arms, giving Kate an apologetic look. "I'm afraid I need a quick shower though. Sorry."

She smiled. "No worries. I'm fine."

Cooper watched Gavin disappear into the camper, his stomach deflating. And once again he sank into the chair.

10

Cooper seemed a little twitchy tonight. Maybe it had something to do with the current that ran between them. They definitely had chemistry. Katie had been aware of it from the beginning.

But let's face it, Cooper probably had chemistry with a mailbox. She obviously wasn't the only woman to feel it. Those eyes and that uniform . . .

"Are you in a hurry to get somewhere?" she asked.

"Just the paperwork I mentioned before."

"Don't feel as if you have to stay. I can go inside the camper if you're worried about me."

He eyed the tin can where Gavin was getting ready to step into the shower. "That's all right. I don't mind."

Silence settled in. The walls of the camper were so thin she could hear the shower kick on. She hoped Gavin wouldn't be long. She really did like him. He treated her like gold, and he had a lovely family. Everything was great between them so far.

Except she seemed to be a wee bit attracted to his brother. She winced. This wasn't like her at all. She kept telling herself it was just the connection of their shared experience on the cliff. But she was starting to wonder if it was something more.

Cooper broke the silence. "How do you like living in Riverbend so far?"

"I like it a lot. I'm not used to living in such a small town though. Recognizing people I know everywhere I go. After living here all your life it must feel like you have a giant extended family."

"Complete with drama, disagreements, and general meddling. Not to mention the grapevine."

"Oh yes. The grapevine. I've heard a little here and there." Cooper seemed to have his very own vine.

"Okay . . . What have you heard about me?"

"What makes you think it was about you?"

"Oh, I don't know, the look on your face?"

"I've heard you're very good at what you do. People depend on you. People know they can count on you."

"And . . . ?"

"And . . . I heard you're the town's most eligible bachelor."

"A gross exaggeration."

"You apparently break a lot of hearts and somehow manage to come out unscathed—and still well liked by the women whose hearts you've broken."

His lips tilted at the corner. "Is there an insult in there somewhere?"

"Not at all. But what skills you must have."

His gaze sharpened on her as he hiked a brow.

Her cheeks went warm and she chuckled. "Not those kinds of skills. Jeez. I just meant it takes a special kind of talent to remain friends with the women whose hearts you break." Though she imagined those lips of his could do some real damage.

Her face was probably lit up like a Christmas tree. "Anyway, your reputation is intact. That should help your campaign. Your family name works in your favor too—everyone seems to love the Robinsons."

"Our roots are deep here. Jeff's family goes back a long way—his father was responsible for bringing the Appalachian Trail through town. It really revived the town's economy."

"So you're basically a shoo-in for sheriff?"

"Not at all. Riverbend is just one town. I need to convince the rest of the county to vote for me."

"How do you do that? Attend pancake breakfasts, Little League games, all of that?"

"You got it. It's been a busy summer, and I'm sure it'll get busier as Election Day gets closer. Can we change the subject? All this talk of glad-handing is stressing me out."

"Sure. What do you want to talk about?"

"How's your job at the clinic going? Having a dictator boss can't be easy."

Katie laughed. "You must be kidding. Avery's

a great boss and a wonderful doctor. She really cares."

"I was teasing. But she's driven, our sister."

"You have to be to get through med school and open your own clinic. You're really lucky to have a big family." There was a forlorn note in her voice she'd tried and failed to avoid. When she glanced at Cooper, she found him studying her face and couldn't look away.

"You're welcome around anytime. Everyone likes you a lot."

Something pleasant bloomed inside her. The Robinsons seemed like the kind of close-knit family she'd always wanted. To be included as one of them would be a dream come true. But they barely knew her. And she and Gavin were a long way from that kind of commitment.

From inside the camper the shower kicked off.

Gavin would be out soon. Katie found herself both anticipating and dreading Cooper's departure. He was just easy to talk to. Like Avery. If things progressed with Gavin it would be good to have solid relationships with his siblings.

"I gotta take this," Cooper said.

She hadn't even heard his phone ring. "Sure."

He said very little to the person who called, but she could tell by his professional tone it was business.

He ended the call and stood. "I've got to go. There's an accident on 209."

84

"Duty calls. I'll tell Gavin you said good-bye."

And then he was gone. Katie waited for her boyfriend to rejoin her—but somehow she felt as though the night had already ended.

11

Downtown Riverbend was busy this Friday evening. Hikers wandered in and out of the Iron Skillet and the Trailhead Bar. Later they'd bed down somewhere that didn't include a sleeping bag and would wake up to a warm shower. Cooper loved that the town was a respite for weary travelers.

He strolled down the sidewalk, drawing in the summery scents of freshly mowed grass and the marigolds the garden club had planted in the terra-cotta pots along Main Street. He greeted neighbors and tourists alike as he passed by.

When he reached his campaign office he pulled up short at the dozen or so signs on the plate-glass window. The red-and-blue signs featured white print that read Robinson for Sheriff. He was taken aback every time he saw them. It still didn't seem possible he could be running for sheriff of Madison County—at the age of thirty no less.

Yeah, the Robinson family had deep community roots and a good name. But Cooper also had his birth dad's reputation to contend with. Over the years Cooper had tried to live it down, set himself apart. He'd made the grades in school, never caused trouble. He'd become a public servant, for crying out loud. A person usually had reasons for becoming a deputy—Kate had really hit the nail on the head with her assessment. That burning drive to win the sheriff's seat made more sense than ever now. There was more to lose here than an office.

He spied his sister behind the plate glass and entered the building, the stuffy air an assault to his senses. His sister's hair was still up from work, and her small earrings glittered under the fluorescent lights.

"The buttons are here," Avery said by way of greeting, holding one up for his perusal.

He wasn't sure it was necessary—the buttons, the pens, the bumper stickers. This was small-town stuff. But Avery didn't do anything small. And Sean Curtis wasn't exactly lying down and playing dead. Last week he'd provided cupcakes for the Rotary meeting.

"They look great," Cooper said.

"We can take them to the Bluegrass Festival in Marshall tomorrow. Also, you'll be happy to know we got two more volunteers."

"That's wonderful." The volunteers met on the first Monday of the month to make phone calls and spread literature on his behalf. They were doing a great job. He showed up with donuts and provided decent coffee to keep them fueled and made sure they knew how much he appreciated them.

"And guess what? Last night David Logan contributed five hundred toward your campaign."

"Hey, that's terrific news." He gave Avery a sideways hug. "You're a good sister—I don't care what Gavin says."

"Just remember that next time my Jeep battery goes dead."

"It'd help if you remembered to turn off the lights."

Campaigns cost money—Cooper hadn't realized how much. Mailings, yard signs, buttons, and bumper stickers; it all added up. He was thankful and humbled that the people of Riverbend believed in him. Now if he could only get the rest of the county on board.

"Help me unbox all these postcards. The volunteers will start canvassing the county next Monday."

"Sure."

"Dad would've been here, but he's helping a friend move. And your mom had a meeting with the garden club."

Cooper grabbed one of the box cutters and got started. "They do plenty. I'm thankful for all the help." He wasn't sure how Avery was doing it— running his campaign *and* her new clinic. But then she didn't have a social life to speak of.

"I'm surprised you don't have a date tonight," Avery said. "You didn't forget it's a Friday night . . ."

"I don't have a date every weekend, you know."

"Practically."

"Well, you could take a lesson." He couldn't even remember the last time Avery had brought a guy around. "Rodriquez asks about you all the time. When are you going to put him out of his misery and go out with him?"

"I'm too busy to date. I'm trying to get my brother elected sheriff." Avery sliced through the box tape and took out the packets. "What do you think of Gavin's new girl?"

"Everyone's asking me about her. You, Gavin, Mom."

"Well, of course we are. Gavin's finally coming out of his funk, and it doesn't take a genius to see why. We're hopeful."

"Sure. But this is pretty new. Relationships come and go. This one may not last forever."

"Gavin's not like you."

Cooper scowled at Avery.

"That didn't come out right. I only meant Gavin tends to have long-term relationships."

"Well, he got married when he was twelve so . . ."

"Twenty-six is not that young."

"Fine, but he was young when they started dating." Gavin had gotten Laurel pregnant, and they married soon after in a small ceremony at Riverbend Community Church. Her parents, long-time residents, weren't happy about the order of events, but they came around eventually.

Of course, all of that had changed when Jesse died in a car accident two years ago while Gavin was at the wheel.

As they worked Cooper and Avery talked about the campaign, the clinic, and the family. When the boxes were unpacked, Avery went over the financials with him. There were a lot of rules about campaign funding, and she was fastidious about knowing and following them. He was grateful as spreadsheets weren't his cup of tea.

The sun had set by the time they were finished. On their way out the door, Avery grabbed a box of buttons and shoved it at him. "Run these by the church office on your way home. Mrs. Doolittle said she'd have her husband pass them out at the Better Business Bureau meeting. That'll be good exposure to other parts of the county."

"Sure." He didn't have anything better going on anyway. Avery was right. He was used to dating on the weekends when work allowed. But this was his second weekend without a date, and he didn't have to think too hard to figure out why.

He locked up the building, said good-bye to Avery at her Jeep, and continued down the side-walk toward the church.

As he passed the darkened hardware store, a text buzzed in. It was Amber, the hairstylist he'd gone out with twice. They'd texted on and off since their last date a couple weeks ago— the night before Kate's accident. Cooper hadn't decided if he wanted a third date with her. He should do that soon so as not to string her along, but his feelings about Katelyn were clouding his thought process.

Feelings. He didn't like the way that sounded. Could he really have feelings for someone he'd known only two weeks? For his brother's girl?

He rejected the idea, slowing to text Amber back. She was a nice woman. Avery's words lingered in the back of his mind along with Kate's, regarding his reputation. He did date around a lot. Maybe he moved on too quickly. Maybe he didn't open up enough. The thought of being that vulnerable scared him. What if he went all in with someone only to let her down? There were probably reasons he worried about that, but he didn't want to unpack them right now.

He tapped in a response to Amber's text. He needed some time to get his head on straight. Then he'd ask her out again.

After berating herself all week for chickening out at the AA meeting, Katie showed up at the next meeting with fresh determination. It was going basically the same way it had last week, just with a few new faces and stories.

She was still nervous about encountering her mother, but this time she also felt a pang of guilt. She was intruding on other people's pain for her own selfish reasons. She didn't belong here.

This would be her last meeting. She would find another way to get to know her mother.

But she'd nearly made it through the whole meeting, and there was no point in giving up now. Her mom sat in the front row again. Katie studied the graceful curve of her neck, so much like her own. Her heart pounded. She would hang around after the meeting. Maybe even get up the courage to greet her mother.

When the meeting finally ended Katie took her time gathering her purse and standing. Her legs quaked beneath her. Several people had darted out the door right away, but others stayed in their seats and chatted with their neighbors.

A few people, her mother included, approached a table containing a coffee urn and cookies, lined up like soldiers on cafeteria trays. Katie made her way over to the coffee. She filled a Styrofoam cup and added a heaping teaspoon of powdered creamer, which hardly even lightened the brew.

She lifted the cup to her lips.

"Careful, that stuff is hot as a tin roof."

Katie glanced up to her mother's face, catching on eyes the same shade of blue as her own. Up close she saw lines at the corners of the woman's eyes and on her upper lip.

Would Beth Wallace recognize the daughter she'd basically abandoned?

Over the years Katie had thought of all kinds of things she wanted to say to the woman. All the questions she wanted to ask. But the words were lost to her now. She'd waited too long to respond. The silence had turned awkward. She hoped her nerves would be attributed to the AA situation.

"The taste isn't so great either," the woman offered kindly. "But at least it's caffeinated."

Get it together, Katie. She cleared her throat. "That's all that really matters, I guess."

Her mother extended a hand. "I'm Beth, director of the group."

"Katie." She shook her mother's slender hand. There was no recognition in the woman's eyes. Katie was both relieved and profoundly disappointed by that.

"You were here last week, I think."

Katie didn't think Beth had noticed, the way she'd slunk in and out. "I probably should've said something."

"It's not like that around here. Come and go as you like. No pressure at all."

"Okay." Katie didn't know what else to say. Her palms were sweaty, and her mind spun with things to say—none of them appropriate for the occasion.

Instead she took a sip of coffee—and yes, it burned her tongue. But she welcomed the distraction of pain.

Beth checked her watch. "I'm afraid I have to run. I'm late to meet someone."

"Well, it was nice to meet you," Katie said automatically.

Her mother withdrew a card from her purse and held it out. "I'd like to give you this. Feel free to call me anytime, day or night."

"Oh." Katie inched backward. "I don't think—I'm not—"

"Just take the card, Katie. Please. No pressure at all to use it."

Katie did as she said. "Thank you."

"I hope you come back next week."

Katie didn't reply, and her mother scooted out the door as though she was, indeed, late for an appointment.

Katie's hand was shaking so badly, coffee sloshed over the lip of her cup, burning her. She had to get out of there. A young woman who couldn't have been more than twenty frowned at her as she darted toward the door. But Katie couldn't bring herself to care. She was just trying to remember how to breathe.

She exited the room and slammed into something hard. "Umph."

Katie looked up into Cooper's brown eyes. He was just inches away, steadying her with his big hands.

"Katie."

"I'm so sorry. I wasn't paying attention."

He glanced down to her shirt. "You spilled your coffee. Did it burn you?"

Only then did she realize that, yes, she had spilled her coffee all over her chest. And yes, it did burn. The empty Styrofoam cup was crushed in her hand.

"Come on." He took the cup from her, led her one door down, and ushered her inside. He flipped on the lights, revealing a large industrial kitchen, everything stainless steel and clean.

Cooper opened the freezer door and withdrew a large bag of ice.

Katie glanced down at her chest. The area above her V-neck shirt was red and starting to hurt.

She looked at Cooper's shirt. "Are you okay? Did any of it spill on you?"

"No, I'm fine." He was transferring ice into a Ziploc bag, his big fingers working efficiently.

She pressed her hand to her chest, but the heat of her palm only made her skin burn worse.

"Here you go."

She took the ice pack and pressed it to her skin. "Thanks. I promise I don't normally injure myself at every turn."

"I shouldn't have been walking by so fast."

"What are you doing here? Is this where you go to church?"

"Yes. I was running a campaign errand—official business."

His crooked smile made her heart tilt. She just noticed the box he'd set on counter.

"What are you doing here?" he asked.

She opened her mouth but couldn't think what to say. Did he know AA met in his church building on Friday nights? "I, uh . . . I'm—"

Something shifted in his eyes. His gaze darted toward the doorway before it returned to hers.

Yes, he knew about the meetings. Katie's mouth went dry.

"Sorry. None of my business."

Boy, she'd had a busy five minutes. After twenty years she finally had her mother's phone number in her pocket along with an invitation to call, and Cooper Robinson thought she was an alcoholic. And she couldn't really explain without divulging very personal information.

He gestured to the ice pack. "How's the burn?"

"Better. I should go home and get something on this."

"Yeah, good idea. I'll clean up here." In his hurry to help her, he'd left out the ice bag and Ziploc box and a knife he'd used to chisel the ice.

She held up the ice pack. "Thanks again."

Their eyes connected, and she saw so many things there. Affection. Concern. Questions. But she couldn't return his affection, and she wasn't ready to give him answers—so she just turned and left.

12

"Happy birthday, Mom." Cooper kissed her on the cheek as she set a dish of something on the picnic table. The smell of grilling burgers carried across the backyard. "You don't look a day over sixty."

She swatted him on the back of the head. "I'm only forty-nine, smart aleck."

"We should have a big bash next year for the big five-oh."

"That's what I told her," Jeff said from behind the grill.

Avery set down a bowl of potato salad. "We should rent out the Trailhead and invite the whole town."

"That's what I'm talking about." Jeff's laugh lines fanned out as he smiled.

"There's only one thing wrong with that plan," his mom said. "It sounds like torture."

"Wouldn't hurt you to be the center of attention for once in your life." Cooper got it, he really did. But his mom gave so much to the town, worked so hard behind the scenes serving as a trail angel, organizing fund-raisers, overseeing the children's program at church. He'd love to see her recognized for everything she did.

"Where's Gavin?" Cooper asked.

Avery grabbed a handful of SunChips from the bag. "Running a few minutes late."

Mom was on her way back to the kitchen for more food. Cooper followed her and gave her a hand. He was setting the condiments on the picnic table when Gavin came around the side of the house.

And right on his heels was Katelyn.

"Hey, guys!" Gavin said. "Happy birthday, Mom."

They exchanged greetings, and Kate's gaze met and held Cooper's for a long beat when they said hello.

Mom stopped fussing with the tablecloth long enough to hug Gavin and welcome Kate. She welcomed everyone with open arms—it was her way. Kate seemed to blossom like a flower under her attention.

Next to Gavin, Kate seemed so petite. So cute. Her hair swung from a ponytail today, her long neck exposed. Her sunny yellow top showed off tanned arms, and the denim shorts she'd paired it with made the most of her shapely legs.

He pulled his gaze away. The unexpected sight of her was a sucker punch. He hadn't seen her since last week when he'd literally bumped into her at the church. He'd thought about that night a lot. About Katelyn being an alcoholic. He hated that for her. And he wished he didn't know because he wasn't sure she'd told Gavin—and it was kind of a big deal.

"Dinner is served." Jeff set a platter of thick burgers in the center of the table.

"Do we have great timing or what?" Gavin said.

Avery nudged Gavin. "It's like you have a sixth sense or something. Every time he stops by my place, I'm just getting dinner out of the oven."

"You mean out of the take-out bag," Gavin said.

"She's a busy working woman," Kate said. "She doesn't have time to cook every night."

"That's right. But I do cook on certain days." She pointed at Gavin. "And I'm not telling you which ones."

"Aw, give a poor bachelor a break," Gavin said. "Have you seen the size of my kitchen?"

Avery rolled her eyes. "As if that's the problem."

Everyone found a seat at the table, and Jeff said grace, thanking God for his wife and praying for many more years with her. As soon as he finished they all dug in.

Cooper helped himself to a burger, smothered in melted cheddar, and avoided looking up. Why did it seem like Kate was always seated directly across from him? He took a heaping spoonful of potato salad and passed the bowl to Avery, then went to work on the condiments.

Gavin got up and grabbed a couple drinks from the cooler. When he returned he placed a wine cooler in front of Kate.

She glanced at Cooper. "Oh, um . . . could I just have a water please?"

"Sure thing." Gavin fetched the water.

Clearly she hadn't told his brother. And given their family history with alcoholism, that might be an issue for Gavin.

None of your business.

He blocked Kate from his mind and tuned in to the conversation going on around him. The family caught each other up on their work lives.

Jeff owned Trailside Market. That was where he and Mom had first spoken. His mom asked if they carried Band-Aids, and the rest was history.

The campsite was keeping Gavin busy, and the clinic was bursting with patients. Cooper told about a repeat caller, all hang-ups. It turned out the couple's four-year-old son was good with a cell phone and wanted to hear the sirens.

"I got my hair done yesterday," Mom said during a break in the conversation.

"Looks nice, Mom," Gavin said. "I thought something was different about you."

"Yeah, looks great." His brother wouldn't notice if their mom had shaved her head.

"I wasn't fishing for compliments." Mom nudged Cooper. "I saw Amber Clarke there, and she asked after you."

"So?"

"So, she's clearly interested, honey, and she

seems like a nice girl. She's gorgeous and she comes from a good family too. You should ask her out."

"He's already gone out with her twice," Avery said. "Once for coffee and once on a picnic."

He spared Avery a look. "I don't recall mentioning that."

She shrugged and stuffed a spoonful of potato salad in her mouth.

"I heard the picnic went well," Gavin said. "There was definitely kissing involved."

Cooper scowled at him. Stupid grapevine.

"Well," Mom said, "it was clear she was interested, that's all."

"Thank you, Mom," he said facetiously.

"I'm not butting in—just trying to be helpful."

"I can handle my own love life, thanks just the same. What about you, Avery? Are you seeing anyone these days?"

She pushed her mahogany hair over her shoulder. "I'm having an extended affair with my clinic, and we're very happy together."

Mom glanced at Jeff. "How'd we raise these two? Didn't we provide an adequate example of happy married life? One of you is a workaholic and the other can't seem to make it past three dates."

"Give me credit for trying," Cooper said. "Besides, I have a demanding job, and there is the small matter of my run for sheriff."

"And between the clinic and Coop's campaign, I've got all I can handle."

Mom picked up her burger. "I give up."

"Finally," Cooper muttered, earning him a frown.

"You should join a dating website," Jeff said to Cooper. "Broaden your horizons."

"And disappoint all the single ladies of Riverbend?" Avery took a bite of her burger.

"That seems to be the way all the kids are doing it these days."

"I'm not joining a dating site." Cooper's eyes connected with Kate's, and he caught the little twitch of her lips. The irritation drained right out of him, and his own lips tilted upward.

"Anyway, I told Amber you'd give her a call," Mom said.

That caught his attention. "What?"

"She wants to volunteer for your campaign and after all, you can hardly have too much help."

Amber wanted to be more than a volunteer for his campaign. But at his mom's prolonged look, he sighed. "Fine, I'll call her."

"Don't sound so begrudging. She's a lovely girl."

Cooper let the subject drop and thankfully Jeff changed the topic.

Katie tossed the beanbag, which landed on the slanted wooden board right next to the hole.

"Nice," Gavin said from across the grassy lawn. Her last shot arced through the air and sank into the hole.

Gavin punched the air. "Yes!"

"Good one," said Avery, who stood next to her.

"We're up by four." Gavin collected the red and blue bags with Cooper.

"Did we mention Coop and Avery are undefeated this year?" Lisa asked Katie from the picnic table.

"Oh boy." Katie rubbed her hands together. "Pressure's on."

"And they hardly lost last year," Jeff said. "They're the team to beat."

"We're going to take 'em down, Katie," Gavin said. "Let's go!"

Jeff got a call and slipped away from the family.

Katie couldn't miss the humor in Cooper's eyes. Gavin clearly took the game more seriously than his brother. Their eyes clung for a long moment. Why did it always seem like an invisible thread connected them?

The moment was lost when Gavin handed Cooper the red bags. Cooper lined up his body, a frown of concentration slicing his brows. He sank his first shot. The second came close. Avery cheered him on.

Gavin's family was so fun. So welcoming. They rooted for each other and bickered lightheartedly, much like she and Spencer had done. But they were a whole family, complete with mom and dad, something she'd always craved. Even though they were actually two families patched together, it didn't feel that way. And every time she was with them, they made her feel as if she was one of them.

Katie's gaze caught on Cooper, thinking back to the conversation over dinner. To the way his mom had butted in on his love life. He obviously objected to her interference, but Katie thought it would be wonderful to have a mother who cared so much about the details of her life.

She couldn't help but wonder who Amber was and if Cooper was interested in her. He must be if he'd kissed her on their picnic date. At the thought of his lips on another woman, jealousy pricked hard. She had no right to feel that way— she was dating his brother.

What would've happened if Avery had set her up with Cooper instead of Gavin?

She was a terrible person. Gavin was a great guy, and he treated her so well. He'd been through such a hard time—she couldn't imagine the pain of losing a child. And then a divorce on top of it.

She needed to put these ridiculous thoughts of Cooper from her mind.

Cooper's last bag thunked on the board, and she gave Gavin a bright smile. "We only need six points. You've got this."

Gavin winked at her, sure in his ability to pull it off. His first three bags plunked onto the board. The fourth hit the ground. And the last one sailed through the air and flopped through the hole. "Yes! We did it."

"Great job," Katie said as Lisa applauded from the table.

"Lucky shot," Cooper teased.

"Lucky shot, my—"

"Be nice, Brother," Avery said.

Katie and Gavin met in the middle for a high five, then he pulled her into his arms for a hug.

"We should play girls against guys," Avery said. "I'll bet Katie and I could wipe the floor with you two."

"What about Mom and Jeff?" Cooper said.

They turned toward the table.

Jeff had just gotten off the phone, and Lisa was watching him with a frown. "What's wrong, hon?"

Sensing that something was afoot, the family converged at the table.

"That was Louis Parker from the Trail Conservancy," Jeff said in a sober voice. "They called a special meeting and—they're shutting down the Main Street Bridge for repairs. The trail won't be coming through town again until it's repaired."

What's wrong with the bridge?" Cooper's mind spun with the ramifications. If the bridge was down, hikers couldn't come through. Most of the town's businesses were set up to accommodate them: the outfitters, the market, the hostels, the campground, and the motel. No hikers, no business. Even the coffee shop and restaurants would struggle.

"That last storm we had," Jeff said, "the logjam did some damage. They're leaving it open for the next month—long enough to reroute the trail, then they're shutting it down till the repairs are done."

"Reroute the trail where?" Mom asked.

"Through Silverton."

"That's seven miles away." Cooper's stomach took a dive. Hikers wouldn't come this far out of the way. Why would they even hitchhike if they found everything they were looking for in Silverton?

"But Silverton isn't set up as well as Riverbend," Mom said. "And the town isn't exactly known for putting out a welcome mat for hikers."

"There's really no choice. Anyway, Louis thinks their attitude will change once business starts flooding in."

"But clearing a new trail will cost a lot of money," Gavin said.

Jeff shrugged, sinking onto the bench beside Mom.

Cooper joined his parents at the table and so did the others. Quiet descended as the news settled. This would not only mean economic hardship for the community but also for Jeff's store, which had been around since the early eighties when his parents opened it.

"But wait," Avery said. "They'd still have to get the hikers across the river, and there's no bridge in Silverton."

"No, but they have that old railroad truss," Jeff said. "In the next month they're planning to make it into a footbridge."

"How long will our bridge repairs take?" Cooper asked.

"Up to six months, they think."

Cooper's shoulders sank. "Six months? That's the rest of the season."

The winter months were hard enough without losing half of tourist season too. It would be like a ghost town without the tourists. Would the businesses make it through this?

"There has to be something we can do," Mom said. "Some way to bring business to the community."

"What about an event of some kind?" Katelyn said. "A festival or something?"

Mom sat up straight. "That's a brilliant idea! It's too late for a summer festival, but we could do some kind of fall celebration. One last big hurrah before winter."

"It's already the end of August, Ma," Gavin said.

Avery leaned in. "If anyone can throw together

an event in short order, it's Lisa. And she's on the city council."

"They'll see the need for this," Mom said. "I know I can get them on board. And the town will be eager to follow suit. If we're going to count on good weather, we should schedule it no later than Halloween."

Jeff shook his head. "But that'll take us right up to the election. That's a lot for this family to contend with."

"Cooper and I can keep our focus on the campaign, and the rest of you can put your heart into the festival," Avery said. "Maybe we could even use the festival to benefit Coop's campaign in some way."

"Great idea," Cooper said. "And I've got plenty of volunteers, Mom. You don't need to worry about that."

"Now we just need to figure out what kind of shindig we should have," Mom said.

Gavin tilted his head to the side. "What about a harvest festival?"

"Or maybe something related to the trails?" Kate suggested.

"I love that." Mom threw an arm around Kate. "You're a genius, sweetheart."

Kate's cheeks bloomed with color.

"We could call it Trail Days . . ." Jeff said. "And it could celebrate the history and culture of the trail."

Cooper nodded. "I love it."

"It's perfect," Gavin said.

The mood around the table had shifted from despair to excitement.

Eyes sparkling with resolve, Mom leaned in. "We'll make Trail Days the best festival this area has ever seen. It'll bring the revenue this town needs to make it through."

Catching the spirit, Cooper smiled. "We'll do whatever it takes to survive. And so will the rest of the town."

13

Just a few more hours and it would be the weekend—a hard one. Tomorrow morning Katie would leave for Max Patch bright and early. She'd honor Spencer by making the journey he couldn't make himself and scatter his ashes at the summit.

She was both anticipating the trip and dreading it. She was grateful to have Gavin accompanying her; she'd been nervous about making the trip alone. But she worried about involving him in such a private, emotional moment. She wasn't sure she wanted to share that with him. It felt . . . too early in the relationship.

Katie took a quick break between patients, slipping into the office for a sip of stale coffee. The week had passed quickly.

Avery had been distracted by the news of the rerouted trail. The town alone wasn't big enough to sustain the clinic—it depended partly on the illnesses and injuries of hikers. Would the clinic survive the coming lean months? Avery was concerned business would suffer and she'd have to let Sharise go.

Was Katie's job also in jeopardy? She winced at the selfish thought. The Robinsons—the whole town—had so much more to lose.

Katie took another sip of coffee, grimacing at the taste, then headed to the next paticnt. When she reached the exam room she tapped on the door and entered at the sound of a woman's voice.

"Good afternoon, how are—?" She stopped short at the sight of the older blonde woman seated in the plastic chair beside the desk.

Beth Wallace beamed. "Well, hello. How nice to see you here."

Katie's birth mother wore a bright-pink top that gave her an airy, happy appearance. White capris and strappy sandals completed her youthful outfit.

Pull it together. Katie stretched a fake smile across her face and took a seat in front of the computer. "Likewise. What brings you in today"—she glanced at the file—"Ms. Wallace?"

"Beth, please. I did something to my wrist while I was gardening of all things."

Gardening. Katie must've gotten her green thumb from her mother. She forced herself to focus on the computer screen.

"It hurts when I twist it to the right. It's probably just a sprain, but it's my dominant hand so I wanted to be sure."

"Of course." Katie went through the list of questions, somehow maintaining a professional demeanor. Her mother's only meds were vitamins and supplements. She seemed remarkably healthy for a forty-six-year-old recovering addict.

"Do you like to garden?" Katie asked.

111

"It's a hobby. Something to keep my hands busy, you know? I used to smoke and . . . well, do all kinds of things I shouldn't. I find I fare best if I stay busy. My yard looks like a botanical garden." Her laughter was melodious.

"I like gardening too."

"Well, I've been here enough seasons to know what grows well and what doesn't, so if you need any tips, let me know."

Katie offered her a tremulous smile.

She'd never considered that the woman might show up at her workplace. Her heart thumped. Next she'd have to take the woman's vitals, and her hands were trembling.

But she couldn't put it off any longer. She stood, grabbed the blood pressure cuff, and slid it onto Beth's arm. As Katie removed the stethoscope from her neck, she fumbled with the tubing, almost dropping it. *Seriously, Katie!* Finally she put the diaphragm under the cuff and inflated it.

"How have you been, Katie? I haven't seen you lately."

She hadn't been back to AA since Beth gave her the business card. Katie slid her gaze up into eyes so like her own. How could her mother not recognize her own eyes staring right back at her? "I, uh, I've been pretty busy with work and getting settled in to my new place."

"You're new to town, aren't you?" Beth chuckled. "I've been here long enough to

112

recognize most everyone, even if I don't know them by name."

"I moved here in May." She didn't want to mention Asheville, so she removed the cuff a little early. The Velcro gave a loud *rip*. "One hundred ten over seventy. Perfect."

She placed the oximeter on her mother's finger, then put the stethoscope's ear tips in her ears and placed the diaphragm on her left lung. Katie went through the task, trying to keep her expression blank as her mind spun. *This is my mother's heartbeat. I grew inside this body. This heartbeat was my lullaby.*

She blinked away the thoughts, hoping the woman couldn't tell that her hands were shaking or that her heart was about to thump out of her chest.

She recognized the clean citrusy scent of Beth from the time they'd spoken two weeks ago. It was pleasant and subtle, probably a body wash or shampoo instead of a perfume.

Katie went about her work, taking the time to surreptitiously observe her mother. Crow's feet fanned from the corners of her eyes. Her lashes were short and light, her eyebrows nicely arched. Her nose was small and dainty like Katie's, but her lips were thinner. Had Katie gotten her full lips from her father? Katie had her mother's square shoulders and thin build, and the woman's skin tanned to a warm golden brown the way

Katie's did. What else had she inherited from this stranger who was also her mother?

"Everything okay?"

Katie jumped. She hadn't moved the stethoscope for a while. Her face grew warm as she curled the instrument around her neck and backed away. "Everything's fine. The doctor's running on schedule, so she should be in shortly."

Eager for escape, she headed to the door.

"Katie . . ."

She turned and tried for a smile, but her lips wobbled, and the rest of her face felt masklike.

"I was wondering if you might like to grab a coffee sometime. It can be difficult coming into a little town where everyone knows everyone. When I got here I didn't know a soul, and it took me a while to find friends."

"Oh." Katie blinked. Beth must be trying to befriend her. Alcoholics Anonymous was a supportive group, and the woman did head it up after all.

And a coffee date would give Katie a chance to find out just who her mother was. Find out if she might welcome her long-lost child back into her life before Katie risked rejection by telling her who she was. This was the chance she'd been waiting for, wasn't it? Why was she suddenly so nervous? So hesitant?

"I didn't mean to put you on the spot." Beth laughed, a sudden tinkling sound. "Look at me, coming into your place of business and pushing myself on you."

"No, not at all."

"Listen, no pressure. You have my card. Give it some thought, and if you decide you'd like to grab a coffee, give me a call."

If she gave it some thought she'd chicken out for sure. "No, that's okay. I—I'd like to grab a coffee sometime."

Her mother's eyes lit up. "Wonderful! Are you familiar with Millie's Mug and Bean? It's just on this side of the bridge."

"I go there almost every morning."

"Perfect. What day would work best for you?"

"I'm off on Saturdays, but I have plans this weekend." *I'm scattering your dead son's ashes.* Did she even know Spencer had died? Would she even care? "But I'm free next Saturday. Maybe nine o'clock?"

The woman's wide smile reminded her so much of Spencer's, her knees almost buckled.

"Wonderful. It's a date."

Cooper shifted in his desk chair. He was almost finished with his paperwork, hands down the worst part of his job. There'd been a domestic situation on Cherry Street. The woman had a bruised cheek but refused to get checked out. Said she'd hit herself with a cabinet door. That she'd accidentally dialed 911.

Cooper scowled at the memory of her husband's smirk and condescending tone. The human in Cooper wanted to slug the guy. The professional knew he could only advise the woman of her rights and acquiesce when she insisted it was an accident.

The couple was only visiting the area, staying in a rental. They were from Asheville, and Cooper could see there'd been two other "accidents" in the past. Times like this, his job sucked hard-boiled eggs.

"Getting all trained for your cushy job as sheriff?" Rodriguez strolled into the office, appearing every bit the confident deputy.

"If being a sheriff means more time behind a desk, kill me now."

"You should be so lucky. Why the sour face? You're off this weekend, aren't you?"

"Yeah, just finishing up here."

"Heading up the mountains on your bike?"

"You know it."

"When you going to let me borrow that thing?"

"You've never even ridden a bike."

"I could learn." Rodriguez sank into his chair. "Chicks dig motorcycles."

With his jet-black hair and ripped muscles, the guy didn't have any trouble getting "chicks."

Cooper finished the form and slid back from his desk. Freedom. He'd spent much of last weekend in Mars Hill and White Rock, pressing

116

flesh at various events. He was ready for some downtime. "I'm out of here."

As he headed down the hall toward the exit, Sean Curtis, the other candidate for sheriff, entered the building. He was in his midthirties, average height, and sported a slim build. With Sean's perfect teeth and side-parted brown hair, Cooper thought he looked more like a news anchor than a deputy.

The man tossed him an easy smile. "Hey, Cooper. Headed out for the weekend?"

"That's the hope."

"These weekends campaigning can be a drain, huh?"

"You said it."

Sean held the door for Cooper. "Hard to believe we've got less than six weeks to go now."

"Hard to believe. There's fresh donuts in the break room."

Sean patted his flat stomach. "Gotta watch the figure. Have a good weekend."

"You too." Hot air hit Cooper's face like a furnace as he exited the building, but the heat was preferable to awkward small talk with his opponent. They'd always kept it cordial, but tension was inevitable in a small office like theirs. And it had only gotten worse a couple months ago when Roy Gilmore, the sitting sheriff, publicly endorsed Cooper.

He shook away thoughts of his campaign. He

was headed home where he'd order a pizza and enjoy the game. In the morning he'd sleep in, then head up into the hills for some bike therapy.

His cell rang as he slid into his truck. He started the engine, lowering the windows, then checked the screen. Gavin.

"Hey, Brother, what's up?"

"Hey, Coop. Have a good week?"

"Not bad. Just got off work."

There was a beat of silence. "Um, listen, you're off this weekend, right?"

"Yeah . . ." Cooper sincerely hoped Gavin didn't need an extra set of hands at the campground. "Please tell me you don't need me to dig a drainage ditch for free again."

"Hey, I fed you pizza, didn't I?"

"My back hurt for a week."

"Nah, listen, it's nothing like that. There's definitely a problem at the campground, but nothing you can help with unless you have a plumber's license I don't know about."

"What's going on?"

"The biggest cabin has issues. We have a family coming on Monday, and the boss insists we fix it over the weekend. I got Bleeker Plumbing coming to do the work."

"Okay, so what's the problem?"

"I have to oversee the project, and I promised Katie I'd do this thing with her. See, her brother passed away in December, and she has plans to

118

scatter his ashes up on the trail. I don't want her going alone."

Cooper's face fell. Oh no. This wasn't going to happen. Couldn't happen. "Gavin, come on. That's a private thing."

"She's not a hiker and I don't feel comfortable sending her out there alone."

"What about Avery? I'm sure that would be a lot more comfortable for Katie, and Avery's a capable hiker."

"She has to work. And with the upcoming bridge closure, she can hardly afford to turn away business now."

Cooper bit back an expletive. He had to get out of this. He shouldn't be alone with Kate, not even for the few hours this hike would take. Not with the thoughts and—dare he say it—feelings he'd been having.

Cooper scratched the back of his head. "I don't know, man. She should probably just put it off a weekend, then you could go with her."

"Sunday's her brother's birthday—or would've been. She's been waiting months to do this."

Cooper dropped his head into his hand. *Come on, God. Throw me a bone here. I'm trying to do the right thing.*

"I'm sure she'd be fine," Cooper said. "She'd probably rather go it alone than have a virtual stranger along." He balked at those words. Kate hardly felt like a stranger to him, and he'd be willing to bet she felt the same way. Even more reason to get out of this. "Can't Avery take off work this one time?"

"Come on, Coop. I'd feel a lot better knowing she had a man along."

The trail was generally safe, the hikers friendly and supportive. But a while back there'd been a stabbing. A man died and a woman was gravely injured. Then there were the bears. And the chance of injury. Gavin's fears weren't completely unfounded.

Truth was, Cooper wanted to be with her—and that only proved what a bad idea this was. He'd be better off digging a drainage ditch. Ten drainage ditches. Gavin had no idea what he was asking, but there was nothing Cooper wouldn't do for his brother.

He let out a long, deep sigh. "All right. If she's okay with it, I guess I'll tag along."

"Hey, that's great. Thank you. You're a lifesaver. I've already loaned her my overnight gear so she's all set. You'll just have to pack a—"

"Wait . . . Overnight gear? This is an overnight hike?"

"All the way up to Max Patch."

Max Patch. A wave of relief came over him. They could just drive to the mountain, take the short loop trail, scatter the ashes, and be done—few hours, tops. "Oh, that's great. We could just drive there then and walk up."

"Coop, it's part of the journey. Her brother wanted to do that hike—Riverbend to Max Patch—and now he can't."

"Right. The journey."

"She's had this planned a long time. We already dropped her car up at Max Patch, so you'll be all set for the return home after . . . you know, she scatters his ashes."

Dread swamped him even as guilt pierced his heart. Poor Kate. This had to be awful for her. He'd just have to gut his way through it. He could do that for her, for his brother. Couldn't he?

"All right. I guess I'll do it."

"Thanks, man. You're a good brother."

Cooper hoped and prayed he was good enough.

14

Katie handed the server her menu and settled back in the wooden chair, her mind on that nerve-wracking meeting with her mother. The coffee date was one week away, and Katie was both eager and dreading it. What if that path only led to more disappointment and heartache? What if she discovered her mother was happy to leave her children in the past? Katie didn't think she could handle another rejection.

Across from her Gavin surveyed the specials menu. His dark hair had grown out and flopped over his forehead, giving him a boyish look that tweaked at her heart.

Being a Friday night at suppertime, the Trailhead Bar and Grill was packed. A band was setting up to play in the far corner, and the smell of grilled steak and Parmesan fries hung temptingly in the air.

Gavin leaned forward, elbows on the table. "You okay?"

"Yeah, I'm just . . . Long day, I guess."

"And a long weekend ahead."

"Yeah."

The scattering of Spencer's ashes had been heavy on her heart since she'd collected them from the funeral home. She was actually anticipating it.

Spencer's remains didn't belong in a glossy oak urn, no matter how lovely it was. She was eager to finally lay him to rest at a place he loved, following a hike he'd always wanted but been too sick to do.

Oh, she knew his ashes weren't his essence. His soul was in heaven. But she longed for the peace of having this last sacred rite done.

"So, hey, about this weekend . . . I'm afraid I have some bad news."

She noted the flicker of regret on his face. "What's up?"

"There's been some major trouble with one of the cabins—plumbing issues. I have a large group coming on Monday, a family reunion, and my boss doesn't want to cancel the booking. He's out of town and insisting I stay and oversee the repairs."

"Oh. I see."

"I'm not leaving you hung out to dry though. I don't want you doing this hike alone." He gave her a wary look. "I hope you don't mind, but I asked Coop if he'd accompany you, and he'd be happy to go along."

"Coop?" Katie's mind spun at the sudden shift of events.

"I know you don't know him very well, and maybe you wouldn't be comfortable with this, but I'm hoping you'll consider it." Gavin winced. "I hope I haven't overstepped, but I was worried about you being out there alone. I know you can take care of yourself, but there's no cell coverage for much of the hike, and if you have an accident . . . I'd trust Coop to watch out for you, that's all."

"I'll just ask Avery. I'm sure she'd take the day off if I asked her to."

"It's your decision, of course. But I'd feel a lot better if you had the security of a man since you'll be gone overnight."

"Right." She envisioned two solid days with Cooper. Overnight in the shelter. Scattering her brother's ashes. Katie's heart fluttered and she shifted her gaze away. She didn't hate the idea.

"He's also done this hike before, so he'll know what to do if you run into wildlife."

She imagined how the two days would unfold. Imagined having Cooper's company on what was, admittedly, a very private affair. And she felt . . . okay with it. He had a calm, soothing presence, wasn't one to intrude where he wasn't welcome. He was intuitive. He'd give her space if she needed it. And she couldn't imagine anyone she'd feel safer with.

"Katie?" Gavin's hand covered hers. "Are you mad at me?"

"Not at all. It's sweet that you're concerned. And I really didn't want to do this alone."

A smile pulled the corners of his lips even as his shoulders measurably sank. His blue eyes sharpened on hers. "You're so great, Katie. I've never met a woman like you."

"Thanks. You're pretty great yourself."

It was true. Gavin was handsome and attentive. He didn't have annoying habits she couldn't live with. He was close to his family, but he was also his own man. In short, he was husband material.

His gaze grew intense. "I feel like I can breathe for the first time in a long time."

Her heart constricted at his words, and her eyes stung because she knew what he'd suffered, even if he hadn't told her himself. "I'm really glad. You deserve good things, Gavin."

He squeezed her hand and cleared his throat. The moment passed.

"Are you sure Cooper doesn't mind? It's an awful lot to ask."

"Cooper loves to hike."

"I know but he's giving up his whole weekend. Doesn't he have campaign obligations?"

"Nope. Like I said, this is right up his alley—and there's no one I trust more. I'll let him know to be at your house at seven if that's all right. He has all the gear he'll need. You found the sleeping bag I left on your porch?"

"Yeah, everything's packed and ready to go."

He gave her a fond smile. "Little Miss Organized. I hadn't packed a thing yet."

"I guess sometimes it pays to procrastinate."

"Usually it just stresses me out." He turned his

attention to the stage, where Lonnie Purdy, the Trailhead's owner, introduced the band.

Was it strange that she was a little glad Cooper was coming instead of Gavin? Guilt stung at the thought. She couldn't quite put her finger on why she liked the idea. Perhaps it was only because he was a known entity. While she might know Gavin better in the day-to-day world, she'd already gone through a crisis with Cooper. She trusted him to handle a difficult situation.

She wasn't sure how scattering Spencer's ashes might affect her. She'd lost a lot in her life, but nothing had been harder than losing her brother. She'd already done her share of grieving, of course, but one didn't get over such a loss quickly or easily. She still missed him every day. Still had moments where she started to call him before she remembered she couldn't.

She was relieved when the band struck up their first song, making conversation all but impossible. She had a lot to sort out and didn't want to do it under Gavin's watchful eyes.

She was surprised he hadn't yet told her about his son. After all, they'd both lost someone they loved. Wasn't this a commonality that could draw them closer? Didn't he want that? Maybe he wasn't ready for that kind of intimacy. Was that a red flag?

Well, she had to respect his need for privacy. Obviously the loss had cut deeply. She'd never had a child, much less lost one. She should be patient with him. Her gaze drifted covertly over his features as he watched the band perform. There was a sadness in his eyes that never went away.

Lisa had told her that Katie had brought happiness back into his life, and Gavin's own words seemed to corroborate that. She was glad for it. He deserved to be happy. She hated what he'd been through; she just wished he trusted her enough to open up about it.

15

The next morning Katie put her hair in a pony-tail and strung it through her Yankees cap. She wore lightweight hiking shorts and a white tank top. The first weekend of September would be a hot one. She'd filled her backpack with water bottles, snacks, a change of clothing, and of course, the urn with Spencer's ashes.

As she put on her favorite running shoes, the sound of popping gravel filtered through the walls of her house. Cooper was here.

Her heart thudded in anticipation as she finished tying her shoes and gathered her belongings. She was eager to have this thing done, that was all. At least that was what she told herself as she exited the house and locked the door behind her.

Cooper, similarly attired in a gray ball cap, athletic shirt, shorts, and hiking boots, shouldered his backpack. His biceps strained the sleeves of his shirt as he adjusted his pack. Upon sight of her he stopped abruptly, his face falling. "Oh boy. I guess I can't do this after all."

Katie blinked. "What? Why not?"

He threw a hand up. "A Yankees fan. I don't think we can be friends."

Relief surged through her, coming out as a laugh. "You dog. I thought you were serious."

"Oh, I'm very serious about baseball." He belied the statement with a smile. "People cheer for the Braves around here, you know. But maybe I can overlook your confusion this one time."

"My confusion, huh?" She couldn't help returning his bright smile, excitement for the coming day winning out.

"What else can I blame it on? Maybe I can help you see the errors of your ways." He locked up his car. "You had a good breakfast, right?"

"Lots of protein, as instructed."

"Good girl. It's about thirteen miles to the shelter. Then another six miles or so to Max Patch."

"Today's the challenging day." Physically. But tomorrow might prove to be the more difficult one.

As they walked down the drive, he went through a list of items she should have in her bag. Gavin had already advised her on this, so she was well prepared. Cooper carried a first-aid kit and a few other extras like a knife and sleeping pads.

At the street they turned right, walking toward the trailhead on the south side of town.

"You have a water filter?" he asked.

"Iodine tablets—borrowed from Gavin. That and the sleeping bag."

"You don't own one?"

"What would I need with a sleeping bag?"

His eyes twinkled. "You might want to keep that to yourself. Around here that's considered the eighth deadly sin."

"Oh boy. I have enough trouble with the first seven."

He laughed. "Which one gives you the most grief?"

"I don't even know if I can name them all. Gluttony . . . greed . . . pride?"

"I think envy and lust are in there somewhere."

Heat worked up Katie's neck despite the cool of the morning. "That's only five."

He took off up a steep, grassy slope, leading toward the trailhead. "Plenty enough right there to trip a guy up though."

"Or a girl." She wasn't about to share her Achilles' heel, though in truth it depended on the situation. Currently, his calf muscles bulging as he climbed, that last sin was at the forefront of her mind.

She tore her gaze away and forced her thoughts elsewhere. She was grateful for the cool breeze. Soon enough the sun would beat high overhead, and the humidity alone would make sweat bead on her skin.

Before long they approached the trailhead, passing the bulletin board that displayed a map and town information for northbound hikers coming off the trail.

"This first part is all switchbacks, heading

uphill out of the valley." He moved aside, gesturing her to pass. "It's pretty much a one-lane road. You can set the pace."

Katie took the lead and immediately a canopy of trees sheltered them from the sun. The air was thick with the buzz of cicadas, and knotty roots snaked across the path. Soon the trail inclined sharply, and she was grateful that her jogging routine kept her in good shape.

She took in the dense forest where fallen logs lay covered in moss and damp, decaying leaves carpeted the floor, giving off a rich, loamy scent. The trail switched back and grew steeper. Her lungs worked to keep pace with her heart.

She walked through a web—yuck—and got it out of her face as best she could, hoping a spider hadn't been attached to it. Conversation had come to a halt as they navigated the steep trail. Squirrels scrambled through underbrush, and birds tweeted from lofty perches. Still the trail climbed.

"How are you faring back there?" she asked.

"Doing great. Nice views."

She peered off through the woods toward town and the mountains on the other side of it. "We're getting up there."

She ran through another web. This time she paused to clear its sticky remnants from her face.

Cooper came up behind her. "Hold still."

She peered over her shoulder. "What? What is it?"

He picked something off her shoulder—a black spider—and flung it away.

She shuddered. "Ugh. Disgusting."

"Want me to take the lead?"

"Nobody told me there'd be spiders."

He laughed and eased past her. "Let me know if you want to slow down."

They set off again, their conversation limited to the basics until the ground leveled off a bit.

A slight rustle in the woods provoked a question. "Have you ever seen a bear while hiking?"

"Only once. If you make plenty of noise they stay away."

"Where were you when you saw it? Was it a black bear?"

"Yeah. At a shelter actually. I was hanging out by the picnic tables with some thru-hikers, and it just ambled right on by. Didn't even glance our way."

"Gavin said I wouldn't need bear spray."

"It weighs the pack down and like I said, they mostly keep away."

"It's the 'mostly' that has me concerned."

He tossed her a smile over his shoulder. "If it makes you feel better, I carry my Glock. Just a habit. I've never had to use one on a bear and don't plan to start now."

That did make her feel a little better. "I'm surprised we haven't passed anyone yet."

"It's early, and anyone coming this way

would've spent the night at Deer Park Mountain shelter. We'll probably be passing some folks soon."

The sun had risen a bit, and the temperature was noticeably warmer than when they'd started. The afternoon would be uncomfortable. But the cooler temperatures tonight would be a welcome reward.

How would that be—sleeping in the shelter beside Cooper? Would it be weird? No weirder than sleeping six inches from a stranger, and according to Gavin, that's how it was done.

"So what are these shelters like exactly?"

"Well, they vary. Walnut Mountain is a three-sided log structure. Sleeps five or so. It's right on the trail, and there's a fire pit and a picnic table, plus a privy and water source nearby."

"Will we have company?"

"Most likely. Hopefully we'll get there early enough to get a space."

"And if we don't?"

"We pitch the tent I brought just in case."

"Oh." She hadn't realized they might be sharing a tent. "That was smart thinking."

"Best to be prepared. People are pretty good about making room, especially if there's bad weather, but sometimes they fill up. Some people just hang a hammock, but that's no good in bad weather."

The ground leveled out a bit, and the inclines

grew shorter. The ridge was above the trail, so the views were infrequent. When they reached a spot with a large log just off the trail beside a trickling stream, Cooper slowed.

"Ready for a water break?"

"Sure."

Gavin sank to the log and adjusted the laces on his boots.

She shrugged off her pack, pulled out a water bottle, and drank in sips. Nature carried on around them: squirrels nattering, birds tweeting, wind rustling the treetops.

And still the pervasive anticipatory feeling Katie had awakened with persevered. What would tomorrow feel like? Would scattering her brother's ashes be the closure she needed? Or would the rite only pick open the scab over her heart?

Cooper grabbed a water bottle from his pack and quenched his thirst. "Don't hold back on the water. You don't want to get dehydrated, and there are plenty of water sources between here and Max Patch."

"Okay. I'm grateful for the shade. It's going to get hot today."

"About three in the morning you'll wish for a little warmth."

Cooper was enjoying the hike. Enjoying the company. Kate was easy to talk to. She didn't complain or focus on the negative. Even though she'd had a difficult childhood, she remained optimistic. He admired that.

He'd been glad to take the lead earlier. Her shapely form was a distraction he didn't need. And with her hair up and that long, graceful neck exposed, she was a tempting sight. What was it about her neck? And why did he feel like that *Twilight* dude all of a sudden?

He looked away. She was Gavin's girl. He took another swig of water, his thoughts going back to the night he'd run into her coming from the AA meeting. As of a week ago, she hadn't yet told Gavin about her issue. It was a constant worry in the back of Cooper's mind. Maybe an addiction wasn't something you shared on a first or second date. But surely things were starting to get serious between Kate and Gavin. After all, he was bringing her around the family.

Gavin had a right to know about her addiction, even if she did have it under control. He had a right to make a decision about the relationship before he was too deeply involved. Maybe it was time to ease his worry. And when would he have a better chance?

Cooper took a quick slug of water as he formulated his thoughts. "Listen, Kate. I know you might think this is none of my business, but I was wondering if you'd told Gavin about . . ." He struggled with the wording, not wanting to sound overly harsh or judgmental.

She gave him a quizzical look. "What?"

He sighed. "It's the drinking thing . . . It's a big deal. I mean, I'm sure you have a handle on it, and I'm glad you're going to meetings and everything but—"

Kate let out a laugh, covering her mouth to hold the water in.

He frowned at her. "I don't see anything funny about this. It's a serious problem, and Gavin's already been through a lot. It's not fair to let him—"

She waved his words away. "No, no. I'm not— This is not the way it seems, Cooper. I'm not an alcoholic."

He stared into blue eyes that were as convincing as any he'd seen. But he also had an alcoholic dad, and he knew they were capable of lying to themselves—not to mention others—quite convincingly.

"No, really." She clearly struggled with something. Finally she sighed. "Okay, I guess I'll have to explain. You know I was a foster child. Well, my mom was an addict. Because of that, I've never touched drugs or alcohol."

Kate took another drink and capped the bottle. "After Spencer died I did some searching online and discovered our mother was living in River-bend Gap. I found out she was a leader at the local AA group."

Ahhh. He tipped his head back, relief rolling

136

through him. "You moved here because of her."

"Stupid, really. I mean, our mother never sought us out, even though we never left Asheville. We would've been easy enough to find. She'd obviously straightened out her life, but she still hadn't bothered to find us."

"You attend the meetings to see her?"

"I went to two meetings—and I did meet her."

"Would I know her?"

Kate considered for a moment. "Beth Wallace?"

"Name sounds a little familiar, but I don't know her."

"She seems like a nice enough woman. She gave me her card and told me to call anytime."

"Have you?"

She gave a wry huff. "I didn't have to. She turned up at the clinic yesterday and invited me to coffee."

"Did you tell her who you are?"

"No, not yet. And she didn't recognize me either. She looked me right in the eyes—which are the same shade of blue as hers, by the way—and didn't even know her own child."

"I'm sorry. That must've hurt." He shifted his foot in the dirt, feeling her pain. "I know a little about having an alcoholic parent. About being rejected by said parent. It leaves its scars."

"Gavin told me about your dad. It was a connecting point for us. And yes, all the above can shape who you are." She shook her head. "I set up a coffee date with Beth for next Saturday, and I don't know what I'm doing."

"I suspect you're trying to get to know who she is before you risk heartache by telling her outright."

"*Yes*. That's it exactly. Is that stupid? I moved my life here on a whim, and if she rejects me . . ."

"It's wise to get to know her a little first. She's given you no reason to trust her. But if she ultimately rejects you, it's no reflection on you, Katelyn. You're a terrific woman. You're beautiful and smart and kind. Look how far you've come from the mess your mother left you in."

Her eyes caught on his, and Cooper felt the jolt down to the soles of his feet. Heat washed through him. Had he given himself away with those emphatic words? He broke eye contact and scratched the back of his neck.

"Thank you, Cooper. You're pretty wise yourself."

"Not beautiful and kind? I'm hurt."

She chuckled, just as he'd hoped she would.

"Does Gavin know? About your mom being here?"

She sobered. "Not yet. He knows I was a foster kid and that my mom had to give us up, but the rest of it . . . no."

"Your call, of course." Why hadn't she told him? But this wasn't information that would

138

hurt his brother. Just something Kate needed to sort out. He thought of telling her Gavin was an excellent sounding board. He had a good head on his shoulders. But for some reason, Cooper held back the words.

"Wallace . . ." he said. "You have a different last name than your mom."

"I changed it when I was eighteen." She shrugged. "I guess I felt the need to cut ties with her. And I knew this girl in high school— Jennie Loveland. I always thought it was such a wonderful last name."

"It has a nice ring to it." He leaned into Kate's shoulder and gave her a nudge. "No matter how this works out with your mom, you're going to be just fine."

He wanted to tell her she was strong enough to get through this. That she could handle anything life threw her way. But he was afraid he'd already said too much.

16

Sweat beaded on Katie's skin. But even as the sun rose higher in the sky and the air thickened with humidity, Katie found herself smiling. The morning had passed with surprising speed.

Cooper was right; they'd passed a few hikers heading north on the trail. They stopped for a moment to chat with a couple from Kentucky who had been hiking one segment at a time. After ten days on the trail, they were eager to reach Riverbend, where warm showers and comfy beds awaited them.

Her conversations with Cooper were light and fun, their laughter frequently cutting through the thick forest. She liked his sense of humor. It reminded her of their time on the cliff when he'd tried to keep her from dwelling on the tenuous situation. Now that the circumstances weren't life or death, she was able to fully enjoy his company.

They talked about his run for the sheriff's position and Katie's reasons for becoming a nurse—her brother's heart issues being the biggest factor. She'd been his health advocate and found comfort in being able to *do* something.

When she and Cooper weren't talking due to steep inclines, Katie pondered two questions:

Why did she keep telling Cooper intimate details of her life that she hadn't yet shared with Gavin? And why had she been worried about having Gavin on this trek when she didn't mind having Cooper along?

Her nose twitched at the earthy smell of rain an instant before a drop hit her arm. A moment later another splashed on her hand.

Soon a steady drizzle spilled from the sky.

"Did you bring a rain jacket?" Cooper called over his shoulder.

"No—they weren't calling for rain."

"I didn't either." He scanned the surroundings. "Nothing worse than hiking in wet clothes. Let's find someplace to sit it out."

"Sounds good. We have plenty of time." They'd planned to arrive at the shelter before the worst heat of the day.

"There's an outcropping of rocks just ahead."

As they approached she saw the outcropping was up a steep incline off the path. The rock wall went about twenty feet high and bore an indentation at the base. Not deep enough to be a cave but enough to provide shelter.

"Looks like a good place to hunker down." Cooper scrambled up the incline.

"Looks like a good place for a bear to hang out."

He tossed her a smile as he gave her a hand up the hill. "Should keep us good and dry."

"Hopefully it'll pass quickly. Maybe even cool

things off. It's a good time for lunch anyway. You hungry yet?"

"Starving."

They took off their packs and settled side by side in the cozy enclave. The scent of rain in the air and the gentle pattering on the leafy canopy created a soothing atmosphere.

She unzipped her bag and rooted for snacks. "The sound and smell of rain remind me of lazy mornings as a kid."

"Sounds like a good memory."

"I used to hate getting out of bed on days like this. I probably drove Jill nuts on school mornings."

"Your foster mom, right?"

"Yeah." She pulled out a bag and ripped it open.

"Skittles? That's the sustaining snack you brought?"

"Sugar provides quick energy." She flashed him a cheeky smile and popped a few in her mouth.

"And feeds that sweet tooth of yours. But you need protein and complex carbs, my friend."

She rooted through her snacks and came up with a bag of peanut M&M's. "Voilà. Protein."

"You'll be hungry in an hour. Your choice, but you're welcome to my protein bars. I brought plenty."

"Well, maybe just one." He handed it to her and she set it aside to finish her Skittles. "Thanks."

"I think you've just earned your trail name."

"What—Skittles? I guess I can live with that.

And what about you? How about Soggy Card-board Eater?"

"Don't knock 'em. Three hundred fifty calories and twenty-five grams of protein. And I already have a trail name: Banana Split."

"Okay, you have to explain that one."

"Shortly after my mom married Jeff, we went on a family hike. A bonding experience, I suppose. Well, I was wearing these ugly yellow shorts—a hand-me-down from Gavin—and on the second day when I jumped across a creek, my shorts ripped in the back."

Laughter bubbled up inside. Katie covered her mouth full of Skittles.

"Go ahead and laugh."

"And it stuck—the nickname?"

"Like I had a choice. Gavin and Avery called me that every chance they got."

"You could change it now, you know."

"Aw, it's kinda grown on me." He slid her that sideways smile that made her pulse jump.

They went back to their lunch. Katie wrapped up the rest of her Skittles and opened the protein bar, which tasted a little better than cardboard. The rain continued pattering the forest floor.

"I won't be in the way tomorrow." Cooper's voice seemed deeper in the quiet little hollow. "I realize it's a private moment, and I'll give you your space. Just wanted you to know."

She met his gaze, that thread pulling and

buzzing with something that made her heart flutter. "I had no doubt. That's why I didn't mind you coming along."

He had really nice lips, the bottom one just thick enough and the top one dipping distinctly in the middle.

She dragged her eyes away and took another bite of the bar. Why in heaven's name was she thinking about the man's lips?

"What was it like growing up in foster homes? You don't have to answer if that's too personal."

"No, that's okay. There were a lot of kids around, so we always had someone to play with— that was good. But we didn't have much space of our own. Our toys and even our clothes were often shared. Nothing was *mine,* you know? We had one bicycle we all shared. Silly, but I think that's the thing that bothered me most. I loved to ride that bike."

"Must've been difficult."

Her mind drifted back. "There was a girl who lived down the street—only child. She had this beautiful mint-green bike she rode by our house every day, ringing the bell. It had a white seat and handlebars and a white basket on the front she always carried her cat in. I wanted that bike so badly."

He gave her an empathetic smile. "How was school life? You must've done well. I hear nursing school is rigorous."

"I liked learning and I excelled academically. But the kids . . . They weren't always kind. Being a foster kid was embarrassing for me. I felt like something was wrong with me because my parents didn't stick around while everyone else's had."

"I get that. Because of my dad—I felt embarrassed. Everyone knew who he was, and I always felt his behavior reflected on me."

"Why do we take on our parents' issues?"

Cooper shrugged. "We shouldn't. We had no control over any of it."

They chewed in silence for a while. Katie peeled down the bar's wrapper, the cellophane loud in the enclosure. "I always had Spencer though. Our caseworker was really good about keeping us together."

"He was lucky to have a big sister like you. You were all each other had. Losing him must've been hard."

"Still is. Looking out for him had become my life." Her throat thickened, making her laugh wobble. "About the time he turned eighteen, he started getting pretty annoyed by that."

"You'd probably become like a parent to him."

"I was. And when he balked at that, I had to loosen the apron strings. Balance out the relationship a little."

"Become his sister."

"That was hard, though, because of his health

issues. At times he needed me even if he didn't want to. He was always trying to do too much, and I was forever holding him back."

"I'll bet you were a great sister."

She needed something from him in that moment. She didn't know what it was until she soaked in the certainty in those deep brown eyes. He believed what he'd said. And maybe he was right.

The knowledge loosened the knot in Katie's throat. "Thanks. I feel bad that I sometimes tuned him out—he used to go on and on about certain things."

"Like what?"

"Music, nature, hummingbirds . . ."

"Hummingbirds?"

"He loved them, was fascinated by them. I could sit here and bore you with all the tedious facts I learned over the years. When he was twelve he asked James and Jill for a hummingbird feeder for his birthday. He loved that thing. Kept it filled with sugar water and sat inside by the window, watching the birds whenever they came. Their hearts can beat twelve hundred times a minute. Did you know that?"

"Really?"

"Maybe that's why he admired them so much. They have strong hearts."

Cooper nodded. "Makes sense."

She considered telling him the rest. He was

such a good listener, it was impossible not to. "Since he died, hummingbirds have been kind of a thing with me. My first day back to work after his death, a patient of mine, a twelve-year-old girl, found out my brother had died, and she drew me a picture. It was a hummingbird—she knew nothing about Spencer."

"That's really cool."

"They've shown up a few times since he passed. Just when I need him most, there's a hummingbird." She stared at the ground a few seconds. "Silly, I know."

"Not silly at all. My grandpa and I used to play Monopoly, and he always chose the top hat. At his funeral, after everyone had left, there was a top hat on one of the chairs. Everyone thought someone left it, but no one remembered anyone wearing one. I was sure my grandpa had put it there."

They shared a smile—no words required. He understood and that was so comforting.

They ate in quiet for a moment. She was all talked out.

"Listen to that," he said a few minutes later.

Katie stopped eating and listened. A beam of sunlight split through the treetops, dappling the forest floor. "It stopped raining."

He crumpled up his wrapper and slipped it into his trash bag. "Whenever you're ready . . ."

"I'm ready." She bagged her trash, emerged

from the enclave, and shouldered her backpack. She was ready. Ready to reach Max Patch, where she could finally lay her beloved brother to rest.

By the time they reached Walnut Mountain shelter late in the afternoon, Katie's legs were trembling. They'd been in no rush, stopping to wade in a stream along the way after they refilled their water bottles. They took a couple of selfies by the creek and one on a peak with the mountains in the distance. They took rests in the shade and carried on conversations that made her oblivious to the miles they covered.

Her legs noticed though. She had stamina but she was used to jogging on flat terrain. Her calves and hips and quads weren't used to climbing mountains.

After a quick visit to the privy, she wasted no time slipping off her pack and sinking onto the picnic table. Her back muscles released painfully. "Yikes. I thought I was in shape."

"We've been hiking for hours. You did great."

Cooper seemed to have enough energy to continue to Max Patch tonight. Even now, instead of resting he was gathering kindling for the fire. "You're going to have a real campfire supper tonight."

"And what, pray tell, does that consist of?"

"Ramen noodles and beef jerky, among other things."

She made a face. "Sounds interesting?"

"It's tasty enough. I wouldn't mind waiting till it's cooled off a bit before starting a fire."

"I'm fine for now."

The shelter area appeared just as Cooper had described. The three-sided log structure wasn't very big. It sported a raised wooden platform where, presumably, everyone would stretch out side by side. In front of the shelter, a sitting log rested by the fire pit, and a picnic table sat off to the side of it. The dirt paths, marked with the white blazes of the Appalachian Trail, branched out into the woods going both directions.

It was only the two of them so far, but it was early yet. Would others join them soon, or would they have the shelter to themselves? Did she want them to?

She shook the thought away and gestured toward the lines above the sleeping platform. "What are those for? To hang wet clothes on?"

"Yeah and to keep, ah, animals out of the food."

"Oh, right, the bears."

Cooper let the assumption slip. They were actually mice lines, but he didn't want to worry Katelyn. Sometimes mice weren't a problem at the shelters. Other times they scuttled over you in the night in search of food. Hopefully they wouldn't be a problem tonight.

By the time he finished setting up the fire, a

family had come up the trail from the south. The Cooks consisted of a mom and a dad, a twelve-year-old daughter, and a ten-year-old boy. They were hiking from Max Patch to Riverbend and peppered Kate and him with questions about where to stay and the best places to eat.

As was tradition they introduced themselves by their trail names: Daddy Bear, Mama Goodstuff, Topknot, and Dragon Slayer.

They went about supper preparations, Cooper cooking up his beefy noodles alongside Daddy Bear. Kate chatted with Mama Goodstuff at the picnic table while Topknot and Dragon Slayer played cards in the shelter.

Cooper hoped no one else showed up. Six would probably be the limit, and that was squeezing in pretty tight. He could always set up his tent, but it was pretty small. And while the idea of Kate nestled up against him was tempting—it was tempting.

"You're a good brother." Gavin's words rang in his ears.

He'd noticed the looks Kate gave him today. Was he only imagining the affection in her eyes as she laughed at his jokes? Did she really hang on to his hand an extra moment as he helped her over logs and streams, or was that only wishful thinking?

He gave his head a sharp shake. *Knock it off, Robinson. You're feeding the fire.*

They were definitely sleeping in the shelter tonight. If someone showed up without a tent, he'd lend them his, but he wouldn't put himself in that position.

The evening had cooled as the sun sank in the sky. They'd both changed into tomorrow's clothing, wanting to sleep in something clean.

When the onions and greens were sufficiently cooked through, he removed the pot from the fire and set it on the table.

Kate's smile was like a rainbow after a storm, bright and hopeful. "Smells good."

"Hope you don't mind eating from the pot. I usually don't bother with plates."

"Fine by me. I'm starving." She blew on a bite before she stuffed it into her mouth. "Mmm. Delicious."

"Eat plenty—you earned it."

The Cooks joined them a few minutes later with their beef hash.

Daddy Bear gave Cooper's dish an approving glance. "Not bad, Banana Split. You'll have to share the recipe with me."

"Sure thing." While they tucked into their supper, Cooper quietly leaned over and whispered to Kate, "When are you going to stop doing that?"

"Doing what?"

"Twitching your lips every time someone calls me that."

She gave a helpless shrug.

The group finished their supper and made pleasant conversation. Then they washed the dishes and readied for the night.

Kate checked Topknot's wrist, which had been giving her a little trouble. She wrapped it with an Ace bandage, diagnosing a minor sprain, and suggested the girl get it checked out once they reached Riverbend.

On the trail, sleeping schedules went by sunrise and sunset. The Cooks hung their food bags on the mouse lines, then arranged their sleeping bags, leaving space at the end for Kate and Cooper.

Cooper set his bag along the wall, hoping to spare her from the mice that tended to scamper along the perimeter. This put her beside Mama Goodstuff, whom Kate had hit it off with. The two kids were next on the platform, and Daddy Bear bookended the bunch.

When it grew dark the Cooks doused themselves liberally with insect repellent, visited the privy one more time, and bedded down.

Cooper and Kate sat at the picnic table awhile. The glow of the campfire flickered on her pretty face as they talked about everything from religion to politics to all the places they wanted to visit someday.

But as time wore on and as much as he was enjoying their conversation, he could see the day had taken its toll. Her eyes grew heavy and her chin rested on her fist. Tomorrow would be difficult for her, and she needed her rest.

"You about ready for bed?" he asked.

"I'm bushed."

They quietly made their way up the platform and to their sleeping bags. Kate squirmed into hers, but Cooper left his open, enjoying the coolness of the evening.

"Good night," he said, once they'd settled.

"Night."

Nocturnal sounds were loud. Cicadas buzzed, a cricket chirped nearby, and somewhere in the distance a lonely owl hooted.

"Cooper?" Kate whispered a few minutes later.

"Yeah?"

"Thanks again for coming with me."

Warmth flooded through him at her heartfelt tone. "You're welcome."

Sometime later Cooper turned onto his back, trying to be quiet to avoid waking the others. He wasn't used to going to bed at nine thirty, but apparently the Cook family was.

Though Kate had tossed and turned a bit, there hadn't been so much as a rustle down the row for the last half hour. The smell of burning wood hung in the air and the oscillating call of insects filled the forest. The moon had risen above the treetops and glowed white beyond the shelter's opening.

It had cooled considerably, but he still had no use for his sleeping bag. Kate, on the other hand, was snuggled up in hers.

She rolled over, facing him. A quiet sigh escaped.

"Doing okay, Skittles?" he whispered quietly enough not to wake her if she was asleep.

"Just thinking about tomorrow."

The moonlight kissed her face with a faint glow. "How are you feeling about it?"

When a long pause followed he said, "We don't have to talk about it. You're exhausted."

"I don't mind. I can't sleep anyway. Mostly I'm looking forward to laying him to rest where he wanted to be. I've been thinking about this a long time."

"Closure?"

"Yeah, I think that's it."

He waited for her to continue, but she didn't. She just sniffed quietly.

Was she crying? And if she was, what should he do?

Someone stirred a few sleeping bags down, then settled once again.

Katelyn sniffled again.

She *was* crying. His fingers tingled, aching to touch her. He gave in to the urge, just a feather touch on the shoulder in the darkness. "I'm sorry, Kate. This can't be easy."

She didn't say anything but the sniffles came closer together.

His chest constricted. "You want me to leave you alone?"

"No . . ." The word escaped on the sob.

Ah, jeez. Without thought he pulled her closer. She came willingly, rolling onto her side. His arm went around her. His other hand went to the curve of her neck—that beautiful neck he'd been eyeing all day.

He shouldn't have done that. But since he already had . . .

He moved his thumb, tentatively grazing her skin. It was soft and silky, and her pulse thrummed beneath it. Her hair smelled of oranges. A stray strand tickled his cheek, but he didn't brush it away. She was warm and soft in his arms, weeping softly.

He wished he could change things for her. Wished he could bring back her brother or at least say something that would take the sting out of the loss. He'd only lost his grandparents and his nephew. Those had been difficult, but he still had family, whereas Kate was alone.

His thumb continued its back-and-forth motion, his palm cupping the curve of her neck.

"I'm sorry," she said between sniffles.

"Don't be," he whispered into her hair. "You're fine."

Fine. Such a banal word. Having Katelyn in his arms didn't feel *fine.* It felt right. It felt as if she belonged here. He should put distance between them, but instead he chased the unwanted thoughts from his mind. She was hurting and he was comforting her. There was nothing wrong with that.

"Do you want to tell me about him?"

She was quiet so long he wasn't sure she'd heard him. Then she drew a breath and began. "There were so many things he wanted to do with his life. He wanted to travel and write music and learn everything he could about nature. He was so full of dreams and ambitions, and now all those hopes are gone. He'll never be as old as I am right now. He'll never marry and have children. He'll never meet our mother. His life was only just beginning. I don't know why I'm crying, now of all times."

"You're allowed to feel sad, Kate. You're still grieving the loss of all those things."

She tilted her head to look up at him. Moonlight flickered in her eyes, gleamed off the tears dampening her cheeks. "You always say just the right thing."

"Do I?" He swept a thumb across her cheek, wishing he could eradicate her pain as easily as he did her tears.

"Yes."

Could she hear his heart pounding? Did she sense that he longed to offer more than comfort with his touch? Did she know he wanted her for himself?

He couldn't avoid that truth anymore. Not now that she was in his arms. He didn't want to let her go. He wanted to lower his head and kiss those sweet lips.

Would she return the kiss? Maybe she'd take the comfort he offered, but it would be wrong on multiple levels. He wouldn't take advantage of her emotional state, even if she was finished weeping, her breaths steadily rising and falling against his ribs.

With the last vestiges of control, he forced himself to think of his brother. Kate was his girlfriend. Cooper had no right to hold her. No right to think of her this way. Certainly no right to kiss her.

"We should get some rest." His words scraped like gravel across his throat.

"You're a good man, Cooper Robinson." With one last smile tilted up at him, she moved away, settling into her sleeping bag.

Was he? Because right now he just felt like a terrible person.

17

Something stirred Katie from slumber. She opened her eyes and surveyed her surroundings. All was quiet on the shelter's platform. The air held a chill, and sometime in the night she'd sought warmth—from Cooper.

Last night surged back to mind. He'd been so sweet to listen. To comfort her. She hated to admit it, but she'd enjoyed being in his arms. Apparently she liked it so much she'd come back for more.

She was currently curled up to his side, arm slung around his waist, head resting on his chest. The delicious weight of his arm rested on her shoulders, and his hand cupped the back of her head.

Judging by the slow, steady rising and falling of his chest, he was still asleep. Would it be wrong to stay here just for a moment, absorbing his solid strength? She had a difficult day ahead. It was Spencer's birthday—he would've been twenty-three today.

A minute ticked slowly by, and she still didn't want to leave the warmth of Cooper's arms. But she probably should. Perhaps she could just slip away without him ever knowing she'd been wrapped around him like a Christmas ribbon.

His breathing stuttered and his heartbeat quickened beneath her ear.

Too late. She drew up onto her elbow, meeting his gaze. His heavy-lidded eyes made her pulse kick up a notch. She was suddenly conscious of her snarled hair and makeup-free face. Her eyes were probably swollen too.

"Good morning," she whispered.

"Morning."

She glanced back at the Cook family, more to escape Cooper's perceptive eyes than anything else. They still slumbered.

Katie rolled onto her back, staring up at the food bags, just shadows really, hanging on the lines above them in the predawn light. She snuggled deeper into her sleeping bag until it was up to her nose.

"Sleep okay?" Cooper asked quietly.

"Like a baby. You?"

"Not bad. But that coffee's sure going to hit the spot."

"That sounds so good."

"You cold?"

"Freezing."

He sat up, rubbing the sleep from his eyes, then he quietly got up and settled his sleeping bag over her. "It's early yet. I'll stoke the fire and be back with some coffee."

Almost five hours later Katie's calves ached as they made the steady ascent to Max Patch. They'd passed many hikers on the way.

"Max Patch is a popular camping spot," Cooper had said. "You can't beat the stargazing up there."

They were mostly quiet on the trek, enjoying the views. Katie suspected Cooper was giving her time to prepare herself mentally.

They'd spotted a few deer near a creek, and a couple salamanders had scurried across their path. At one juncture they'd come upon a half-empty crate of water bottles and snacks.

"Where in the world did these come from?" Katie asked.

Cooper reached in and helped himself to a bag of almonds. "Trail magic. Go ahead and grab something."

She did as he suggested. "What's 'trail magic'?"

"Basically it's an act of goodwill. People in nearby towns do little favors for hikers. The people who do this sort of thing are called trail angels. My mom and Jeff have hosted hikers for supper, given them rides to town or to the grocery, and even given them a place to bed down."

"Is that safe?"

"People do it all the time. It's a different culture here. That five-to-seven-month thru-hike is a real challenge. People want to cheer them on."

They continued climbing steadily for miles until they broke out of the woods. A broad summit rose before them, the breeze blowing the tall grass and wildflowers.

"Is that Max Patch?" Katie asked.

"That's it."

As they walked up the dirt path, Katie's heart quickened. She could hardly believe the moment was upon her. It seemed as though she'd been waiting forever for this day.

Cooper stopped about fifty paces from the peak. "I'll wait here. Take your time, okay? I'm in no hurry to get back."

Her gaze sharpened on the top of the mountain, her mind on what lay before her. "All right."

Breath hitching, she continued up the short incline. The summit was broad and flat with a 360-degree view of the surrounding mountains. She continued walking until she reached the other side of the summit. There was not a soul around, making her feel as if she were the only person on the planet.

"Are you here, Spencer?" She took in the misty blue ridges of the mountains in the distance. "It's so beautiful. You would've loved this view."

Moving on, she stopped by a rock, removed her ball cap, and shrugged her bag off her shoulder. Her hands trembled as she unzipped the bag and pulled out the vessel containing Spencer's ashes.

When she had it in hand she sat on the rock and gazed at the majestic view. The wind tugged at her ponytail. The sun beat down, warming her skin as anxiety stole the saliva from her mouth.

"Happy birthday, Spencer." Her voice wavered with emotion. "I wish you were here. I'd take you to Happy Burger and bake you a German chocolate cake even though coconut has a nasty aftertaste and the texture of those little shredded papers in a gift basket."

She stared off into the distance, not really seeing. Was this really it? Would she finally be able to let him go—her baby brother?

She wasn't ready.

Her throat tightened and her eyes stung with tears. "God, I don't know how to let him go. Help me to trust You with him. I know he couldn't be in better hands. I know he's at peace now. I know he wouldn't come back even if he could, and I wouldn't want him to. He's better off now.

"It's me who needs to let go. Help me do that. Give me peace over this so I can truly move forward with my life."

From her peripheral vision a movement caught her eye. A hummingbird. It fluttered over the field of flowers, not ten feet away, pausing at a pink bloom.

Was she seeing things? She blinked. The bird remained.

A shiver ran down Katie's arms, gooseflesh popping everywhere. "Spencer?"

She came slowly to her feet, not wanting to frighten the bird away. Her legs quaked beneath her. The hummingbird hovered there for a long, wonderful moment, its beating wings humming quietly.

Katie's heart thrummed in her ears. Her vision blurred as tears filled her eyes.

And then the tiny bird fluttered away. Katie watched it until she couldn't see it anymore. The moment expired like a long-held breath. She sucked in a deep lungful of air as peace stole over her like a mist, enshrouding her.

Had that really just happened? She laughed even as a tear slipped down her face. She stared into the bright-blue expanse of sky. "Thank You."

That was just what she'd needed. Now she was ready. She removed the top of the vessel. And in one sure, deft movement she emptied the contents into the air. The ashes floated away on a breeze, a dark cloud slowly dissipating, disappearing into the vast valley below.

Spencer wasn't gone. He was just someplace else. But someday she'd see him again.

Her throat tightened as tears flooded her eyes again. "Thank You for Spencer. Thanks for making him my brother and giving me twenty-two years with him." She let the emotions sweep over her. Let the tears fall. "Tell him I love him."

At the sound of footsteps Cooper looked up the path. He'd been praying for Kate since she disappeared over the rise some half hour ago.

She approached. Silhouetted by the sunlight behind her, he couldn't read her expression. But there was a lightness to her step.

He dropped the strand of grass he'd twisted until it was frayed and rose from the ground. As she grew closer he could make out her features. Her face was flushed, her eyes swollen, her lashes wet.

His chest tightened. *Aw, jeez.*

But just then her lashes swept up and, catching sight of him, her lips split into a broad smile.

His soul gave a heavy sigh. He opened his arms and she stepped right into his embrace. He wrapped his arms around her, cradling the back of her head. He buried his face in her hair and breathed her in. He'd been worried about her. It had been hard to stay here, knowing she was up there alone, hurting.

"You okay?" he asked softly.

"Oh, Cooper—there was a hummingbird. I was praying, staring out at the view, not really seeing anything, then there it was." She gave a choked laugh. "A hummingbird. It floated around some flowers for a minute and then it was gone."

Cooper had been up here two dozen times, and he'd never seen a hummingbird. "Oh, honey."

"Isn't it crazy?"

"Crazy wonderful."

"It really was. I just feel so . . ."

"What?" he asked when she didn't continue.

"Good," she said finally. "At peace, I guess."

"I'm so glad." He dropped a kiss on the top of her head, his throat tightening at God's goodness.

He held her for a long moment, letting her decide when she'd had enough.

When they drew apart they shared a smile. He glanced at the top of her head. "Where's your hat?"

She looked around, frowned at her bag. "I must've left it up there."

"I'll get it." Before she could argue he jogged up the path and onto the summit. He found the hat lying near a rock. The hummingbird was gone. There were no signs of ashes in the air. Just a lonely breeze rustling through the meadow of flowers.

He grabbed the hat and took in the panoramic vista, Mount Mitchell to the east, the Smoky Mountains to the southwest. No matter how many times he saw it, the sweeping view was still breathtaking.

God, whatever You did up here . . . Thank You.

After a moment he made his way back down the dirt path and found Kate waiting where he'd left her. He set the cap on her head.

From beneath the brim she gave him a saucy grin. "Thought you didn't like my Yankees hat."

"I don't." His lips curved of their own volition. "But I like the woman wearing it."

18

Cooper took his time driving Katelyn's car down Max Patch, not because the gravel road was windy and bumpy—although it was. But because his time with her was ticking down one second at a time. He was already thinking ahead to when he might see her again. This coming Friday at the family supper?

When they finally reached the paved road, he increased his speed. She checked her phone and must've had a signal because she started typing. Probably letting Gavin know they were on their way back.

"How are you doing over there?" Cooper asked when she put her phone away.

"I feel really good. Today was just what I needed." She shifted to face him. "Thank you again, Cooper. I mean it. You gave up your whole weekend for this, and I really appreciate it."

"It's nothing. It was good to get out and hike again." He glanced her way, just long enough to catch and hold her smile for an exhilarating moment. "Quite a week for you. I'll be praying about your meeting with your mother Saturday."

"Thanks. I should see you before that, though. Family supper Friday?"

That seemed so far away. "Right."

Their relationship had deepened significantly over the past two days. Despite his best efforts, Kate had wormed her way even further into his heart. He didn't know what to do about that. But he didn't want to waste these last moments alone fretting about it.

"What's on tap for the rest of your day?" he asked.

"I have no idea. I could hardly think beyond this morning. Maybe I'll do a little gardening." She stifled a yawn. "Or maybe I'll take a nap."

"You could probably use one. The weekend took a lot out of you, physically and emotionally."

She dropped her head back against the headrest. "I'm so tired all of a sudden."

"We've still got a bit of a drive. Feel free to doze off if you want."

As if weighted, her eyelids fluttered closed. "You sure? I don't want to be bad company."

"You could never be bad company." He wasn't even sure she heard him. Her face relaxed and her lips parted as her breathing deepened.

Silly, but it made him a little heady to think she was comfortable enough to fall asleep with him. She trusted him. She'd trusted him with more than her safety this weekend. She'd trusted him with private things she hadn't yet shared with anyone else, not even Gavin.

• • •

Twenty minutes later Cooper pulled into Kate's drive. She must've been sleeping deeply because the popping gravel didn't wake her and neither did the sudden quiet when he turned off the ignition.

Poor thing was tuckered. He hated to wake her. Instead he allowed his gaze to roam over her face.

She'd knocked her ball cap crooked, exposing one delicate eyebrow. Her arresting eyes closed, her other features cried out for notice. Her long eyelashes swept the tops of her cheeks. Her pert nose was perfectly proportioned atop lush, pink lips.

Despite the cap, she'd gotten a bit of sun on her nose and cheeks. Her arms, folded over her chest, were golden brown against the white sleeves of her shirt. Her bare knees were shifted toward him and covered with chill bumps. She had a little scar on the side of her kneecap.

His fingers tingled with the need to touch the old injury. But instead he touched her arm. "Katelyn."

She didn't stir.

"Kate, we're here. Wake up, Skittles."

She shifted, her eyelids fluttering open. She looked around, adorably lost until her gaze landed on him. Then she straightened and ran a hand over her face. "Oh man. I really conked out. Are we already home?"

"I think you're officially beat."

Gravel popped on the drive behind them. Cooper checked his rearview mirror. His stomach sank at the sight of the familiar truck. They were alone no longer. "Gavin's here."

"I told him we were on our way."

He wished she hadn't. Cooper and Kate got out of the car, and she met Gavin as he hopped from his truck.

Behind his open door Gavin pulled her close and lowered his head until his lips met Kate's.

Cooper's breath froze in his lungs. His jaw clenched. The kiss probably lasted only a couple seconds, yet they seemed to drag on like the final minute of an agonizing workout. His hands twitched with the urge to shove Gavin away from her, but what right did Cooper have to do that?

He removed his pack from the back seat and grabbed the empty water bottles from the cup holders. By the time he finished, Gavin was at his side wearing a grateful smile and extending a hand. "Hey, Bro. I can't thank you enough. Really."

Cooper clasped his hand and allowed his brother to draw him in for a shoulder bump. "Not a problem."

When they parted Gavin gave Cooper's shoulder a light shove. "You're a good brother—I don't care what Avery says."

But a few minutes later when Cooper pulled

from Kate's drive, leaving the two of them inside her house, he didn't feel like a good brother. Because he wanted to be the one Katelyn was winding down with. He wanted to be the soft shoulder she cried on, the rock she depended on.

And what kind of brother did that really make him?

19

Katie anticipated this evening so much she wasn't even going home first to shower and change. She turned out of the clinic parking lot and toward Lisa and Jeff's place.

The Robinsons would soon gather for supper. Lisa had asked her to come early to help with the food and brainstorm ideas for Trail Days. She'd already gotten council approval and a bit of funding from local businesses. Katie was eager to spend time with the woman. And, if she was honest, eager to see Cooper again.

She'd thought of him a lot since their return Sunday, had revisited the more poignant moments many times. The enigmatic looks he'd sometimes given her. The smile that seemed just for her. That comment he made after setting her cap on her head. *"I like the woman wearing it."*

That one really resonated.

She'd tried telling herself she felt connected to Cooper because they'd covered a lot of emotional ground together: the harrowing car accident, then the poignant scattering of her brother's ashes. Significant experiences.

She'd tried to convince herself of that on Sunday and Monday, but by Tuesday, she gave up the excuse. Whether these intense moments had bonded her and Cooper or not, bottom line was . . . she felt something for him. Something that was inappropriate when she was dating his brother.

The question was, what should she do about it? The thought of breaking things off with Gavin twisted her stomach. She cared for him. She didn't want to hurt him—especially after all he'd been through.

He wasn't opening up to her as much as she'd hoped, but who was she to talk? She hadn't told him about her mother. She'd been planning to tell him Sunday, honest she had. But when she tried to recap her experience up on the summit—the scattering of the ashes and the hummingbird—Gavin didn't seem to get it.

Maybe it was her fault. She hadn't told him about the significance of hummingbirds before then, and maybe she hadn't adequately explained how powerful that moment had been. His response fell flat.

She kept comparing his reaction to Cooper's. Maybe that wasn't fair.

Even Mama Jill's response hadn't measured up. She'd called right after Gavin left Sunday. But Jill was wrangling six kids and the youngest was battling colic. The woman seemed moved by Katie's experience—she'd loved Spencer, too, after all. But there were so many interruptions, and Jill had to rush off because of the baby.

Now Katie pulled into the Robinsons' drive and stopped in front of the garage door, thankful to put an end to that line of thinking.

Lisa met her at the front door with one of her warm hugs. "Thanks for coming early, sweetheart."

"Thanks for having me." Katie followed her through the living room to the bright, airy kitchen at the back of the house.

"Something smells good." Katie set her purse on a chair and met Lisa at the island where she was chopping a head of lettuce. Beans bubbled in a pot on the stove. "What can I do to help?"

"Would you turn down those beans and give them a stir, please?"

"Sure thing."

When Katie was finished Lisa gestured toward a few ripened tomatoes on the island. "How do you feel about chopping up those?"

"I can handle that." Katie washed her hands, then grabbed a knife and went to work on the chopping block.

Lisa worked across from her with smooth, efficient motions that bespoke many hours in the kitchen. They caught each other up on their weeks as they worked on the salad.

The bridge was closing for repairs today, and that had been the talk of the town all week. Businesses were braced for change, but folks were hopeful the coming festival would help to compensate.

When Lisa and Katie finished setting the table, Lisa launched into the topic at hand. "As you know, we have to attract many people to Trail Days if we want to get this town through the lean months ahead. I'm making flyers to hang around the region, but I just don't know what else we can do to draw people, especially when we're on a tight budget. It'll be the last weekend in October—Friday through Sunday—and we'll have several food trucks as well as regional food for sale. Local artisans will sell their wares. But we'll need a lot of activity and game ideas."

"Since I know so little about the trail, I'm probably the worst person to ask."

Lisa waved away her remark. "Avery says you've had many great ideas for the clinic. And since you have no preconceived ideas you might be just the right person to ask."

"Well . . . tell me a little about the trail's history."

Lisa shared the story of Harvard graduate Benton MacKaye, who was sitting in a tree in 1921 when the idea came to him of a trail running through the Appalachian Mountains from Maine to Georgia. The plan was put into action in 1925, but there were dramatic setbacks. It was maritime lawyer Myron Avery who finally completed the 2,200-mile trail in 1937.

"That's a cool story," Katie said. "What about a skit telling how the trail came about?"

"I love that. Maybe one of our churches could put something together."

"Good idea. The kids especially would love that. And what about having hiking-themed contests for different age groups and maybe throwback events and costumes celebrating the 1920s?"

Lisa jotted down the ideas. "You're so good at this. I think we'll attract hiking enthusiasts, of course. And there's a certain segment that'll probably just come for the food. And maybe others who'll enjoy the small-town atmosphere and mountain getaway."

"Are you just trying to attract people from nearby towns?"

"Mostly, I think. I have a friend working on a website. We'll list the schedule of activities as soon as we have something concrete. I'm working on getting some local bands to perform. They're eager for exposure so they're willing to play for free."

"It's hard to argue with free." Katie scraped the chopped tomatoes into the salad bowl, then went to the sink to wash the board.

"Thanks so much. You've given me plenty to think about."

"I'm happy to help." As Katie gave the beans another stir, the conversation turned to Gavin. Katie bragged on him, telling Lisa how well he treated her.

"He's a good man." Lisa turned off the stovetop and placed a hand on Katie's arm. "Honey . . . I can't tell you how happy I am that Gavin has you in his life. He's a new person since he started dating you. We've been so worried about him. I can't thank you enough."

Katie dredged up a smile. "Of course. I'm glad he's doing so much better."

The front door opened and Jeff entered, followed by Avery and Gavin.

"We all arrived at once," Avery said after the greetings.

"Perfect timing," Lisa said. "Everything's ready."

Jeff pecked Lisa on the lips. "Let's eat."

Katie wondered about Cooper as they took their places at the table. Would it be giving away too much if she asked? She was being paranoid.

"Where's Coop?" Avery finally asked after grace.

"He's attending some benefit dinner in Marshall," Jeff said.

Avery frowned. "And he didn't think to tell his campaign manager? I would've gone with him."

"He knows you've been busy with the clinic." Lisa passed the salad. "He said he could handle this one on his own."

Talk turned to Cooper's run for sheriff, but Katie's thoughts revolved around the staggering disappointment she felt at his absence.

This was silly. She was dating Gavin, and they

made a great couple. Even his mom thought so. Feeding these feelings for Cooper was pointless. Because even if she broke up with Gavin, Cooper would never make a move on his brother's ex-girlfriend, even if he wanted to—and she wasn't sure he did. Sure, she'd caught some vibes, but he loved his brother and he was a loyal man.

If she broke up with Gavin she'd not only lose both men and strain her relationship with Avery, but she'd also lose Lisa and Jeff, whom she'd already become attached to.

She needed to focus on and be grateful for what she already had. She caught Gavin's eyes and gave him a warm smile.

He took her hand beneath the table and gave it a gentle squeeze.

20

Katie's heart kicked against her rib cage as she took a seat at the coffee shop table. She was early. Millie's Mug and Bean was busy this Saturday morning. Patrons sat in groups of two or three, and the line was long with to-go orders. She inhaled the rich scent of freshly brewed coffee and let out a slow breath.

The front door swept open again, making her nerves jangle. But it wasn't her mother.

Katie sipped her decaf coffee, her mind going back to last night at the Robinsons'. It had been a wonderful evening. Gavin's family was fun and delightful. So warm and caring. Did he know how lucky he was to have them?

After a delicious supper and several rousing rounds of cornhole, Gavin had walked her out and given her a lingering good-night kiss. By the time she got into her car and drove away, she was wondering what was wrong with her. Gavin was the ideal boyfriend. His family was a dream. So what if it was taking him a while to open up? That was probably normal for divorced people, right? She should be patient with him.

She had to put this silly infatuation with Cooper from her mind.

She could start by focusing on this morning's

meeting with her mother. She didn't want to lie to the woman, but shc had to be careful which details she revealed. She didn't want Beth guessing who Katie was before she decided if she wanted this woman in her life. Or if Beth would want Katie in her life.

It would be a fine line to walk.

The coffee shop's door swung open and Beth came through. Her gaze swept the room and settled on Katie.

Katie's mouth went dry as they exchanged waves, then Beth went to place an order. The line was nonexistent now, so it wasn't long before Beth received her coffee and joined Katie at the table.

"You're early," Beth said.

"I've been up since five."

Beth slung her purse straps over the chair's back. "Trouble sleeping?"

"Not really. I'm just an early riser."

"Me too, usually. But I didn't get to bed until almost one, so I slept in a bit."

"How's your wrist doing?"

"All better. I was probably being overly cautious."

"We should never take our health for granted." Katie thought of Spencer's weak heart and wished she could mention it. But of course that would give too much away.

"I haven't seen you at group for a couple

weeks. I hope we didn't scare you away."

"Not at all. I've just been busy with work and stuff."

"The clinic's been busy?"

Katie was glad she'd dropped the subject. "Pretty steady. I don't know if you heard about the bridge closure. That'll be bad for all the businesses, I guess."

"I heard. Word's gotten around and people are getting nervous. It's going to be a long six months."

"They're hoping the fall festival will help make up for the loss in revenue. They're calling it Trail Days. I'm helping a bit with the planning."

Beth's face brightened. "That's a great idea. Let me know if I can pitch in somewhere."

"I'll keep that in mind." But Katie didn't like the idea of bringing her birth mother around the Robinsons. Too messy. Especially since she hadn't even told Gavin about her.

"What kind of marketing are they doing for the event?"

"It's pretty minimal, I think. Signs posted in nearby towns, newspaper ads. Things like that."

"Newspaper ads aren't very cost effective. Online is where it's at. They could target specific groups of people who'd most be interested in their event."

"Sounds as if you know a lot about this stuff."

"That's actually what I do for a living—I'm the

director of marketing for a local radio station."

"Oh wow. I'd love to bend your ear about this. We could really use some direction."

"I can do you one better. Let me handle the social media for Trail Days. If you have the funds I can do some direct ads. I can get you a pretty good bang for your buck."

"That's awfully nice of you." As much as Katie didn't want to pull Beth into this, the offer was too good to pass up.

"I care about this town. If I can do something to help get us over this hump, sign me up."

Maybe Katie could be a liaison between Beth and Lisa. "Thank you. I'll talk to Lisa Robinson and see what she says."

"Sounds great."

"So, tell me a little about yourself, Beth. How'd you come to be in Riverbend Gap?"

The woman laughed, and there was that smile that reminded Katie of her brother. "It was a man, wouldn't you know? He's long gone but the town was a keeper. It was all for the best really. I hit rock bottom and ended up finding a great support group here. Once I got myself together, I was able to get a job at WPBR and work my way up."

She talked about her job while Katie listened. Though she was eager to know more personal details, she didn't want to push. Especially when Katie wasn't ready to reveal her own history.

• • •

Cooper had never been less eager for a date. But all week long he hadn't been able to get Katelyn out of his head, and his brother's words last Sunday buzzed like a pesky fly in his ears.

He started his truck and headed toward town. If he really wanted to live up to Gavin's words, he needed to avoid Kate. Which he'd done last night. He also needed to get his mind off of her.

Enter Amber. Or rather, reenter. He'd sort of left her hanging for several weeks, and that wasn't really his style. But he hadn't known what to do about her. Amber was a nice woman with potential, but he'd been distracted by Kate.

No more. He would starve this infatuation by avoiding her and by filling his time and thoughts with Amber. She'd be good for him. He winced. Probably not good that he was thinking of her the same way he thought about brussels sprouts.

He usually picked up his dates, but this morning he would meet Amber because she'd had an early appointment at the Beauty Barn. He pulled his truck into an empty spot and made his way toward the coffee shop. He didn't see Amber's car but she'd probably walked over.

He strode toward the entry, resolved to give her a fair shot. To be attentive. To appreciate her company. No thinking about Kate or comparing her to Kate or wishing he were with Kate.

He'd get to know Amber better. He tried to

remember what she'd already revealed about herself—he didn't want to seem like one of those jerks who never listened. But for the life of him he couldn't remember anything except her occupation and that she had a sister. He couldn't even remember if her sister lived in town.

He probably should've suggested dinner instead of the easily escaped coffee date, but he'd thought it might be better to ease back into the relationship since he'd more or less ignored her the past few weeks. Maybe he really was a jerk.

When he opened the door the delicious aroma of java filled his nose. He searched the room for Amber's Marilyn Monroe hairstyle. His gaze snagged on the back of a blonde head, but it wasn't Amber. He did a double take.

Katelyn.

Are you kidding me right now? He huffed. No matter how hard he tried, he just couldn't seem to escape her.

She shared a table with a woman he didn't recognize, and their conversation from the trail came rushing back. The meeting with her birth mother. His pulse thrummed in his ears as he claimed the last empty spot, taking a seat that gave him a full view of Kate's table—because he was a glutton for punishment like that.

The woman laughed at something, and he could see her daughter in her smile. He could only imagine how nervous Kate must be. He said a quick prayer that the meeting would go well.

"Hey, stranger!" Amber approached from behind and squeezed his shoulders.

"Hey, yourself." Cooper stood and embraced her. The woman's hair and makeup were expertly done as always, and she wore a cute sundress that made the most of her trim figure. "You look nice."

"Thanks. Did you already order?"

"No, I waited for you."

She tilted a flirtatious grin. "Such a gentleman."

Truth was he couldn't remember what she liked even though he'd had coffee with her twice. They moved to the register and ordered their drinks. *Skinny chai latte*—he drilled the order into his thick skull.

They settled at the table while the baristas made their drinks. He glanced at Kate's table. The woman—Beth, he remembered—was talking and seemed to be enjoying the conversation.

"So, Mr. Sheriff-to-be, how goes the campaigning? I've seen the yard signs up everywhere. I talked Cheryl into putting one in front of the salon."

"Thanks. It's going pretty well. A lot of events, a ton of glad-handing."

"That doesn't really seem like your thing. Not that you aren't a friendly guy, but you seem like an introvert at heart."

"True enough. But I want to be sheriff, so I'll do what's necessary."

She flashed a saucy grin. "And do you always get what you want, Deputy Robinson?"

He thought of Katelyn and just barely stopped himself from glancing her way. "Not always."

"Well, you'll get your way this time. Everyone around here loves your family."

Amber had come to town after his dad had left. Cooper hadn't mentioned the stigma his old man brought him and didn't feel like getting into it now.

"It's more the surrounding towns I'm worried about. That's why I've been out of town so much."

"I'm glad you've finally managed to fit me into your busy schedule," she teased.

"Come on now. It's not like that."

"What's it like then?"

"I've just been busy. Distracted." That was the truth if ever he'd heard it. He glanced at that nearby table. Beth was still talking.

"What do you make of all this bridge repair stuff?" Amber took a sip of her drink.

"It'll be hard on the town without the hikers coming through."

"When I was doing Barbara Jean McCafferty's hair, she told me the bridge might be closed into next season too."

"That's not true. It'll take no more than six months."

185

"Hope you're right. I mean, the salon will be fine—we don't get many hikers. But the town needs that income. It'll put the hurt on your family's store for certain."

"It'll be hard on pretty much all the retailers, motels, hostel, and campground."

"How is Gavin doing these days? I saw him in town the other day and he seemed better. He was friendly."

"He's doing pretty good. Just needed a little time, I think."

Her lips curved knowingly. "And maybe a certain woman?"

He hiked a brow.

"I do Donna Jenkins's hair. She was venting last time she was in."

Donna was Gavin's former mother-in-law. She was no doubt bitter Gavin was moving on with another woman even though the divorce had been final for a year. Anyway, Cooper didn't want to hear a bunch of gossip. "Well, I'm sure you get that a lot."

"For sure. But hey, I think it's great about Gavin. He deserves to be happy. How's your sister doing? Is the clinic going well?"

"She's fine. Clinic seems to be clipping right along, and she's been pouring herself into it."

"It's good to have a doctor on hand. When Gretchen Miller's husband had that stroke over the winter, Avery saved his life."

Pride welled up inside. His sister had busted her butt to get through med school and she made a fine doctor. Even if she did pretty much leash herself to the clinic. "That's my sis."

Laughter from the other table snagged his attention. With the discipline of a saint he took a sip of his coffee and forced himself to focus on Amber's doe eyes. "How's your sister doing?"

"Danielle? Oh, she's fine. Knee deep in diapers and baby food. I don't know how she does it."

Danielle. That's right, her sister was married with a few kids.

"I mean, some days I think being on my feet all day is going to kill me, but I love what I do. I love doing hair and chatting with different people. If I had to be holed up with kids all day I'd go mad."

"To each her own, I guess."

"I do want kids though, don't get me wrong. Kids are great. I love my little niece and nephews. I'm over there all the time."

Sister lives in town.

He gazed at Kate's table. Beth leaned in, listening intently, elbows on the table.

Amber glanced over her shoulder to see what he was looking at.

Get it together, man. "Um . . . did you get to take a vacation this summer?"

The distraction worked. "I'm saving for a hair

conference in Orlando next year. It's like the who's who of stylists. Gotta keep those skills sharp."

He couldn't imagine the folks around here benefiting from the latest in hairstyles, but what did he know?

"What about you? Go anywhere fun?"

"Between work and the campaign I couldn't get away this year."

Her eyes twinkled. "You work too hard—always off protecting and serving."

It was a police motto, but he didn't bother correcting her. "Somebody's got to prowl the streets of Riverbend."

A chair screeched nearby. Kate and Beth stood. Kate shouldered her purse and turned toward the door. Her gaze caught on Cooper, her eyes widening slightly before they swung across the table to Amber. Her smile wobbled.

Beth and Kate said their good-byes, then she stopped by his table. "Hi there."

"Hey, Katie." Cooper stood and gave her a brief hug. As he inhaled her familiar scent, his heart gave a traitorous whimper. He was dying to know how her conversation with Beth had gone. He sorely wished Amber weren't here. He'd invite Kate to sit down and have a nice long chat.

Then you'd be right back to square one, moron.

He pulled away and gestured to the other woman. "Katie, this is Amber. Amber, Katie."

"Hi there." Amber's gaze raked quickly over Kate, no doubt taking in her freshly made-up face and long, shiny blonde hair.

"Hi." Kate returned Amber's tight smile with a friendly one. But the tense set of her shoulders and her hand clutching her purse in a white-knuckled grip gave her away.

He couldn't resist asking about Beth. "How'd your meeting go?"

"Good. I think it went fine."

He wanted to ask her so much more. Wanted to hear every detail. But now was not the time.

As an awkward silence crept in, Kate glanced between Amber and him. "Well . . . I don't want to interrupt your, um, date. And my garden awaits."

"It's supposed to rain later," he said.

"I'd better get on it then." With one last bright smile she left the coffee shop.

Amber didn't even wait until the door swung shut before she said, "Who was that? I don't think I've seen her around here."

"Katie." He took a sip of his coffee. He probably shouldn't bait her, but he couldn't seem to help himself.

She gave him a tolerant look.

"Gavin's new girlfriend."

Her face brightened. "Oh. She seemed nice."

The obvious relief on Amber's face was off-putting—and worrisome. Because he just wasn't as invested in her as she seemed to be in him.

But he had to make an effort if he was ever going to get over Katelyn. Now that she'd left the shop, he could focus on Amber. And before they left today he was going to ask her out again—this time for supper.

21

Katie settled back into the cushions on Avery's sofa. They'd just watched the newest Scarlett Johansson movie and were enjoying the homemade brownies Lisa had brought over.

"These are so good," Katie said. "Must have recipe."

"No need. Lisa makes them all the time."

"I like to bake though. And you never know when you'll need a brownie fix. Plus there's the batter."

"Excellent point, my friend. I need milk. Want some?"

"Actually, I could use some water. I feel like I'm still dehydrated from last weekend."

"Hiking in the heat will do that to you." Avery slipped into the kitchen only a few steps away.

Boots, Avery's black-and-white cat, jumped onto the sofa and curled up against Katie. Her fur was the softest thing Katie had ever touched.

Avery's flat above the clinic was small and homey, decorated mostly in neutrals with a pop of color here and there. It suited her friend. It was neat and tidy except the dining room table, which was cluttered with Robinson-for-Sheriff promotional materials.

Katie's mind went back to this morning as it had done all afternoon while she gardened and caught up on chores. It wasn't even the meeting with her mother that claimed her thoughts, though that had gone better than she'd expected.

It was seeing Cooper with that woman—Amber. Katie remembered Lisa mentioning the hairstylist's interest. Cooper had apparently decided to take Lisa's advice and move things forward.

But seeing him with Amber had gutted Katie. Even now the memory of them together made her feel hollow inside. She had no right to be jealous. But that didn't negate the fact that she was. Amber was beautiful and she practically radiated confidence. No wonder the woman had caught Cooper's eye. Katie had felt like a slouch even though she'd taken care with her appearance. She pulled Boots into her arms and cradled him against her stomach.

"What's wrong?" Avery set a glass of ice water on the coffee table for her.

Katie dredged up a smile and took the last bite of her brownie. "Nothing. Just getting tired, I guess."

"It's not even ten, but I'm tired too. We must be getting old. Have another brownie."

"I've already had two. Remember how late we

stayed up at college? We were just getting started at ten."

"Yeah, those all-night study sessions while everyone else partied."

"That's why you made it into med school and I made it into the nursing program."

Avery raised her milk in a toast. "To hard work paying off."

Katie clinked her glass. "Hear, hear."

They reminisced about college awhile, then the conversation turned to the clinic and some of the patients who had come in that week.

"Can I ask you a question?" Avery said after they'd exhausted the topic.

"Sure."

"If a serious genetic disorder ran in your family . . . would you want to know if you carried the gene?"

"I'm not sure. It's difficult to know something like that until you're faced with it. Are you talking about one of our patients? I didn't come across anything like that in the files."

"She, uh, wants to keep it private for now."

Fair enough. It was a small town, and Avery probably knew the patient personally. "Is it a serious condition?"

Avery gave a nod. "Huntington's disease."

That was serious. "Has she had genetic counseling?"

"Yes."

"Well, I don't think there's a pat answer for everyone. It's something each person has to decide for him or herself."

Avery popped the last of her brownie into her mouth. "You're right."

"And further complicated if she has children to take into consideration."

"Children definitely complicate the issue."

It was a heavy decision to make, and Katie was glad the woman had confided in Avery. Especially if she didn't have anyone else to talk about it with. Huntington's disease was a fatal genetic disorder with an onset of symptoms in the thirties or forties. The probability of offspring inheriting the disorder was 50 percent, and there was no cure.

"It's me," Avery said.

"What's you?" Her gaze locked on Avery's, and the meaning of her words hit Katie like a tidal wave. A sudden coldness swept through her. Avery's dad was almost sixty, but her mom had died when Avery was a child. Katie couldn't remember Avery ever telling her how.

Katie's breath tumbled out. "Your mom had Huntington's?"

"Yes." Avery's hand was steady as she took a sip of milk.

Katie couldn't wrap her mind around the fact that Avery might have this horrible disease. "Oh, Avery."

"It's not like I haven't known this all my life. I just couldn't decide what to do about it. I thought the counseling would help—I went through that after undergrad—but the pros and cons of knowing the truth seemed equally balanced."

"I can't even imagine what I'd do. On the one hand, if you did the test and found out you hadn't inherited the gene, you'd be free and clear."

"But if I found out I did have it . . . I'd know exactly what's in store for me. I watched my mom go through it. The depression and personality changes, the involuntary movements, and inability to care for herself . . ." Avery swallowed, then her gaze met Katie's. "In the last year I've finally come to a conclusion: I don't want to know if I have it. It feels a little cowardly."

"Not at all. I can completely understand that. It would be hard not to spend your life dreading its onset. What does your family think?"

"We don't really talk about it. They don't want me to feel pressured to make a decision. I haven't told anyone else I'm not taking the test, so I'd appreciate it if you wouldn't mention it to Gavin. I'll tell them when I'm ready."

"Of course. And Avery . . . I'm here for you whenever you need to talk."

"Thanks."

Katie met her friend's smile with one of her own. But inside her heart felt as if it had been crushed.

22

It had not been a good day. Cooper hunched over the report on the cheap metal desk, scrawling as quickly as he could. The aroma of popcorn and stale coffee permeated the space, and the window air conditioner hummed over the intermittent calls coming in to Jackie's office down the hall. Six deputies shared two desks and two computers in the tight ten-by-twelve space, but he was the only one in the office at the moment.

This afternoon's traffic accident was still fresh in his mind. A man texting while driving had caused two likely totaled cars and three injuries, one of them a child. It wasn't a pretty ending to his workweek.

Earlier in the day he'd been called to the hardware store where an eighteen-year-old man was causing a ruckus. Cooper arrested the guy on a disorderly charge and found a stash of heroin in his pocket.

Following that, he'd had to serve divorce papers to a woman who had three young kids huddled around her legs. Upon sight of him at her front door, she burst into tears.

Cooper's mom entered the office, startling him from his thoughts. She gave him that pointed look mothers everywhere had down pat. "All right, out with it. What's going on?"

"Hi, Mom. Just finishing up some paperwork. How are you doing?"

"That's not what I meant and you know it. I haven't seen you in three weeks."

"Sorry. I meant to stop by, but I've been busy with work and the campaign." It wasn't a lie. A week ago the *Herald* had endorsed Sean Curtis, raising the stakes yet again. There was so much more riding on this than a county office. Katelyn had helped him see that.

"I'll make it over sometime this weekend."

"No, you'll make it over tomorrow night for supper like everyone else."

He opened his mouth with a ready excuse.

"And don't tell me you have a campaign obligation because Avery already told me you don't. I'm not taking no for an answer this time."

"What if I have a date tomorrow night?"

"You're going out with Amber on Sunday so that's highly unlikely."

Darn that grapevine. Why hadn't he made a preemptive stop to see his mom and Jeff before now? Now he had no choice but to see Kate again. Not that avoiding her had done much good. She was constantly on his mind. Maybe she wouldn't come.

He signed the report and set it aside. "All right. I'll be there."

"What is it with you? Why have you been avoiding us?"

"I'm not avoiding you."

Her gaze sharpened on him. "Is there something going on between you and Gavin?"

"Why? Did he say something?"

"No, but something must be up. You never miss the chance for a home-cooked meal, and now you've missed supper three weeks in a row. Gavin won't even be there if that makes a difference."

It made all the difference. If Gavin wasn't there, Kate wouldn't be there either. "It's not that. There's just a lot involved in running a campaign." He held eye contact. He was pretty good at being unreadable—it came with the job—but when it came to her sons, his mom had some kind of superhero radar.

"If you need more help, you know the family's here for you."

"I know you guys are busy with Trail Days. Anyway, Avery and I have it covered."

Rodriguez entered the office, his eyes going straight to Lisa, his lips lifting in a cheeky smile. "Hello, Mrs. Robinson. You sure are a sight for sore eyes."

"Oh, you're too sweet, Ricky. Is there a serious girlfriend on the horizon yet? If not, you should let me set you up. I'm pretty good at it, despite what Cooper might think."

"Aw, I'm still too brokenhearted that you're taken. Why'd you have to go and get married before I grew up?"

Cooper rolled his eyes at Rodriguez's familiar antics.

His mom laughed and patted his shoulder. "I'm practically old enough to be your mother."

"You don't look a day over twenty-five."

"Listen to the lies coming out of your mouth, young man. I should tell your mother."

"If you ever change your mind—"

"Did you come here to work or flirt?" Cooper asked.

"I don't see why a man can't do both."

"You're too much, Ricky." His mother hitched her purse higher on her shoulder and gave Cooper another pointed look. "I have to run now. I'll see you tomorrow night."

"Yes, Mother."

"It's a carry-in this time so bring a side dish." She smiled at Rodriguez. "You're welcome to come, too, Ricky. That is, if you don't have a hot date."

"He's busy," Cooper said.

As soon as Mom left, Cooper grabbed the stress ball off his desk and hurled it at Rodriguez, who was watching her walk down the hallway.

The ball thwacked the deputy on the shoulder. "Hey!"

"Stop hitting on my mom."

. . .

Katie's heart gave a start when the knock came at the door.

"Would you mind getting that, honey?" Lisa called from the kitchen where she was pouring iced tea into glasses.

"Not at all." Katie's legs trembled as she stood from the armchair and approached the front door. For three weeks she'd managed to keep Beth and Lisa apart. But Lisa more or less insisted on meeting the woman who was heading up the online marketing for Trail Days, and resisting would've seemed odd.

So here she was, about to introduce Lisa to her birth mother, only no one—except Cooper—knew who she really was. How did she get herself into these messes?

Katie arranged her features into a welcoming expression and pulled open the door. "Hello, Beth."

The woman's lips split into a warm smile. "Hi, Katie. I hope I'm not late."

"You're right on time. Come on in."

Beth swept past her, that citrusy scent now familiar in a pleasant way. They'd met up last week to go over the social media plan Beth had put into place. Katie had tried to explain it to Lisa, and that's where she'd gone wrong. Marketing wasn't her forte, and she'd done nothing but confuse Lisa.

As soon as Beth and Katie took seats in the living room, Lisa swept into the room with a tray of drinks, ice clinking in the glasses with each step. The women exchanged pleasantries as Lisa handed each woman a glass, then they got down to business.

"It's so nice of you to pitch in like this," Lisa said. "I've already seen an uptick in visits to the Trail Days website."

"I'm glad to hear that. There's been a lot of interest in the posts. You won't regret diverting your advertising budget to online ads. Newspaper ads are something we refer to as 'spray and pray,' meaning that you're targeting a lot of people but no one in particular. Online ads allow us to target people with specific interests like hiking, the Appalachian Trail, or festivals in general. I've also narrowed down the target audience geographically. And all those people who visit your website . . . I'm retargeting them with ads."

"Well, that just sounds wonderful," Lisa said, "even if I don't have the least idea how you're going about such a thing."

"You don't have to worry about the particulars. That's my job. I just want to give back to this community for everything it's given to me."

"Well, who am I to turn away help?"

Beth spent a while explaining her strategy, and Lisa seemed satisfied with her explanations and the cost of online advertising.

Katie let the ladies talk since she didn't have much to add to the conversation. She shifted in her seat, antsy to have Beth gone. Being with her birth mother was awkward and scary enough without adding other people—people she cared about—to the mix.

"How long have you lived in Riverbend, Beth?" The question jerked Katie from her reverie.

"Seven years this fall."

"What brought you here? Do you have family around these parts?"

"No, unfortunately. My parents have passed and I never married."

Katie tensed, waiting for a mention of children.

But just then Jeff came through the door. He greeted the women, gave his wife a kiss on the cheek, then excused himself to shower.

"Goodness." Lisa glanced at her watch. "That hour sure slid right on by. Why don't you stay for supper, Beth? We always have more than enough."

Katie's stomach twisted in a knot. She'd been so careful in what she mentioned to Beth. She wasn't ready to reveal the truth to her mother. The Robinsons knew she was from Asheville and that she'd been a foster child. What if someone gave away too much? Sweat broke out on the back of her neck.

"Oh, I don't want to be in the way," Beth said.

"Nonsense. The more the merrier. Katie's

staying—she's dating our son. Our daughter, Avery, will be here and our deputy son, Cooper, is coming too—he's running for sheriff."

"I've seen the signs around town," Beth said. "How wonderful. Well, if you're sure. I don't have any other plans, and I set a mean table."

"We'll put you right to work then. It's only a Chinet kind of occasion though."

"My favorite kind," Beth said.

Since it wasn't too hot outside, they set the picnic table on the back porch, working together as they chatted about a little bit of nothing. Katie's pulse raced as she waited for the other shoe to drop. She should have at least told Avery about her mom. They'd grown closer since Katie had moved to Riverbend. And after all, Avery had confided in her about the possible genetic defect. But it was hard for Katie. There was still some part of her that felt deeply ashamed that her mother had chosen substance abuse over her.

She wished she could come up with an excuse to leave, but that wouldn't fix anything. At least if she was here she had some control over the conversation.

By the time the table was set, Avery had arrived and Jeff rejoined them. Beth remem-bered Avery from the clinic. Cooper was the last to arrive. Katie hadn't seen him since the coffee shop run-in two weeks ago, and her heart stuttered at the sight of him.

He must've gone home to shower because the hair at his nape was damp. He looked fresh in a crisp white T-shirt that stretched over his broad shoulders. When his eyes locked on hers and his lips tipped in a smile, she could hardly breathe.

"Hey, Katelyn."

Oh, she'd missed that voice. "Hi."

He set his dish on the table and came up beside Katie, catching sight of Beth. He shot a glance at Katie and back, recovering quickly. "Hi there."

"Cooper," Lisa said. "This is Beth Wallace, a friend of Katie's. She's doing wonders for our online marketing for Trail Days."

"That's great. Nice to meet you, ma'am."

"My pleasure." Beth glanced between Katie and Cooper. "Well, don't you two make the cutest couple."

The temperature in Katie's cheeks shot up by ten degrees. "Oh . . . no, we're not—"

"Together," Cooper finished.

"She's dating our other son, Gavin, who can't make it tonight." Lisa patted Cooper's shoulder. "We're still working on getting this one to settle down."

"I'm so sorry," Beth said. "I just thought . . ."

"No worries," Jeff said.

Avery dropped an arm around Katie's shoulder. "Katie fits in around here so well we're always happy to have her, Gavin or no."

"She's like family already." Lisa beamed. "All right, the food smells great. And Cooper even made an actual dish."

"Well, well." Avery took her place at the table. "Green bean casserole. Where's the standard bag of chips?"

Cooper sat across from Katie and gave Avery a mock scowl.

"Your recipe repertoire is expanding," Jeff said. "Must be getting tired of pizza and Hot Pockets."

"I can follow a recipe."

"But it's ever so much easier to have a woman cook for you," Avery teased.

He probably had women inviting him over for meals all the time. Trying to impress him with their culinary skills.

After Jeff said grace they all dug in. As usual conversation flowed easily, quickly hopping from one topic to another. They did a good job of including their guest in the exchange.

After they finished eating there was a brief lull in conversation. Avery pushed back her plate. "Do you have any kids, Beth?"

Katie's fork froze halfway to her mouth. Would her mother admit to having children? Or would she deny Katie's existence? She was suddenly unsure if she wanted to know the answer.

Beth's face had drained of color. She cleared her throat in the sudden silence. "I do, actually. But . . . I'm afraid it's a little complicated."

"Don't mind Avery," Cooper said. "She's too inquisitive for her own good."

Katie could've kissed him for smoothing over the moment. But she couldn't help but wonder if Beth would've continued the story if pressed.

"Sorry," Avery said. "Didn't mean to be nosy."

Beth gave her a warm smile. "Not at all."

"It's her curiosity that drove her into med school, I think," Lisa said. "She loves solving problems. Katie, honey, would you mind getting the banana pudding from the fridge?"

"Of course not." She wasted no time getting up from the table. Her face felt like it was on fire, and her legs trembled as she made her way up the steps and through the back door.

23

Cooper frowned at Kate's back as she retreated. He couldn't have been more surprised to find her birth mother here, and judging by Kate's nervous demeanor, it hadn't been her choice. Conversation at the table resumed, but he could only think about what Katelyn must be dealing with.

His mom fetched another water bottle. "Oh, Cooper, could you run inside and get the dessert cups? They're above the stove. Katie won't be able to reach them."

"Sure, Mom." Relieved for the chance to check on Kate, he made his way across the patio and up the steps. The patio door swung open silently.

He found her hunched over the sink, head hanging low. "Hey, you okay?"

She whirled around, bearing a forced smile, and reached for the fridge handle. "Yeah, of course. I'm fine."

He placed a hand flat against the door. "Don't do that. You don't have to pretend with me. I know this must be hard for you."

Her face fell and her shoulders sagged a good two inches. "I didn't intend for this to happen. For her to get in the middle of your family. It's so awkward. She volunteered to help with Trail Days, and your mom wanted to meet her, then she invited her to stay for supper and—"

"It'll be okay. Nobody knows a thing."

"That's the problem, though, isn't it? What if someone says something and she figures out who I am? It'll ruin everything." Kate's eyes grew glassy.

He slid his hand over hers. "Come on now. That's not going to happen. Let's just get through the meal. It's almost over and I'll help out where I can."

"But what about next time? She'll be working on Trail Days for the next month, and Lisa will want updates. This is getting so messy."

"Let's not borrow trouble. Mom doesn't know anything about you that would give you away."

"I should've at least told Avery about her. She's going to be hurt when she finds out I kept this from her."

"This is your private business. It's up to you when to share it—not anyone else."

"I haven't told Gavin yet either."

"Well, he hasn't told you about Jesse yet, has he?"

Relief washed over her features. "No."

He loved that he could read her so well. She wore her feelings like a neon sign. "Try not to take that personally, by the way. He doesn't talk about Jesse with anyone. He's still dealing with a lot of guilt."

He was still holding Kate's hand. He should

probably let go, but he couldn't seem to make his muscles cooperate.

"Your relationship with your mom is intensely personal—I can see that. Childhood wounds go deep. She broke your trust in the worst way, and you have a right to get to know her at your own pace. If you find she's worthy of your trust, you can tell her who you are. If not . . . you don't owe her anything, Katelyn."

A weight seemed to fall away from her. "Yeah. Thanks. I seem to keep forgetting that."

"For what it's worth, she seems pretty nice."

"Not at all like a woman who would abandon her kids and never look back, huh?"

"Drugs do terrible things to people." Unfortunately he saw it all the time on his job. "But she's off them now."

"She admitted she had kids . . ." Kate's gaze clung to his, impossibly blue. Impossibly hopeful.

If that woman hurt Kate again, he'd hunt her down himself. "She was honest. That's something, I guess."

"I was so afraid she'd say no. I didn't think I could take it if she just . . . acted like we never even existed."

"Well, that didn't happen. But even if it did, you're a strong woman, Kate. You can handle whatever comes your way."

She offered a tiny smile. Her eyes beamed at him with warmth and affection that soaked right through his skin. "You always say the nicest things."

Of its own volition, his hand palmed her cheek. He was only a breath away. He took in her lovely features. Those almond-shaped eyes, the smattering of freckles on her nose, the sweet curve of her mouth. How had he made it two weeks without seeing her? It was like coming up for oxygen after holding his breath for five minutes underwater. Suddenly he could breathe again.

"It's the truth," he said softly.

Somewhere behind him feet shuffled to a stop.

He stepped away and glanced over his shoulder.

Avery stood on the kitchen threshold, gaze toggling between them. "What's going on?"

"Nothing." He turned and opened the cupboard over the stove. "Just helping Kate with the dessert dishes."

She arched a brow at him. "'Kate,' huh?"

The fridge opened behind him with a sucking sound. "Oh wow. This looks delicious."

"Need some help?" Avery's voice was tight.

"I got it." The air stirred as Kate brushed past him. A moment later the door clicked shut behind her.

Cooper pulled down two stacks of glass dessert dishes. He wasn't looking forward to the coming confrontation. He knew how that moment with Kate must've seemed. And he couldn't even admit she was in the middle of a crisis because Avery would want details.

"What was that about?"

"What was what about?"

"Don't insult my intelligence. You were holding her hand and touching her face, and she was staring at you like . . ."

It was a sad state of affairs that he desperately wanted her to finish that sentence. "You don't know what you're talking about. Here, make yourself useful." He handed her one of the stacks.

When he tried to pass she grabbed his arm. "Cooper, you need to answer me. That's our brother's girlfriend you were ogling."

"I haven't forgotten, Avery."

"Well, excuse me, but it kind of seems like you have."

For crying out loud, he was doing his level best. How many times had he resisted pulling Kate into his arms and kissing her senseless? Didn't he get any credit for that?

He jerked his arm away and headed toward the door. When he reached it he turned. A question burbled in his throat until he couldn't hold it back any longer. "Just tell me one thing, Avery. Why'd you set her up with Gavin and not me?"

She gave her head a shake. "Seriously?"

"What? I'm not good enough for her?"

"Come on, Cooper. You run through women like I run through latex gloves."

He flinched. "Maybe I'm just particular, ever think of that?"

"Cooper, please. You can't do this to Gavin."

"I'm not doing anything, Avery. There's nothing going on." He pinned her with a long, unswerving look, then proceeded outside.

As Gavin walked Katie to her car, quiet chatter carried from neighboring campsites, and crickets chirped from someplace nearby. She crossed her arms against the breeze that brushed her skin. She felt bad staying only an hour, but she was tired.

At the car she turned, yawning. "Sorry. I promise I'll be more lively tomorrow night."

"You've had a long day. How'd that meeting go with Mom and the marketing lady? You never said."

"It went well, I think." This would be a great time to mention that Beth was actually her mother, but it was late and she didn't want to get into it tonight. "She seems to be drumming up a lot of interest in Trail Days. Your mom's pretty excited about it."

"I appreciate everything you're doing to help her."

"Your mom's a doll. I might just be willing to walk through fire for her."

Gavin chuckled as he set his hands on Katie's waist. "She has that effect on people. Look out . . . We Robinsons are pretty addictive."

"I noticed that." She gave him a cheeky smile but found herself thinking of Cooper instead.

"You did, huh?" Gavin leaned close and gave her a sweet, lingering kiss. As usual it was technically perfect, soft and slow, never sloppy or rushed. Altogether pleasant.

He eased away. "Go home and get some rest. I'll see you tomorrow night."

On the way home Katie reflected on her fireside chat with Gavin. There'd been a moment when he brought up the end of his marriage. He mentioned Laurel by name and referred to the mounting tension that preceded their divorce. He stared at Katie, the glow of the campfire flickering in his sad eyes, and she was sure he was going to tell her about Jesse. But he looked away, his jaw knotting with emotion.

Katie's heart squeezed tight at his struggle. Poor guy. He was trying. She kissed the back of his hand and said a little prayer that God would give him peace.

Even as Katie turned in to her driveway, the melancholy lingered in her mind. Once inside her house she checked her phone. A text from Avery had come in while she was at the campground.

Can I swing by tonight?

Gravel popped in Katie's driveway, rattling her nerves. It didn't take a genius to figure out what

213

this impromptu visit was about. A moment later she opened the door as Avery ascended the porch steps.

Her friend's tepid greeting was less than encouraging.

"Come on in." She moved aside as Avery brushed past. Katie decided to cut to the chase. "I can guess why you're here, but let me assure you, there's nothing to worry about."

"I know it's none of my business, but I can't seem to help myself."

"Have a seat. Want something to drink?"

"No, I want you to put me out of my misery." They settled on the sofa. "All I can think about is Gavin getting his heart broken again and you—my best friend—right in the middle of it all."

"That's the last thing I want."

"I saw the look on your face, Katie. And the way Cooper was touching you. And in case I haven't warned you, he has commitment issues."

Katie resisted the urge to defend him. Maybe he did date around, but he was as authentic as any man she'd ever known. "I won't deny that there's a connection between Cooper and me. We've been through a couple of emotional events together."

"Okay . . . That's true enough. I can see where that might engender some kind of bond."

"Exactly. But nothing's going to happen between us."

"So . . . are you saying you feel close to him but just as a brother?"

Katie opened her mouth to respond. But nothing came out. She didn't think of him that way at all. But she couldn't find the words to articulate it in a way that would reassure Avery.

The silence drew out between them, tension growing as it lengthened.

Avery's face fell. "Oh boy."

"No, there's no 'oh boy.' Everything is fine. I care for Gavin, I really do. I would never betray him." She meant that with everything in her. His expression tonight when he'd almost brought up Jesse had a powerful impact on her.

She'd deal with her feelings for Cooper. She'd avoid family gatherings awhile. Suffocate these futile feelings simmering for Cooper until there was nothing left but cold ash.

"It's just that—he's been through so much, Katie."

"I know that. You don't have to worry about this. Really."

Avery held her gaze steadily for a long moment, then let out a breath. "Okay. I'm so relieved. Ever since I walked into that kitchen tonight, I've been worried sick our family was about to implode."

"I would never do that. I love your family. And you have plenty on your plate right now without dreaming up concerns."

"You're right. Sorry. I should've trusted you

more. I know you'd never cheat on Gavin or anyone else for that matter."

Katie smiled but guilt pinched hard. Because even though she hadn't actually cheated on Gavin, her mind had already gone places that made her unfaithful.

24

The Trailhead Bar and Grill buzzed with conversation and excitement tonight. Silverware clinked and clattered against plates, and the scent of grilling burgers made Katie's stomach growl. Music pumped through the speakers, but a local band was almost finished setting up. They were playing to a packed house tonight.

Gavin leaned over the four-top. "Know what you want yet?"

"It's definitely the campfire burger for me."

Gavin glanced around for their server, but she was scurrying back to the kitchen as fast as her legs would carry her.

"They're understaffed tonight," Gavin said. "But that's okay. We'll be here awhile. Let's get an appetizer. I'm starving."

"Sounds good."

Gavin waved at someone across the room. The Robinsons seemed to know everyone. Since she'd started dating Gavin she met so many people, and she loved feeling like part of the community. It seemed when you were accepted by the Robinsons, everyone else accepted you too.

More people flooded into the restaurant's foyer. It was already standing room only, and the band hadn't even started yet.

"Seems like half the town turned out tonight," she called across the table.

"Silver Spurs is a favorite. They always draw a crowd. What's Avery doing tonight?"

"I don't know. Probably getting some paperwork done."

"She never goes out anymore. She used to love this band."

"She's busy with the clinic and campaign," Katie said even though she had the same concerns about her friend. Especially now that she knew more of Avery's struggles.

"We should set her up with someone. I'm worried about her. When she's not working or campaigning she holes up in her apartment. And as far as I know she hasn't had a boyfriend since college."

Katie gave him a pointed look. "Not that she needs a boyfriend to be happy."

"Of course not." He winked at her. "But having someone you care about sure doesn't hurt."

"Fair enough. But Avery doesn't seem interested in dating right now. She's busy building her business."

"She could do both at once."

"You know your sister . . . She's focused and driven."

"Maybe you're right." Gavin glanced around the room. "I don't see our server anywhere. I'm going to run up to the bar and grab us some drinks."

Katie watched him weave through the tables, then glanced around the packed restaurant, the busy bar, and the teeming lobby. Her eyes doubled back to a familiar face in the crowd.

Cooper. And right at his side—because the universe just couldn't resist sending happy little surprises her way—was Amber Clarke.

This night was not going his way. Cooper frowned at the crowd in the lobby. It would be at least an hour before he and Amber got a table—if that, since everyone would hang around for the band. He couldn't even locate the hostess to put their name in.

And something was going on with his date tonight. Amber had seemed distant since he picked her up fifteen minutes ago. He asked if she was okay, and she said she was "fine." On the way over he tried to make small talk, tried to draw her out. But all he knew so far was that she wasn't "fine" and that he had no clue what the problem was.

"Coop!" a voice called out.

He spotted his brother several feet away in the queue at the bar and inched closer, Amber in tow.

Gavin greeted them and turned back to Cooper, all but shouting over the music. "You guys staying?"

"We were hoping to but . . ." Cooper looked pointedly around the crowded lobby.

"We've got room at our table. Come sit with us."

Us. Cooper scanned the restaurant and his gaze homed in on Kate. He opened his mouth, a refusal on his lips.

But Amber spoke first. "That'd be so great. My feet are killing me."

"Perfect. We haven't even ordered yet."

Gavin took their drink orders, then Cooper and Amber headed toward the maze of tables. On the way they passed groups of people he knew, and he paused briefly by each table to chat a minute, introducing Amber, who actually did seem "fine" when she was talking to other people.

By the time they reached their table, Gavin was already seated. When Kate spotted him, her smile didn't quite reach her eyes.

"Hey." Cooper glanced between the couple. "Sure you guys don't mind the company?"

"Glad you showed up. Right, Katie?"

"The more the merrier." The words were more welcoming than her tone.

This would be fun. Fortunately, the band was about ready to play and would serve as a nice distraction.

The server showed up a few minutes later, harried and distracted. They gave their orders as the band kicked into their first rousing country song, and the noise level went up several decibels. He was all kinds of grateful that conversation would be almost impossible.

Gavin and Kate pulled their chairs together and turned them to better see the stage. He slipped an arm around her, cupping her bare shoulder, and his thumb stroked her neck.

Cooper clenched his teeth.

They listened to the band awhile, Cooper attempting to keep a tight rein on his attention. Otherwise, it drifted automatically to Katelyn. He cursed his excellent peripheral vision because he could still see every touch, every glimpse. Sitting at their table had been a mistake. He should've taken Amber someplace else. But then he'd be suffering through this cold-shoulder business without any distractions.

When the band segued into a slow song, Gavin pulled Kate to her feet. They headed toward the dance floor where he drew her close. Gavin slid his arm around her waist, settled his hand low on her back, and positioned his foot between hers. As the lead singer crooned about a broken heart, Kate rested her head on Gavin's shoulder.

Cooper forced his gaze away from the couple, but he couldn't unsee that cozy picture. Couldn't stop the jealousy twisting his gut. For about two seconds he entertained the idea of asking Amber to dance, but given her current mood he didn't think she'd consent. He did, however, need to get to the bottom of this.

He scooted his chair closer and leaned in. "Are you going to tell me what's bothering you?"

She ignored him for several long seconds.

Was she just going to pretend she hadn't heard him? If so, this would be their last date. He didn't care for the silent treatment much less outright disregard.

But a few beats later she spoke, her eyes still fixed on the band. "Megan Taylor came into the salon this afternoon." Her tone was conversational.

Okay . . . He'd gone out with Megan a couple times in April, and as he'd told Gavin, it had ended badly. "I thought she moved to Mars Hill."

"She did."

He wasn't sure where Amber was going with this. She couldn't be jealous, could she? When he'd gone out with Megan he didn't even know Amber. Maybe Megan knew he and Amber were talking now and had baited her somehow. It was possible she was that spiteful.

Finally Amber turned to him, but her sunny smile was nowhere to be seen. "When were you going to tell me, Cooper?"

"Tell you what?"

She gave him a withering look. "I know about the baby. For heaven's sake—she's *showing*."

Cooper blinked. "What?"

Amber rolled her eyes. "Save the innocent act. I know we only just barely started dating, but this isn't a small thing. I don't even know why I came out with you tonight." She started to get up.

He grabbed her. "Wait."

She sank back onto the chair and stared pointedly at his hand.

He loosened his grip. "First of all, I don't have any idea what you're talking about. If Megan's pregnant I didn't know anything about it. I haven't spoken to her since she moved away. And why would you just assume the baby's mine? We went out two times. We sure didn't sleep together."

She leaned forward, pinning him with an accusatory glare. "I know the baby's yours, Cooper. She said so. Everyone in the salon heard her."

Cooper fell back in his chair. Coldness swept through him even as sweat broke out on the back of his neck. *"What?"*

Her eyes glittered. "You're seriously going to sit here and deny it?"

"Because it's not true!"

"Wow. I thought you'd at least man up. I knew you had a problem with committing, but I thought deep down you were a good guy."

"Are you serious right now?"

"I was willing to hang in there. I mean, mistakes happen, and I really thought we might have something here."

Anger blazed inside him. He leaned toward her. "I did not sleep with Megan."

"I never took you for a liar, Cooper." Amber jerked her arm from his grip and stood. "I can find my own way home."

He watched Amber storm off, his head spinning. Had Megan really told Amber he'd gotten her pregnant? Could she be that dishonest? That spiteful? Or was it possible Amber had misunderstood somehow?

"Everyone in the salon heard her."

Cooper's gut clenched at the ramifications. He ran a hand over his face. If Amber was telling the truth—and he had no reason to disbelieve her—the rumor would be all over town in days.

His reputation would suffer. Not that it was a crime to get a woman pregnant out of wedlock, but folks around here were a little old-fashioned. Shoot, *he* was old-fashioned. He couldn't imagine getting a woman pregnant out of wedlock—but if he did he'd sure enough own up to it.

But he hadn't done anything!

Heat swamped him from the inside out. Sweat trickled down his spine.

The server appeared and began unloading her tray. But when she set his rib platter in front of him, the tangy scent of barbeque sauce only made his stomach turn.

25

As the last strains of the ballad drew out, Gavin pressed a kiss to the top of Katie's head. Beyond his shoulder she had a clear view of Cooper. He hunched over the table, brow furrowed, jaw clenched. His date had just stormed off. What had upset Amber so much?

"Food's at the table." Gavin led her through the throng of people on the dance floor.

Once they reached the table Katie paused. "I have to use the restroom. Don't wait for me."

"Hurry back," Gavin said.

Cooper frowned at his plate, seemingly unaware they'd even returned.

She skirted the people and tables, heading toward the short hall on the other side of the room. Where had Amber gone and why? Had she and Cooper broken things off? And why was Katie so buoyed by the other woman's departure?

Inside the restroom the bass guitar thumped through the wood walls, and the cloying scent of sweet perfume hung in the air. She couldn't get her mind off Cooper. He'd been so distracted when they returned to the table. Maybe he had real feelings for Amber despite the newness of their relationship. Otherwise, why would he be so upset by her departure?

The thought rankled.

As she washed her hands she found herself wishing Gavin wasn't there so she could talk to Cooper. She glanced at her reflection in the mirror, noting her flushed cheeks and sparkling eyes.

Stop thinking about him. He'd probably had the server box up his food so he could leave. He was probably on his way out the door right this minute.

She dried her hands and left the restroom, the music reverberating in her ears. She stopped short at the sight of Cooper standing in the hall a few feet away, frowning at his phone.

"What's wrong?"

He startled. An instant later the crease in his brows smoothed as he pocketed his phone. "Nothing. You ready to eat?"

"You don't have to pretend with me." She repeated his words from yesterday, holding his gaze.

His facial muscles slowly relaxed. He glanced down the hall, the dim light from the adjoining room glowing on his features. "Amber just told me something that—Never mind. It's absurd."

"What is it?"

A shadow flickered in his jaw. "Λ woman I went out with back in the spring, Megan Taylor, came into the Beauty Barn today where Amber works. She's pregnant—and she's apparently telling people the baby's mine."

Katie's stomach bottomed out. Someone else was pregnant with Cooper's child. That was a game changer. Not for her, of course, but for him. But if that were true, why did she feel as if he'd just punched her in the heart? "I see."

He pinned her with an intense look. "No, you don't see. It can't be mine. I never even slept with her."

A wave of relief washed through her—big red flag. But there was no time to pick apart her feelings. "Have you talked to Megan? Maybe it's some kind of . . . misunderstanding?"

"I was just about to call her. I can't believe this is happening."

"Are you sure there's no possibility that you could've . . ."

"Not unless it's another immaculate conception."

"Right." Katie's cheeks went hot. "Well, then you have nothing to worry about."

A group of women passed by, talking loudly.

Once they were inside the restroom, Cooper leaned closer, the furrows back in place. "She's telling people I'm the father. Everyone at the Beauty Barn heard her say it."

Katie frowned. "Why would she do that?"

He withdrew his phone again, scowling. "That's what I'm about to find out."

This had to be hard for him. She knew he cared about his reputation more than most because of the way his father had embarrassed him. She placed a hand on his arm, noting the delicious feel of hard muscle beneath flesh. *You're a terrible person, Katie Loveland.* "Maybe you should call her from someplace more private."

As if to underscore her point, a man pushed past on his way to the restroom.

"You're right. I'd go to her house if I knew her new address. I guess it's a good thing I forgot to delete her from my phone. I can't believe she's doing this."

"Maybe there's some kind of reasonable explanation."

"I can't think what it would be." He stared at Katie, his expression shifting subtly before he stared at the floor.

"What?"

His gaze returned to hers, his expression adorably uncertain. "Do you believe me?"

"Yes, of course I do." She'd never known him to be anything but honest. "Why wouldn't I?"

"Funny you should ask. Amber took off like a bat out of hell when I denied it."

Her heart squeezed tight. "I'm sorry. I'm sorry this is happening to you."

"Thanks. I knew there was something about Megan . . . I don't think this is a mistake."

"Well, you'll know more after you make that phone call. Did you tell Gavin?"

"Not yet. I want to find out what's going on first."

"Okay, I won't say anything."

"Thanks." He tried for a smile and came up a little short. "And thanks for talking it out with me."

"I'll be praying it all works out."

As Cooper drove home anger churned in his stomach. He took several deep breaths. He had to calm down, keep his head when he talked to Megan.

He tried to give Megan the benefit of the doubt. Maybe Amber had misheard Megan. Maybe she was desperate for a baby daddy. Maybe she was mentally ill and actually believed he was the father. Maybe *Amber* was mentally ill and made the whole thing up. Maybe it hadn't been Megan at the salon at all but her long-lost twin sister out for revenge. He gave his head a shake. He'd wandered into soap opera territory with that one.

He recalled the moment Katelyn had found him in the hallway. He almost didn't tell her. He only now realized why that was: he was terrified she wouldn't believe him. Amber's disbelief had made him angry, but Kate's disbelief . . . That would gut him.

But she did believe him. The thought soothed him, and the anger that had flared up burned a little dimmer.

But a few minutes later when he got home and called Megan, his fury ignited again. The woman's number had been disconnected.

26

Katie was dying to know how Cooper's phone call had gone.

She changed into her pajamas and slid into bed, her thoughts spinning. It had been so hard sitting at the Trailhead, trying to be a good date, when she wanted nothing more than to reach out to Cooper. But Gavin wanted to stay until the band played two sets, and now it was almost eleven thirty. Probably too late to call Cooper or even text.

She grabbed her phone off the nightstand, propped her pillows, and stared at the home screen—a photo of Spencer and her. Should she text Cooper? She only had his number because she'd called him once about returning a shirt she'd borrowed on their hike. She'd ended up dropping it off on his porch.

Her fingers hovered over the texting app. She was worried about him. He'd been understandably upset. She opened the app, clicked on his name, and began typing.

Hi, it's Katie. How did it go?

He was probably asleep. After all, it was a work night and he had to be up early. Yet so did she, and here she was.

Three dots appeared in the text box. Katie waited, her pulse kicking up a notch.

Hi Kate. It didn't. Her number was disconnected. I know someone who might have it though. I'll try again tomorrow.

Why would she do this to you? Was there an ugly breakup or something?

We only went out a couple times. But yes, it was a little ugly. I caught her in a lie and called her on it. She got nasty with me.

Oh no. Would she do this out of spite? That seems extreme. Maybe she just changed her number when she moved.

I don't see why she would. I just hope the rumor doesn't spread before I can get a handle on this.

She'd been here long enough to know the Riverbend grapevine was alive and well.

Have you told anyone in your family yet?

I'd like to talk to Megan before I do that. Make sure there hasn't been some kind of misunderstanding on Amber's part.

Is there anything I can do?

Three dots appeared in the space. They blinked
and blinked. Was he going to respond?
Finally his reply popped up.

> You've been great Kate.
> I could use your prayers.

Her heart gave a tug.

You've got them.

27

The sun was barely up when Cooper knocked on Megan's apartment door. He'd awakened at o-dark-thirty this morning and couldn't go back to sleep, so he showered and dressed in street clothes. It only took a few minutes on Google to locate Megan's new residence in Mars Hill.

He didn't let the early hour keep him from knocking hard and loud on the door. It was possible she wasn't home but unlikely; her white Camry was out front. He didn't care if he woke Megan up. He didn't even care if he woke every neighbor in the building.

The apartment building was located in a questionable part of town. Its dingy walls needed a fresh coat of paint, the brown carpet had seen better days, and the dim fluorescent lights cast an unflattering glow around the space.

He had yet to hear a noise from inside Megan's apartment. He pulled out his phone and punched in her new number—he'd looked that up too. The phone rang and rang, no way of leaving a voice mail.

Frowning, he knocked a third time on the peeling brown door. A dog barked from inside the apartment behind him. And still not a peep from Megan's.

He hadn't driven all the way over here for

nothing. He pounded again. He briefly considered shouting out his credentials, but he wasn't on duty and this wasn't official business.

The door behind him cracked open, chain still attached. An old lady peered through the gap. A dog yapped at her feet and its wet nose protruded through the crack in the door.

"Sorry about the noise, ma'am. I need to speak with the woman who lives here. Do you know if she's home?"

"I don't know." She didn't move from her spot. The dog continued to yap.

He continued to stare at the woman, hoping the prolonged silence would compel her to fill the void.

"She doesn't always come home at night," she said.

"Does she work night shift?"

"Don't think so. Maybe she has a boyfriend or something."

"Any idea when she might come home?"

"Nope."

He'd gotten about all the information he would get from the nosy neighbor. He dug for a card and extended it. "I'd appreciate it if you could give me a call when she returns."

The woman took the card, saying nothing.

He didn't expect to hear from her. Megan was a woman living alone, and he was just some stranger knocking on her door.

"Thank you. Have a good one." Cooper turned and left. When he exited the building he made a right and continued around the building. Megan's apartment faced the backyard—if you could call it that. But when he got there, her drapes were pulled tight.

He still had an hour before he needed to be at work. Time for a stakeout. He headed back to his truck and moved it to the side lot where he could keep an eye on the building's only door without being spotted.

He hoped he could catch her this morning. If Amber had been honest about what had happened, he needed to find out so he could help squelch the rumor. His stomach turned sour at the embarrassment and humiliation that would result. It reminded him of how he'd felt when his dad was the town drunk. Cooper had managed to live that down, to become someone people respected, and now some woman he barely knew was going to send him right back to that place he hated.

Not only that, but a rumor like this could have an impact on the election. If Megan had done this out of spite, that might've even been her intention. She knew he needed every Riverbend vote he could get. He couldn't even think about that right now.

He glanced at Megan's Camry. It was possible a boyfriend had picked Megan up, and she'd spent the night with him. It was more likely she was in her apartment and had ignored his knocking the same way she'd ignored his call. Hopefully she'd make an appearance before he had to leave for work.

In the meantime he'd see if he could get information elsewhere. He knew Cheryl Davies, who owned the Beauty Barn. She cut his hair sometimes when he couldn't get in at the barbershop. She might be more forthcoming about what had gone down yesterday.

The salon wouldn't be open yet, but Cheryl might be there. He looked up the number and called it, keeping watch on the apartment building.

Four rings later Cheryl answered. "Beauty Barn, how can I help you?"

"Hi, Cheryl, this is Cooper Robinson. How are you?"

"Hey, Cooper. You need an appointment, honey? I'm afraid we're pretty booked up today, but I could probably fit you in tomorrow."

"That's not why I'm calling. I was wondering if you could help me with something. I heard Megan Taylor was in the salon yesterday. I heard she said some things about me."

"Well . . . that's true enough."

"I don't mean to put you in an awkward position, but I was told she was telling people she's pregnant." He forced out the words. "And that I'm the father of the baby. Is that true? Did she say that?"

"That's what she said—heard it with my own ears. And I want to assure you, I haven't repeated a word of it to anyone. I respect your family too much for that. I can't speak for the others who were here though."

"I appreciate that, Cheryl. I really do. And I want you to know what she said isn't true. I've been trying to reach her, but she's avoiding me. Are you sure she was pregnant?"

"Well, sure enough, she had a little baby bump. 'Bout five months along, I'd say."

He did the calculation and flinched. Perfect. That was exactly how long ago they'd dated. "Did she say anything else? Anything at all?"

"Mostly she whined and complained. Said you were denying the child. That you weren't there for her."

He grated his teeth. "Because it's not my baby. I didn't even know she was pregnant."

"I wondered. I don't know the woman—never darkened our doorstep while she lived here, mind you. But it didn't sound like something you'd do."

"I appreciate your faith in me, Cheryl. And the information. I'd be grateful if you'd continue to keep the rumor to yourself."

"Of course, honey. What's going on, you think? Why's she saying these things about you?"

"I don't know but I intend to find out."

When he disconnected the call he tried Megan's

number again. This time it disconnected right away. She must've blocked his number.

Someone exited the apartment building, but it was only a man and a child.

Cooper settled back in his seat, staring at the door as Cheryl's words rang in his ears. There'd been no mistake. Megan was out to ruin him.

He wanted to talk through this with someone, and he didn't feel like facing his family just yet. He thought of the texts Kate had sent last night. She always had a way of making him feel better.

It was early. The clinic didn't open until nine, and Kate probably wasn't even awake yet. He opened his text app and sent her a message.

You awake?

A moment later her reply popped up.

Yes.

They could go on as they had last night, texting back and forth. But it would be more efficient if he just called. He found her in his contacts and tapped her name.

After two rings she answered. Her raspy voice dredged up a tempting image of her, tousled and sleepy eyed.

"Good morning," he said.

"Morning."

"Sounds like you just woke up."

"I've been awake awhile. I just haven't spoken yet."

"Not in the habit of talking to yourself?"

"Only at the grocery store."

"Ah . . . you're one of *those* women."

"Afraid so." A smile laced her voice. "How'd you sleep?"

"Not well, I'm afraid. I got up early and drove down to Mars Hill to confront Megan. Her car is here, but she won't answer the door."

"You're still there?"

"I'm hoping to catch her when she leaves for work. She'll have to leave soon though. I'm on duty at nine. If she does come out, I'll have to hang up quickly."

"Understood. Maybe you can find her new phone number and reach her that way."

"Already did. No answer, no way to leave a voice mail. I think she blocked my number."

"She's definitely avoiding you then."

"Like the plague. I called Cheryl from the Beauty Barn a minute ago, and she confirmed what Amber had said. She added that Megan was complaining that I hadn't stepped up and taken responsibility for the baby."

Kate gave a huff of outrage. "Of all the nerve. What kind of woman does something like that?"

At her defense, satisfaction sprouted deep inside him.

"You know, Cooper, maybe she had stronger feelings for you than you realized. Maybe she instigated this rumor out of revenge for breaking her heart."

"Oh, she's definitely looking for revenge, but not because of any feelings she harbors. She was really upset when I called her on that lie."

"What'd she lie about exactly, if you don't mind my asking?"

"We were talking about her job at the motel, and she mentioned she'd turned down a clerk position at the courthouse. I knew for a fact it wasn't true. I have a lot of contacts there, and that position requires a degree, which Megan doesn't have. I wouldn't have said anything to her, but I was pretty sure she'd already lied to me a couple times."

"Yikes."

"She was really uncomfortable when I called her out. She turned it around and blamed me for accusing her. I thought she was going to throw her drink in my face."

The apartment door opened and a middle-aged woman exited holding the leash of a mixed-breed dog.

"Sounds like a toxic personality," Kate said. "Sometimes there's no understanding that kind of person. I hope you can convince her to set the record straight."

"If she doesn't leave soon that won't be for a

while." He suddenly didn't want to talk about Megan anymore. "What about you? Busy day ahead at the clinic?"

"We never really know. Business has slacked off a little since they closed the bridge, but it's still steady enough."

"It's already affecting everyone. Jeff said business at his market is down over 50 percent." It had only been two and a half weeks since the bridge closure.

"All the more reason to make Trail Days a success."

"Speaking of that . . . How's it going with your mother?"

"I haven't talked to her since Saturday, but she texts me occasionally to update me about the marketing campaign."

Cooper held his tongue because he sensed she had something else to say.

"I still feel guilty not telling Avery about her. There was a long gap after undergrad where we didn't talk much, but we've gotten closer since I moved here."

"If you want to tell her, you should. She's trustworthy."

"I know that. But I don't feel ready to tell Gavin yet, and I'd feel guilty confiding in Avery and not him. But this matter between my mother and me—it's a real tender spot inside me. I can't explain it."

241

Her pain was palpable. "I'm sorry. This is a difficult situation. But you have to do what's best for you and trust they'll both understand when the time comes."

"You really think so?"

"I do. And I think you can count on them to be in your corner if and when you do decide to tell them."

"I keep thinking I should be ready to confront my mother with the truth by now. She's obviously kicked her drug habit. I've had several meetings with her and multiple phone calls and texts. She seems like a genuinely nice person. You and your mom seem to think so too."

"Go at your own pace. You're the one bearing all the risk here." The ultimate risk for her, he believed: rejection.

"Thanks." She gave a wry laugh. "You always make me feel so much better."

A warm wave flushed through him and his lips melted into a smile. "Right back atcha, Skittles." He checked the clock. "Unfortunately, I'm out of time. I'll have to head to work now."

"I'll be praying all of this works out, Cooper."

He started his truck. "Thanks. I appreciate that."

They said good-bye, and with one last glance at the apartment door, Cooper pulled from the parking lot. He only hoped the rumor didn't spread far and wide before he could get Megan to set it straight.

28

Cooper was sliding into his cruiser when his phone buzzed for an incoming text. He'd been called out to a Poppy's Pizza, which had alarmed. Turned out the manager was getting forgetful and couldn't recall the password. Cooper's ears were still ringing from the piercing alarm, but the security company had finally helped him shut it off. The manager, Helen, had been upset and disoriented at first. He stayed, offering comfort and reassurance, until Poppy showed up.

Cooper started his cruiser, jacked up the air, and checked in with the office. When he was all caught up he checked the text that had come in. Mom.

> I need to talk to you. Can you stop by or meet me for lunch?

Dread rippled through him. The pregnancy rumor had definitely gotten back to Mom and before he'd had the chance to warn her. He slammed a palm against the steering wheel. He should've known it wouldn't take long, not for something this juicy. He didn't want to talk about this at the station, and he sure didn't want to discuss it at the diner, surrounded by prying ears.

I can grab lunch and meet you
at the house about 12:30?

Sounds good.

He scowled as he pulled from the parking lot. So much for getting on top of the rumor.

Cooper held no grand hopes that his mom's favorite chicken salad sandwich would soothe her ruffled feathers—but that hadn't stopped him from waiting in the deli line for fifteen minutes. The speculative stares from the deli workers and a stilted conversation in line with Gus Ferguson confirmed Cooper's suspicion that the rumor had circulated.

The minutes ticked by slowly as he waited for his food. His face flushed and his skin prickled. The air seemed thick and stuffy. By the time his order was in hand, he was relieved to leave the crowded shop behind.

The drive to his mother's house was short. She met him at the door, uncharacteristic frown lines drawing her brows together. "Hi, honey. Come on in. I already have the table set."

He kissed her cheek as he passed, then headed to the kitchen, where he set the bags on the table. They sank into chairs on opposite sides of the table, unbagged their lunches, then Cooper offered a quick prayer.

"I heard a rumor when I was in town this morning," Mom said.

Cooper held up both hands, palms out. "I'm sorry. I should've called you earlier, but I got busy and I didn't think it would spread that fast. I already know all about the rumor—and it's not true."

"You're my son. I already know that. Now start from the beginning."

Cooper told her about Amber's accusation on their date Sunday night. Then caught her up to speed through this morning when he'd gone to Megan's apartment, making sure she understood he'd never gotten physical with Megan. "Things did end on a bad note though. I suspect she might be a chronic liar."

"Well, you know how I feel about lying." She set down her sandwich. "This rumor sounds like the spiteful work of a bitter woman to me. And I know you said it ended because of that lie, but . . ." Mom gave him a pointed look. "Maybe she actually had feelings for you. Sometimes women take relationships far more seriously than men do."

The comment stung as it hit its target, especially since she wasn't the first to mention it. Did he play a little too fast and loose with women? Maybe. He was definitely noncommittal, but he made a point of not drawing things out if he wasn't feeling it. It was how he managed to maintain the friendship after he ended things.

Mom was still giving him that disapproving look mothers everywhere had down pat. This was not the first such warning she'd extended, and it was as close to an *I told you so* as she'd ever give.

"Point taken," he said.

"I'm not saying this is your fault. Clearly she has a problem, and her behavior is inexcusable. I could just wring the girl's neck."

"The rumor's making the rounds. I could tell by the way people treated me at the deli."

"You should tell Avery and Gavin what's going on. I'll let Jeff know, of course, but your siblings should hear it from you first. That way if someone brings it up, they won't be caught off guard and they'll have a ready answer."

"I will." He'd tried to call Megan today from Rodriguez's phone, but Megan hadn't picked up from an unknown caller either.

"The people who know you won't believe the gossip. I've already done a few things to help put the rumor to rest. I certainly set Shirley Black straight, and I'll do the same to whoever has the nerve to spread the rumor."

"Thanks. But plenty of people will believe it. Or they'll at least question it, and I don't like having my integrity questioned."

"Of course you don't. You have to find Megan and get her to make this right."

"I found out where she works now—she's a sales rep for the *Herald*. I'll go over there after work."

"Maybe you shouldn't wait that long. Why don't you just call her at the paper and straighten this out?"

Cooper's neck muscles tightened at the thought of what the woman had done. "I want her to look me in the eye and explain why she's doing this. And I have a feeling that convincing her to retract her statement won't be easy."

"Fair enough. But you need to nip this in the bud. I'd hate to see a false rumor impact your campaign. You've worked so hard to make this happen."

"I don't plan to let it go that far." The rumor might spread around town, but the locals were likely to support him—weren't they? In other towns, though, he was largely unknown outside the people he'd met briefly at events. But the rumor wasn't likely to travel that far.

They ate in silence awhile. The whole Megan debacle weighed him down so much he hardly tasted his club sandwich. He bagged his chips for later when his stomach wasn't twisting with worry.

He needed something else to think about. "How's the planning for Trail Days going?"

"Pretty well. I was going to see if you and Avery wanted to hang flyers in a couple of the

247

towns we haven't hit yet, but you have enough on your plate right now."

"No, I'd rather stay busy. Maybe Saturday after the clinic closes? Besides, it's always beneficial to show my face and shake a few hands."

"That's what I was thinking. I'll try and find another volunteer or two to go along. The more people you have, the less time it'll take."

"Sounds good. Thanks."

They finished lunch, then she loaded him up with a box of flyers and gave him a big hug at the front door. "This, too, shall pass, honey. Let me know how it goes with Megan."

"I will. Thanks, Mom."

Later, after a day that seemed to drag on and on, he sent Kate a text.

Headed to Megan's work to confront her. Prayers please.

Her response came a moment later.

You got it.

29

Katie was patting the dirt around a new hydrangea plant when Lisa Robinson's Tahoe pulled into the driveway. Sitting back on her haunches, Katie swept the back of her gloved hand across her forehead. She'd put her hair up in a messy knot and dressed in her gardening clothes. But when Lisa gave a hearty wave, Katie felt a rush of delight at the woman's beaming smile.

"Hey, sweetie. I was going to call, but I was in the neighborhood so I just decided to pop by. Hope that's okay."

"More than okay. You're welcome anytime. I'd get up and give you a hug, but I'm covered with grime and sweat."

Lisa's gaze drifted over the two other hydrangea plants sitting off to the side. "Need some help? I'm no plant whisperer, but I know how to get one in the ground."

"If you don't mind getting dirty. The game comes on at seven, and I'd like to get these planted before that."

"Jeff's already got the chips and dip out. Cooper and Gavin are coming over." Lisa squatted and grabbed one of the plants. "Where were you thinking of putting it?"

Katie pointed. "Right about there, I think."

"Good choice." Lisa grabbed the spade and went to work on the hole, and Katie moved to her other side where the last hydrangea would go.

"Your new picket fence looks great. Really makes for nice curb appeal."

"Thanks. Honestly, it was more of a project than I'd anticipated. I was planning to fence the whole yard, but after spending an entire afternoon on this one stretch, I decided a section of decorative fencing would be just fine."

"It's the perfect touch. You should've had Gavin put it up for you. He's very handy."

"I'm too independent for my own good."

"Well, there's nothing wrong with that either." When Lisa was finished with the spade she handed it to Katie. "I just love hydrangeas—the blue ones especially. Mine are white though."

"The pH of the soil determines the color of the bloom. Hydrangeas grow purple in acidic soil—at least they should."

"Well, aren't you clever. I had no idea."

Katie warmed under the woman's praise. "Well, we'll have to see if it actually works—they won't bloom for a year or two."

A breeze whispered across Katie's skin, cooling her flesh and stirring the fine hairs at her nape. The wind chimes tinkled out a pleasant melody.

Lisa looked over her shoulder. "I just love wind chimes. They're so . . ."

"Soothing," both women said at the same time, then laughed.

"The kids got me those wind chimes I have hanging on the back patio. When I hear them tinkle I pray for them."

She was such a great mom. Katie's heart squeezed. "I just love that."

"Well, once your kids are grown, that's about all you can do for them. Of course I'd love to give them advice at every turn, but unless they ask my opinion I try to keep my big mouth shut."

"I'm sure you're being too hard on yourself. You seem to have a great relationship with all your kids."

Lisa's eyes twinkled. "That's only because I've learned to butt out and let them make their own decisions."

"Well, you seem to handle it with great aplomb."

Lisa waved away her words. "Jeff's always nudging me under the table when I'm about to blow it. He's the savvy one. He does this thing—when the kids are sharing a problem with him and he has something to say, he pulls two pennies out of his pocket and sets them on a table. If they want to hear his two cents, they pick up the pennies. If they don't, they just move the conversation right along, no harm no foul."

Katie's mouth spread in a smile. "That's genius."

"My husband is a wise man." They worked in silence for a minute, then Lisa spoke again.

"Well, how was your day, honey? The clinic seems to be holding its own."

"Business is down a little, but it's been pretty steady despite the bridge closure." She gave Lisa a sidelong glance. "Last Friday someone tried to convince Avery to treat their dog."

"What? How did I not hear about that? For heaven's sake, we have a perfectly good vet in town."

"I guess the lady doesn't get along with him too well. Avery sent her packing though."

"Well, I should hope so. Goodness."

"How's the planning for Trail Days going on your end?"

"Well, that's actually why I came by. The online marketing is going great, but we're a little late getting the flyers up in a few of the nearby towns. I'm trying to get a group of people to do that on Saturday. Interested?"

"Sure. I don't have anything better to do."

"Terrific. So far I have you, Avery, and Cooper. If I can get a few more, you can split up and hit different towns."

"Sounds good." Katie's bright smile belied the sudden tension in her shoulders. Katie, Avery, and Cooper. After the awkward moment in Lisa's kitchen two days ago, that sounded like a fun afternoon. But maybe it was a chance to show Avery there was nothing to worry about.

Her conscience twitched at the thought.

By the time they finished planting and watering the new shrubs, it was ten minutes till game time. Lisa gave her a good-bye hug, and Katie waved as she left. She loved that the woman felt comfortable dropping by her house. That might annoy some people, but Katie had always wanted a family that was close enough for impromptu visits.

As she put away her gardening supplies and took a quick shower, it wasn't the game she was thinking of. It was Cooper. How had his confrontation with Megan gone this afternoon? Would he let Katie know, or should she reach out to him?

She'd no sooner settled in front of the TV than her phone rang. Cooper.

"Hello?"

"It's me. Are you busy?" His rapid speech revealed agitation.

"No, I was just watching the game and wondering how things went with Megan."

"They didn't. She wasn't there. Worse than that, she won't be around for another week—she went on vacation."

"Vacation? How convenient."

"Isn't it? She starts a nasty rumor and leaves town."

"I'm sorry, Cooper. What are you going to do?"

"I don't know. They wouldn't tell me where she went, of course. But the rumor is spreading.

My mom knows everything now. I called Avery a while ago and told her. Gavin is next. I'm on my way to Mom and Jeff's to watch the game. Gavin will be there."

"I'm so sorry this is happening. I know what your reputation means to you."

"And Megan knows what this run for sheriff means to me. A small-town rumor may not seem like much, but most of my votes will come from Riverbend—I hope."

"Sabotaging your campaign seems so extreme."

"Mom thinks she must've had deeper feelings than she let on."

"Someone who really cared about you wouldn't want to hurt you."

"I'm guessing Megan doesn't think like you do."

"Then she doesn't know that caring for someone means you put their needs ahead of your own."

"I suspect that's true."

"Should you make some kind of public statement?"

"Avery and I talked about that, but we don't want to blow it out of proportion or give the rumor more credence than it's due. I really can't see it spreading outside of Riverbend, so there should be minimal damage to my campaign. But I'd like to avoid dragging my family's name through the mud if I can."

"Maybe it's not as bad as you think. Pregnancies outside of wedlock happen all the time."

"It's not the pregnancy that's so damaging. It's the fact that I've supposedly turned my back on Megan—never mind that it's not true."

"There's a DNA test—but of course we'd need the mother for that."

"Yeah, Avery mentioned that." The heavy sigh on his end of the line conveyed that this burden was weighing him down.

Katie didn't know what to say, so she whispered a quick prayer. There must be some reason God was allowing this to happen. It was always confusing when bad things happened to good people. When bad *people* happened to good people. Her stomach was in knots for Cooper.

"I shouldn't be calling you," he said quietly. Honestly.

His words ushered in a new kind of tension. The kind that existed because they were tiptoeing around the feelings growing between them. But with that one little statement, he'd stepped right on a land mine. Maybe he regretted it now.

She threw him a lifeline. "There's no crime in needing to talk to someone, Cooper."

"We both know I could be talking to my mom or Avery right now. I should be."

Then why aren't you? The words gathered in her throat, the question begging for release. She wanted the answer more than she wanted her next breath. Wanted to hear him admit he had feelings for her. After all, she'd offered him a lifeline, and he hadn't taken it . . . But it wasn't a fair question when she was dating his brother.

Silence lengthened between them, and the line buzzed with tension. It had always gone unmentioned, this thing simmering just under the surface. If she'd thought she was imagining it or the feelings were one sided, that idea had just been obliterated. Because at the moment, that thing between them wasn't just simmering—it was boiling.

"I'm sorry," he said. "I've put you in a difficult position. I won't call you again, Kate."

His words made her insides shrivel up tight and hard. She opened her mouth to rebut his statement. Because as much as she hated that this rumor was tearing him up inside, she loved being the one he counted on. The one he called.

But his family could take it from here. They *should* take it from here. As much as she wanted to get closer to Cooper, this thing between them was a disaster waiting to happen.

She closed her eyes and squeezed out the words. "Whatever you think best. I'll be praying for you. I'm sure God will work all of this out."

"Thanks, Kate." A beat of silence followed. "I guess I'll . . . see you around."

Her chest tightened at the despair in his voice. She pressed a palm to her heart. "See you, Cooper."

30

The call came well after ten on Wednesday night just after Cooper had dozed off. He rolled over in bed and snatched his buzzing phone off the nightstand. "Hello?"

"Is this Cooper Robinson?"

"Yes."

"This is Brandon Reed from the *Herald*. I'm following up on a story and wondered if you could answer a few questions."

It was hardly his first interview with the paper, although they were normally scheduled in advance and at a reasonable hour. He sat up in bed and ran a hand over his face. "Um, sure. How can I help you?"

"Mr. Robinson, we have a source who claims you've gotten a young woman pregnant and are denying paternity. Can you confirm if that's true?"

Cooper's mind spun even as his tongue stuck to the roof of his mouth.

"Mr. Robinson? Can you corroborate that?"

"That is a false rumor. What kind of paper are you running over there? This is a personal matter."

"You're running for public office, sir. That makes it the public's business. Is my source correct? Do you deny you're the father of the baby?"

"No comment!" Cooper punched the Disconnect button, barely resisting the temptation to throw his phone across the room. He wished he could grab the guy's collar and lift him off his feet.

This was bad. If a journalist was asking questions, it meant the newspaper that serviced the entire county was planning to print this story. So much for keeping the rumor under wraps. The bad publicity would be devastating to his reputation. To his campaign.

He had to call Avery. As he dialed he scrambled from bed. Adrenaline flooded his system and he needed to move.

His sister answered on the fourth ring. "This better be good."

"The *Herald* got wind of the rumor. They just called me for a statement."

"Oh no." Shuffling sounds came across the line. "What did you say?"

"I denied it—what do you think I said?"

"Don't jump down my throat. It wasn't me who tipped them off."

He scrubbed a hand over his face. "Sorry, I'm just—I can't believe they'd print a rumor. A false rumor. What are they, the *National Enquirer*?"

"I guess we should've put out a statement after all."

"We still can."

"Of course we can, and we will. But they'll go to press with this tonight, and the story will be on porches all over Madison County before folks have finished their first cups of coffee."

She was right. He stopped pacing, a fist tightening in his gut. "Anything we say now will only sound defensive."

"The best we can do is hope the article is buried somewhere under the reader letters."

"Still, a statement might help. I have a right to tell people my side of the story."

"Can you meet in the morning before work? We'll have the paper by then and will know what we're dealing with. I'll have Alice meet us there too. She can put out a press release, and I'll get the statement on all your socials."

"All right." He took a deep breath, feeling a modicum better just having a plan in place.

"It would sure help if you could locate Megan."

"I'll be working on that." He'd start with Megan's neighbors. Try and get the name of her boyfriend. Someone had to know something.

Silence lengthened between them.

"Cooper . . . maybe you need someone with more experience to handle your campaign."

"This is just a sheriff's race, for crying out loud. I shouldn't need a professional campaign manager."

"I know, but . . . I feel like we're getting in over our heads here."

"Hiring some fancy manager at this point would only make me seem guilty. Besides, some city slicker isn't going to believe in me like you do."

"Maybe you're right. I do believe in you, and so does everyone who knows you. We're going to get through this. I'm going to clear this up if it's the last thing I do."

His shoulder muscles loosened at her reassurance. At her conviction. If only everyone who read tomorrow's paper would have the same faith in him.

Cooper sank into the chair at the circular table in campaign headquarters. Avery and Alice, their publicity volunteer, looked like they needed some caffeine. He'd already had three cups and his nerves jangled uncomfortably.

Avery pulled today's newspaper closer, reading aloud. " 'This is a personal matter. No comment.' " She gave Cooper a grim look.

"He completely left out my denial of the rumor!"

"This isn't good," Avery said.

"Someone please tell me how a false rumor makes page one in a reputable newspaper." Cooper had been up at four thirty, waiting for the paper to hit his porch. Both the location of the article and the headline—"Local Sheriff Candidate Caught Up in Personal Scandal"—tied his stomach in knots.

"At least it's below the fold?" Alice, a former publicity whiz, pushed back her bleach-blonde hair and offered a hopeful smile.

Cooper was in no mood for her Pollyanna personality this morning. But at least the woman had the ability and connections that would hopefully get this train back on the track.

Avery frowned. "He didn't give Megan's name."

"I wish he would've. She's got a lot to answer for."

"Well, what's done is done. It's getting late. Let's start to work on a statement."

They worked for an hour on a single paragraph. It was a delicate message. Cooper was no writer, but he knew what he wanted to say. Alice helped wrangle the words into concise and confident sentences that seemed genuine and heartfelt.

After the woman made one last tweak, Cooper read it out loud and nodded. "I think this is it. Nice job, Alice."

Avery slid the marked-up paper back to the woman. "All right. Do your thing. Let's spread it far and wide."

As Cooper left the office, the morning was just getting underway. Daylight crept over the mountains, the birds tweeted—and all across the county his private life was destined to become today's watercooler fodder.

31

Katie had mixed feelings about her afternoon plans.

She strode up the walkway toward her front door, Gavin on her heels. They'd just had a filling breakfast at the Iron Skillet, which was packed this Saturday morning. At the door she turned to him. "Want to come in for a bit? I have a little time before I have to meet Avery and Cooper."

"I'd like to, but I'm needed back at the campground." He settled his hands at her waist. "Let's go somewhere quiet tomorrow night. Someplace out of town where we won't be interrupted."

"Is everything okay?"

He gave her a warm smile and kissed her nose. "Everything's fine. Stop worrying."

Katie watched him go, waving as he pulled from her drive. Would he tell her about Jesse tomorrow night? If he did, she'd have to act as if she didn't already know. Or maybe that wasn't it at all. Maybe he was planning to tell her he loved her. Instead of feeling excited at the notion, the thought only tied her stomach in knots.

Forty-five minutes later Katie pulled into a slot in front of the clinic where she was meeting Avery and Cooper. Since the building was already closed for the day, Katie had to unlock the door before she slipped inside. A welcome rush of cool air washed over her skin.

"Avery?" Since her boss hadn't gotten around to it yet, she went to turn off the lights.

Avery came up the hallway. "Hey. I'm afraid I've still got a patient in the back—family friend. She's got the flu. I'll have to bail on you and Cooper. She's pretty dehydrated, and I need to set her up with an IV."

Katie ditched her purse on the counter. "I can help."

"No, I've got it covered. Lisa would kill me if both of us had to bow out. She's been trying to get these flyers hung for weeks."

Cooper entered the clinic, stopping short at the sight of Katie. "Oh. Hi. I didn't think you worked Saturdays."

"I don't."

"Lisa roped her into passing out flyers with us. Unfortunately, I'll have to bail on you two."

Cooper scratched his neck. "Oh."

Avery's gaze shifted between the two of them, her brow furrowing. "Or . . . I could go with Cooper, and Katie could stay with the patient."

"No, I can tell you're worried about her. We'll be fine, won't we, Cooper?"

"Of course. We won't come back until both towns are covered in flyers," he said, as if that were the real concern here.

Katie looked back to Avery. "Call me if anything comes up."

"I will."

"Let's hit the road," Cooper said to Katie.

They said good-bye to Avery and headed outside. In the last week fall had arrived in Riverbend, bringing cooler nighttime temperatures. The trees in the upper mountains were starting to turn beautiful shades of red and gold, which would soon sweep down into the valley. Katie loved the cool, crisp weather of autumn. But today clouds had rolled in, and rain seemed imminent.

"Okay if we take your car?" Cooper said. "I've got a bunch of stuff in mine, and I don't mind driving since I know my way around."

"Sure." She handed him her keys and glanced up at the dark sky. "I hope the rain holds off."

Ever the gentleman, he opened the passenger door, and she brushed past him, smiling her thanks.

He walked around the front, got in, and started the engine. Awkwardness had crept inside the car with them, the last part of their phone conversation still humming between them.

So much for avoiding each other. The universe seemed to throw them together at every opportunity. She wished she could cry foul, but who was she kidding? A big part of her was looking forward to an afternoon alone with Cooper. Did he feel the same?

"I think you have a headlamp out."

She could tell from the reflection on the car in front of them that he was right. "I'll get it replaced soon."

He pulled out onto the road.

"How far is it to Marshall?"

"About twenty minutes. But we should stop at Walnut on the way."

"Sounds like a little bit of nothing."

"It is. But there are a few places to hang flyers, and folks tend to gather on Saturdays. It'll be good for the campaign to show my face, shake a few hands."

Was he nervous about facing citizens outside Riverbend Gap after the newspaper article? "I saw the statement you put out Thursday. It was very convincing and well written."

"Thanks. I hope people believe it."

"It's the truth. That helps. I'm glad you're not shying away from this today."

"Mom was willing to let me off the hook, but I'm not about to hide away in shame when I didn't do anything wrong."

"That's the spirit." She shifted her knees his way, trying to ignore how close they were in the small confines of her car. "Any luck tracking down Megan?"

"Sadly, no. She seems to have fallen off the face of the earth. No one in her apartment building claims to know anything."

"She hasn't been there long, right?"

"Yeah. But she's got to return soon." He gave her a sidelong look. "Any progress with your mother this week?"

"I haven't seen her. She's still doing her thing online for Trail Days. She's sent me a couple texts, but that's about it."

A beat of silence ensued as he navigated a sharp turn. "I think Avery was a little reluctant to send us out into the wild alone."

At his observation tension thickened in the space. Katie's pulse kicked into a higher gear. "Yeah, I got that feeling too."

His hands tightened on the steering wheel. They were nice, manly hands with long, tapered fingers, squared off at the ends. The memory of that hand holding hers in Lisa's kitchen surged into her mind. The slight roughness of his palm brushing hers. The magnetic sweep of his thumb across her skin. The thought of never again receiving his touch hollowed her stomach.

"She has nothing to worry about." His low voice scraped across the chords of her heart.

"Of course not." But if that were true, why did it take every ounce of her resolve not to look his way?

Three hours later the mood had lightened considerably. They'd hung around Walnut longer than Katie had expected. Though there were few places to hang flyers, those establishments clearly did a robust business.

Cooper chatted with quite a few people, and he introduced Katie as a friend—not his brother's girlfriend as she'd expected. It meant nothing, but she couldn't stop from hoping that it did. *Stupid.*

Cooper knew some of the townsfolk, and those he'd just met seemed genuinely pleased to make his acquaintance. A couple people seemed guarded, but she was thankful no one brought up the scandal.

Having a bit of success in his back pocket seemed to invigorate him. They hit the bigger town of Marshall with renewed energy. There were considerably more stores and offices in this town, and it took hours to hang flyers and canvass the area.

"That went pretty well," Cooper said as they exited the last store and started back toward the car.

"An understatement. You're very well liked, Mr. Robinson, scandal or no."

"That's got more to do with my last name than anything. Is there any place we missed? We have flyers left over."

"I think we got them all. And stop being so humble. You're a good guy and they know that. No one believes that tabloid gossip the paper put out."

"Hope you're right." His features warmed as he slid her a grateful look. "Thanks. I have to admit I feel a lot better than I have all week."

She'd been wondering about something since their last phone call. She strove for a carefree tone. "So, did you ever square things with Amber?"

"Not really. And I don't think I want to be with someone who so easily believes the worst about me."

The realization it was over between them shouldn't have buoyed her spirits so much, but it did. "I don't blame you. You deserve better."

"Campaign aside, I shouldn't care so much what people think."

"You grew up in the shadow of a father who was a constant source of embarrassment. This has childhood trigger written all over it."

"How do you know these things?"

She shrugged. "From paying attention to my own triggers, I guess."

They stopped at a crosswalk, and Katie stapled a flyer to a wooden pole while Cooper held it in place. They'd worked as a team all afternoon and it felt good. She liked being with him. Maybe they could find their way to friendship. Maybe they would outgrow the chemistry that sizzled between them.

When the light turned they crossed the street. She didn't want to worry about this today. She felt better than she had in weeks, and she wanted to enjoy the afternoon.

"You know what sounds good?" Cooper said once the car was in sight. "Ice cream."

"I didn't think you liked sweets."

"Everybody likes ice cream. Have you been to the Dairy Bar yet?"

"I'm surprised they haven't named their chocolate-dipped cone after me yet."

"Does that mean you haven't tried their cookie monster blast?"

"Can't say that I have."

"You don't know what you're missing—it's got Oreos."

She couldn't believe he'd remembered that. "All right. Let's do it—but I'm still getting a dipped cone."

A moment later, as she watched Cooper round the vehicle, Katie was grinning ear to ear.

32

Since it was almost suppertime and dark clouds were rolling in, the Dairy Bar was practically deserted. The drive-up building was just outside town, tucked between Riverbend's only gas station and a donut shop, which was currently closed.

At the window Katie ordered her cone and tried to pay her share, but Cooper was having none of it. Giving in, she left him to pay and headed toward a circular yellow table. As she sat down the table wobbled on the cement slab.

From the service window Cooper flashed a smile at her. Her stomach flopped at the warmth in his eyes. She pulled her gaze away, trying to get her pulse under control.

Friends. We're just friends.

But her gaze quickly returned to him. His biceps bunched as he removed his wallet from his pocket. He sure did nice things to that shirt. She was also a fan of those jeans and the way they hugged his—

Friends, Katie. Come on. She could do this. She wasn't quite finished with her pep talk when Cooper approached the table and handed her the cone.

"Thank you." She licked the dots of chocolate

ice cream that popped through the hardened chocolate shell.

"No problem."

Thunder rolled in the distance as Cooper returned to the window. He came back a minute later with his treat. The vanilla ice cream, filled with chunks of cookies, heaped like a mountain peak over the lip of his large cup.

"You have to try it." He settled beside her and held out the cup, even though he had a spoon.

She leaned in for a bite, but as she closed in he lifted the cup, dabbing her on the nose with the ice cream.

"Hey!" She wiped the ice cream away as he laughed.

"Sorry, couldn't resist." He held up the ice cream again. "Really, have a taste. You'll like it."

"I'm not falling for that a second time."

"I won't do it again."

"I have trust issues now."

He chuckled. "Fine. Here." He handed her the spoon.

Narrowing her eyes at him, she took the spoon and tried a bite. The cool vanilla melted on her tongue, and the soft cookies mingled with the chocolate and peanut butter flavors. "Mmm. That is good." She took another spoonful, this one heaping.

"Hey, save some for me."

"I have a sticky nose, mister. You owe me." She

271

savored the flavors of his treat, detecting an Oreo flavor this time.

A smug look came over his face. "You like me, Kate Loveland."

"Does that arrogant approach work for you?"

He had the grace to appear sheepish. "Sometimes."

"Well, just so you know, it doesn't do a thing for me."

His lips tipped up in a knowing grin.

That smile, on the other hand . . .

He gestured toward her cone. "Are you sharing?"

"Since you paid I guess I should." She held out her cone.

He eyed her over the confection. "Should I trust you?"

"Oh, you definitely shouldn't trust me."

He approached the cone cautiously, then took a slow bite.

Katie shivered as the look in his eyes shifted from playful suspicion to something else entirely. She barely even noticed the drop of rain that landed on her hand.

Muscles in his jaw shifted as he worked the ice cream around his mouth. He nodded approvingly. "Rich. Sweet. Smooth. They really should name it after you."

Her cheeks warmed as she pulled her cone back and took a bite, breaking eye contact.

One moment it was quiet, the air humming

between them, and the next the sky opened up. A deluge of rain dumped on them. They scrambled from their seats.

Cooper grabbed her elbow. "Over there."

Navigating tables, they dashed toward an overhang on the shop's side. When they were under the roof, their gazes met. Cooper's hair lay flat against his head, and water dripped off his chin and nose. His breath came rapidly, and his features held the same stricken expression hers probably did.

Unable to help herself Katie burst out laughing. "That look on your face."

His lips slowly morphed into a smile, then he was laughing too. "Mine? You should see yours."

"Your hair's plastered to your head."

He ran his fingers through it, leaving it in messy spikes. "How did that happen so fast?"

"I guess we should've taken that thunder more seriously." She leaned against the block wall and saluted him with her cone. "At least we still have our ice cream."

His head snapped back toward their table. Cooper's cup still sat on the table in the down-pour. His face fell.

Katie nudged him. "Go get it."

"It's pretty well flooded now, I think." He gave a little pout.

Katie's heart softened. "Aw . . . I'll share mine."

But when he turned back to her, all thoughts of

ice cream fled. Instead there was only the two of them, sequestered behind the curtain of rain. His wet lashes were clumped together, making them impossibly dark. In the shadow of the overhang, his eyes were darker too. Not a hint of gold floated in that molten brown pool.

His breath whispered against her forehead. When had he moved in front of her? When had he gotten so close? She couldn't have looked away if the mayor's house went floating by. The air crackled around them. She couldn't remember how to breathe.

He leaned closer—or maybe it was her. But suddenly they were only a breath apart. Their gazes held, his smoldering. The long, delicious moment hung between them, a prelude to something that promised to be so much more.

He set a hand on the wall beside her. His other hand settled in the curve of her waist. He was giving her time to change her mind. But there was no stopping this. She wanted his mouth on hers more than she wanted her next heartbeat.

He leaned forward, his lips brushing hers, soft and slow. Controlled. Reverent. A breathless pause. Then, mercifully, he tilted his head and came back for seconds. And thirds. Katie responded in kind, her insides melting.

Cooper had only meant to brush Kate's lips once or twice. But he couldn't seem to help himself.

He cupped the gentle curve of her neck and deepened the kiss. It was impossible to stop. Like taking only one bite of an impossibly delectable dish. She felt like a dream in his arms and tasted of heaven.

He'd failed to take her response, and what it would do to him, into account. It stoked the flame inside him. Her mouth was still sweet and cool from the ice cream. He savored her, suddenly desperate to hold on to her, on to the moment.

Her fingers threaded through the hair at his nape, and a shiver passed over him. He touched under her jaw and felt her racing pulse beneath his palm. She was a drug, and he'd been born addicted. How had he ever lasted this long without having her in his arms?

A crack of thunder snapped him back to the present.

He was kissing Kate in broad daylight. He fought the pull of reality, drew out the kiss another moment. Then two. Because, man . . .

A moment later, with the discipline of a saint, he slowly drew back. Their ragged breaths mingled in the space between them. She gave him that sleepy-eyed look, making him want to kiss her all over again.

But a blink later the desire in her eyes shifted to something else. Reality was settling in—for both of them.

Nothing had changed. She was still his brother's girl.

Cooper reluctantly let go of her and put a few more inches between them—just to be safe. There was no going back after a kiss like that. He should say something, but he couldn't bring himself to apologize for a kiss that had felt so right.

Instead he said what loyalty demanded of him. "We can't do this, Katelyn." His whisper sounded harsh even to his own ears.

"I know."

He hated the defeat on her face. The furrow splitting her brows. The guilt shimmering in her eyes. Hated that he'd put those there.

They needed to cool off. "I'll take you back to the clinic."

"I'll walk. You take my car."

"It's raining." But even as he said it, he realized the rain had stopped as suddenly as it had started. In the silence raindrops fell from the overhang.

Katie looked down at her melting cone. The ice cream was dripping onto her hand. She stared at it as if unsure what to do with it.

He took the cone and tossed it in a nearby trash can, then handed her the wad of napkins he'd tucked into his pocket. "Let me drive you."

"It's okay. I need to . . . think."

He'd put her in a terrible position. He did regret that. He'd thought he had the self-control to resist her. He'd been so wrong. "I'm sorry."

She tossed the dirty napkins in the trash and gave him a smile that didn't reach her eyes. "Let's just . . . I should go now."

"What about your keys?"

"Just leave them in the car." She was already backing away. And there was nothing left to say.

33

Katie was glad it had stopped raining because her sanity required a good, hard jog. She needed some space. Some endorphins. Some thinking time. And boy did she have a lot of thinking to do.

Her feet pounded the wet pavement, and her lungs pulled rain-scented air into her lungs. The humidity had broken, leaving the temperature a full ten degrees cooler. She moved through the neighborhood unseeing, her thoughts spinning in a whirlwind.

She'd crossed an unforgivable line, and there was no going back. She wouldn't be able to be around Cooper and not want his kiss. There was no hope whatsoever of keeping things between them strictly platonic.

She had to break up with Gavin. There was no way around it now—she'd have to hurt that lovely man. Her stomach twisted hard at the thought.

She'd also have to leave behind the family she'd grown to love. Avery might very well hate her for a while—even if she didn't find out about the kiss.

She swallowed hard. What had she done? One brush of the man's lips, and she melted like a snow cone in August. But, oh, what a kiss. It made her kisses with Gavin seem downright lame.

The thought plagued her. She should've known it wouldn't work with Gavin. The chemistry had never been there. There was no forcing such things. She should've broken up with him before he'd had a chance to develop more serious feelings. Now she was going to hurt him, and that's the last thing she wanted. She of all people knew the cruel pain of rejection. And now she had to inflict it on someone she cared about.

Furthermore, she wouldn't be seeing Cooper anymore. He would never date his brother's ex-girlfriend. That thought settled like a leaden weight in her stomach. Tears stung her eyes, making the road before her blur. She could hardly stand the thought. How could she live in this little town, run into him, and pretend she didn't—

What? Love him?

She gave a slow blink as reality settled in, clear and palpable. Yes, she loved him. Somehow, while trying to force things with Gavin and after two months of trying to avoid Cooper, she'd fallen in love with the man. All her life she'd been searching for a place to belong, a person to belong to, and she'd finally found him.

But she couldn't have him.

God, how could You let this happen?

She winced at the accusation. *That's it, Katie. Blame God.*

There was no one to blame but herself. She was the one dating Cooper's brother. She was the one who should've handled this much differently. She'd let this go on too long. But she'd been so enamored with the Robinsons, she hadn't been willing to risk losing them.

How sad was that? How selfish?

Now, in one fell swoop, she'd lost Lisa, Jeff, Gavin, Cooper, and possibly, Avery—her boss and, most importantly, her friend. Everything in Katie's life seemed to overlap now. How had this gotten so complicated?

So much for clearing his head. Cooper's long ride through the mountains hadn't helped. His thoughts were still as tangled as last year's Christmas lights.

He pulled into his apartment's parking lot and shut off the motorcycle. Twilight closed in around him as he removed his helmet and made his way into the building. How was Kate doing? What was she thinking right now? Would she break up with Gavin?

He hated the way his heart lifted at the thought—and to what end? Nothing could happen between them now. He hated himself for being disloyal to his brother, and he'd never repeat the mistake.

His thoughts snagged on the last word—how could something that felt so right be a mistake?

Once inside his apartment he kicked off his boots and checked his phone, some small part of him hoping to hear from Kate. He'd missed two calls, a voice mail, and a text—all from Avery.

Surely Kate hadn't told his sister what had happened between them. That wouldn't end well. But he could hardly blame her for needing to talk it out with her best friend.

Avery's text simply demanded that he call her back. The voice mail reiterated the message in a blunt, measured tone.

Oh boy. Kate had definitely told her about the kiss.

Cooper took a minute to gather himself before he dialed Avery's number. She answered on the first ring.

"Oh, you've caused a real mess this time, Cooper Holland Robinson. How could you? She's Gavin's girlfriend, for crying out loud. You said there was nothing going on, but obviously that's not the case."

"I didn't lie to you. There wasn't anything going on—not physically at least. I don't know what Kate told you but—"

"*Katie* didn't tell me anything—the photo pretty much said it all!"

His blood froze. "What photo?"

"Oh, the one someone plastered to the wall of your *campaign page*."

"What?"

281

"Little piece of advice, Coop. Next time you make out with your brother's girlfriend, you might want to find someplace more private than the *Dairy Barn*."

"Who posted that? Take it down."

"I did, genius. But not before it was noticed— and *shared* to the tune of twenty-eight times."

This was out there now. *Gavin.* Cooper closed his eyes, his breath escaping in one long, defeated sigh. This was bad. So bad.

But wait a minute. Avery managed his campaign page. "How can someone even post things on my page without your approval?"

"Are you really trying to blame this on me right now?" The clipped words cut right through him.

He ran a hand over his face. "I'm sorry. This isn't your fault obviously. Was it a clear picture? Could you tell who it was?"

"Oh yeah. You can see for yourself. I'll send it to you now."

She went quiet, presumably doing as she said.

Cooper's mind spun at the possible implications. Was it possible Avery only recognized Kate because she'd already had suspicions about the two of them? He whispered a desperate prayer. Crossed his fingers. Wished on a star. Where was a dandelion when you needed one?

"Who took that photo? No one was around."

"I don't know. The profile that posted it seemed fake so I reported it. There, I sent the picture."

A moment later his phone buzzed. He opened the text and tapped on the photo. It had been taken from the side, perhaps from the sidewalk, though the photographer had zoomed in. Cooper's hand was on the wall beside Katelyn as he leaned in. Their identities were obvious, and the kiss appeared every bit as passionate as it had been.

His last flicker of hope was snuffed out in an instant. "This isn't good."

"You think?"

He gritted his teeth. He could really do without her sarcasm right now.

"And I have to say, the caption didn't help matters much either. Let me read it for you so I don't misquote. 'Could this be Deputy Robinson's mysterious baby mama?' "

He reared back. "What?"

"Yes, Cooper. The general public is now wondering if Katie's the pregnant woman whose baby you're denying."

No. This could not be happening. He paced his living room. "Does Kate know?"

"I don't know. Haven't been able to reach her—I assumed she was still busy making out with you."

"It may seem unlikely," he said in a biting tone, "but that was actually our first and only kiss. I've been out riding around trying to sort out this mess."

"Well, fortunately, the guy who posted the

photo didn't mention Katie by name. But people around here will recognize her, and everyone knows she's Gavin's girlfriend."

She was right. In one fell swoop Cooper had somehow managed to publicly humiliate all three of them. The list of people he owed an apology to was growing by the minute. And it started with his brother.

"You've got some massive damage control ahead of you, starting with Gavin. I recommend you go see him before he gets wind of this. He deserves to hear it from you."

Cooper checked the time. It had only been two hours since the kiss. Gavin wasn't on social media. Still, Cooper should get over there. His stomach knotted at the thought of hurting his brother. What was he even going to say? "I'll go now."

"Do that."

"Can you keep trying to get ahold of Kate? She needs to know what was said about her, and I think it would be best if I kept my distance."

"Fine. We'll talk later about how we're going to handle the publicity part of this."

He couldn't care less about the campaign right now; his family was falling apart—and it was all his fault.

34

Cooper drove down the campground's winding gravel road. Evening was closing in, and being a Saturday night, the property was full. Fires flickered at most of the sites, and families gathered nearby, eating dinner at picnic tables or roasting marshmallows.

Cooper pulled in beside his brother's Sierra Denali and shut off the engine. His feet were like lead as he exited his truck and made his way toward the camper. The lights were on, so at least he'd caught Gavin at home. Relief and dread battled for the lead in his mind.

Cooper had rehearsed what he'd say on the short drive over, but everything sounded so lame. Bottom line—there was no excuse for what he'd done.

As he neared the camper the door burst open. Gavin flew down the steps. "You pig—I trusted you!"

Cooper barely had time to brace his feet before Gavin's meaty fist came flying. Light flashed behind Cooper's eyes. Pain exploded in his head. He stumbled backward, reeling, disoriented.

"My own brother." Gavin's face was a hardened mask. His brows drawn, his jaw flexing, he seemed a little unhinged.

Cooper shook his head to settle the loose marbles and blinked to clear his vision. His ears rang. His brother packed a punch—literally.

Cooper held out his hands, palms forward. "All right. All right, I deserved that."

"You think?"

"I'm sorry, Gavin. It was all my fault."

"How many women do you need, Cooper? Every woman in town wants you, but that's not enough? You had to steal mine?"

He grimaced. "It's not like that. Kate cares about you."

"Kate?" He gave a mirthless laugh and shook his head. "You took advantage of her! You made a play for her like she was just another one of your fans."

Harsh. Cooper pressed his lips together.

"What's wrong? Couldn't stand that there was one woman who could resist your charms? Just had to prove you could get her, too, never mind that she's *my girlfriend?*"

"No, it wasn't like—"

The left hook came out of nowhere. Pain burst through his jaw and cheek. His head jerked back with the force of the blow. He caught his balance and struggled to reorient himself. Something red and hot rose in his chest. He gritted his teeth and sent Gavin a flinty look. "That's your last free punch, man."

Gavin got up in Cooper's face. "You're nothing

286

but a dog! You knew I cared about her, and you went after her anyway."

"I never meant to hurt you," he grated out.

"What'd you think would happen?" Spittle flew. "You're cheating with my girl behind my back. How long's it been going on? Huh? How long?"

"It hasn't—today was the first time I kissed her."

Gavin fisted Cooper's shirt, pulling him face-to-face. "Sure it was."

"It's the truth!"

Gavin pushed him away, as if he couldn't stand to be close another minute. He was all but snarling, blue eyes blazing. "You wouldn't know the truth if it hit you square between the eyes."

It was the cool, measured tone of Gavin's voice that sent fear spreading through Cooper's veins like poison. They'd had many arguments over the years. They'd even come to blows a time or two as teenagers. But Gavin had never regarded him with so much . . . hatred.

Fear compressed Cooper's chest. Gavin's wall of anger protected a gaping wound—a wound Cooper was responsible for. His brother may never forgive him for this. And Cooper couldn't blame him. The red-hot anger dissipated, leaving something much worse in its place.

"I'm truly sorry. It was a terrible mistake, and if I could take it back, I would." He meant those words from the depth of his soul.

Gavin's shoulders slowly sank even as his chest heaved. "Well, you can't take it back, can you?"

Cooper stared into his brother's desolate eyes. He'd done the unforgiveable. Wished he had the words to fix this. But Gavin was right. What Cooper had done could never be undone. It was just as he'd suspected all along. He really was a terrible person—his father's son—after all.

Katie had no sooner emerged from the shower and slipped into sleep shorts and a T-shirt than a knock sounded at her door. Cooper. She hated the traitorous way her heart leaped in response.

But a quick peek through the peephole revealed Avery, her mahogany hair pulled back in the same ponytail she'd worn at noon today. Had it really been less than twelve hours ago?

Katie pulled open the door.

Avery turned a very sour look on her. Her left eye twitched.

Katie hadn't seen the stress-induced tick since finals week their senior year.

Her stomach wobbled. "Hi. Come on in."

"Have you checked your phone?"

Katie shut the door. "Um, no. I went for a jog and left it in my purse. Have a seat and tell me what's wrong. Can I get you something to drink?"

Avery crossed her arms. "I'm just going to get right to the point, Katie. Someone took a picture of you and Cooper kissing and posted it to his campaign page."

Katie sucked in a breath. The ramifications whirled through her mind.

"I took it down but it's been shared. It's out there."

"Does Cooper know?"

Avery's face went harder—if that were possible. "Interesting you asked about Cooper first."

Katie flinched. What was wrong with her? Legs trembling, she sank into her armchair, her gaze falling to her lap. Her breath felt trapped in her lungs.

"Cooper's over at Gavin's right now trying to explain. Though I have no idea what he could possibly say to excuse his behavior."

Oh, dear God. What have we done? "I can't believe this is happening."

"What did you think would happen when you kissed your boyfriend's brother?"

Katie's face went ten degrees warmer. Avery was right. What could Katie even say? "What will this do to Cooper's campaign?"

"Too early to say but obviously it can't be good. We'll meet tomorrow and go over our options."

"Have you talked to Gavin?"

"I thought it best he heard the news from Cooper."

"Right."

"That's not all."

At Avery's foreboding tone, Katie braced for more bad news.

"The person who posted the photo speculated you might be Cooper's mysterious baby mama."

Katie blinked. "What? That's crazy."

"Well, the photo makes it seem plausible, so welcome to the Riverbend rumor mill."

Katie winced at her friend's obvious anger. She couldn't blame her. Katie had come between her brothers. Avery wouldn't be the only one angry with her. Gavin's whole family would probably shun her. Worse yet—she deserved it.

Her chest tightened at the thought of losing the family that had come to mean so much to her. She'd grown close to Lisa, especially, but the woman wouldn't want anything to do with her now. Bad enough she'd kissed Cooper, but now people would think she'd gotten pregnant by her boyfriend's brother.

Her mother.

Katie had taken the relationship slowly, concerned her mom wouldn't pan out to be what Katie needed her to be. But ultimately it had been Katie who'd faltered. Beth would probably believe the worst of her. Why wouldn't she? Katie couldn't even imagine telling Beth who she was now after she'd publicly embarrassed herself. Katie may have just lost her only chance with her mother. If she hadn't been enough when she was a child, she certainly wouldn't be enough now.

Something inside shriveled up at the thought.

But this was no time for a pity party. She needed to talk to Gavin. Needed to apologize to him even though she didn't expect or deserve his forgiveness.

Avery took out her phone and checked the screen, her frown deepening. "Gavin got wind of the photo before Cooper got to him. It came to blows."

"Is he okay?"

Avery raised a sardonic brow. "Which one?"

Shame washed over Katie. She closed her eyes, her pulse throbbing in her temples. "I should go see Gavin."

"You might want to let him cool off awhile. He doesn't lose his temper often, but when he does . . ."

Katie wanted to get it over with, but this wasn't about what she wanted. The least she could do was give him a little time to process this.

"All right. I guess I'll wait till morning."

A few minutes later Katie let Avery out of her house and sagged against the door. It would be a long, sleepless night.

35

Cooper pressed a bag of frozen vegetables to tomorrow's black eye. Great look for a sheriff candidate. He didn't bother with the living room lights, preferring to sulk in darkness.

He'd resolved nothing with Gavin. Five minutes after his arrival, Rodriguez had pulled up in a cruiser—someone had called 911. For once the deputy didn't give Cooper a hard time. Once he saw it was Cooper, Rick quietly left the scene. He probably had no idea what was going on but he would soon.

Cooper's betrayal would be all over town by tomorrow—along with new rumors about Katelyn's supposed pregnancy. Had Avery reached her? She probably hated him now too. He sank deeper into the sofa cushions, wishing he could disappear into the crack with the Doritos crumbs.

Lights swept across the living room. It could be a neighbor returning home, but he couldn't be that lucky. He reluctantly peered through the curtains and spotted his mom's Tahoe. Would this night ever end?

A minute later three sharp raps came on his door. It was futile to ignore her. His vehicles were out front, and Mom wasn't one to give up. He pulled himself off the sofa and ditched the bag of frozen peas. He'd been punched a time or two in the line of duty, but not like this. His ears still rang. His head throbbed. He welcomed the pain as due penance. He only wished it were enough to absolve him from the guilt gnawing away at his gut.

He pulled open the door. His mother took in his battered face, no sign of sympathy in her stern look. She pushed past him into the apartment.

He closed the door and flipped on the lamp, feeling vaguely spacey. Their gazes clashed across the small space. There was nothing he could say in his own defense. He'd pulled a pin from the grenade, and some idiot had thrown it right into the middle of their family. "I already talked to Gavin."

Mom crossed her arms. "I can see that. But now I want you to talk to me. I want you to explain to me how you thought it was okay to steal your brother's girlfriend. Your brother, whom I might add, recently lost his only son and went through a difficult divorce. How does one excuse that?"

Guilt pinched hard. "I can't, Mom."

Her shoulders stiffened and she narrowed her eyes. "Try."

A wave of dizziness passed over him. He blinked against his blurry vision. "Have a seat. Please."

She stared hard at him for a full ten seconds

before she perched on the edge of the sofa.

He lowered his weight into the recliner. "Listen, I didn't intend for this to happen, Ma. When I met her that day out on the cliff, I didn't know who she was. While I helped her through the crisis, there was just some kind of attraction. Strong attraction. Once I realized who she was, I tried to put her from my mind. Tried to fight it. Tried to stay away. And then Gavin asked me to go on that hike with her and—"

"Don't you dare blame this on your brother."

"I'm not. I take full responsibility. You asked what happened and I'm trying to tell you."

"You're saying that's why you avoided the family? Because you were attracted to her?"

It was so much more than attraction. But no way was he throwing that out there. "Yes."

His mom gave an angry huff. "I can't believe you've done this. I can't believe *she's* done this. How could she come between two brothers like that?"

His heart gave a hard squeeze. "It was my fault, Mom. Please don't hold this against Katelyn."

Her gaze sharpened on him, a frown furrowing her brows. "How can I not? There were two people in that lip-lock, Cooper."

And what a lip-lock it had been. He winced at the errant thought. He was a terrible person. "I let things go too far. I thought I could just be friends with her. I thought I could . . . control myself.

She cares about Gavin. She didn't mean to hurt him or our family. Don't hold this against her. She's not like us—she doesn't have a family."

Mom's eyes slowly widened and her lips went slack.

He'd given away too much with that request. He turned to stare out the window, trying belatedly to hide his feelings. Better to play this off the way Gavin believed. Cooper was just an egomaniac out to prove he could have any woman he wanted, and Kate had been his victim.

He faced his mother. "You should stay out of it, Mom. Kate and Gavin can still work things out."

"You're in love with her." Her flat tone rang with certainty.

Cooper tried for a casual tone. "Don't be ridiculous. When have I ever fallen in love with anyone?" His pulse raced, throbbing behind his eyes.

She was quiet so long he thought she might let it drop.

"I should've known. You'd never hurt your brother for some passing fancy."

"Don't blow this out of proportion. I made a mistake but Gavin will have to forgive me eventually, right? Once he and Kate straighten things out this will blow over."

He hollowed out at the thought of it. Would Kate stay with Gavin? And if she did, would he ever be able to come around his family without this crushing feeling in his chest? "I'm sorry I caused a ruckus in the family, Mom. That was never my intention. I won't rest until I fix it."

"Some things can't be fixed, Cooper. And you're not fooling anyone here—least of all me."

He pressed his lips together. She wasn't getting a confession from him. That wouldn't do anyone any good. "Let it go, Ma. Please."

She studied him for a long, painful moment before she gave a resigned nod. She rose slowly to her feet, defeat in her stooped posture. As she walked toward the door, he wished for angry-mom back. Because the distress coming off her in waves was so much worse.

36

How could one little kiss cause so many problems?

Katie balked at the word *little* because there'd been nothing small or insignificant about that kiss. It had been the best one of her life. And if it hadn't completely turned her world upside down, she'd be savoring it over and over. But there was no point in doing that—unless self-torture counted. Because that kiss had cost her everyone she cared about.

Katie turned onto her back and pushed off the covers. As much as she dreaded facing Gavin, she hated being in this state of flux. Once she broke up with him, there would be no going back. She'd lose him and the Robinsons for good. But there was no help for it now.

She grabbed her phone from the nightstand and checked the time. Well after eleven at night and she was wide awake. As if irresistibly drawn to the forbidden, she opened her photos and flipped through them until she came to the ones she was searching for. She and Cooper on the trails. One of him filling his water container at a creek. A selfie of them in front of the shelter. One of him standing on a ledge that overlooked a beautiful vista. And one of her after he swiped her hat. She was reaching for it, laughing, as he snapped the shot with her phone. Then there was his collection of goofy selfies, taken when she left her phone unattended. She couldn't help but smile even as her eyes stung with tears.

She should get rid of these. They represented something she could never have. Looking at them would only bring heartache. Her thumb hovered over the Delete button, her heart kicking against her ribs.

The phone buzzed in her hand, startling her. A notification appeared on the screen. Gavin.

Are you awake?

Her pulse found a new gear. It was time to face up to what she'd done. She thumbed in her reply.

Yes.

His response came a few seconds later.

I'm outside your door.

Oh boy. She tossed her phone aside, jumped from bed, and threw on a robe. In a matter of seconds she was at the door. She paused to compose herself and caught a glimpse of her reflection in the mirror beside the door. Her eyes were red rimmed, her hair snarled. She looked almost as bad as she felt. After taking a deep breath she pulled open the door.

Gavin stood under the golden porch light in a rumpled T-shirt, his black hair tousled, his eyes bloodshot. He wasn't sporting a black eye or any other signs of the fistfight that had apparently happened earlier. But his eyes were sad, his shoulders stooped.

Her heart gave a tight squeeze. This was all her fault. She should've broken up with him long ago. Why was that so clear only now?

Oh, God. Give me words that won't hurt him even more.

But those words didn't exist. She'd made her choice the moment she returned Cooper's kiss. Maybe before that in hundreds of smaller decisions she'd made on the way to that defining moment.

He blurred as tears filled her eyes. "Gavin, I—I don't know what to say. I'm so sorry."

He seemed to take measure of her for a long moment. "Can I come in?"

"Of course." She opened the door.

He brushed past her and turned as she pushed the door shut.

Katie dabbed her leaking eyes, then turned on the light.

Gavin surveyed her from across the small space.

She swallowed against the lump in her throat. "Do you want to sit down?"

"Not really."

"I wanted to talk to you earlier, but Avery suggested I wait a bit."

He shoved his hands into his front pockets. "Probably good advice. I was pretty angry earlier."

"I'm so sorry about this. I feel—I feel just wretched. I never meant for this to happen. I never meant to hurt you."

"I believe you. I mean, I'm angry at you, but mostly I'm hurt."

"I'm sorry."

He scrubbed a hand over his face. "I can't get that picture out of my head. It seemed so . . . Did you at least push him away?"

He gazed at her with such hope, she wanted so badly to say yes. She opened her mouth. But no. That would be a lie, and she'd done enough of that, especially to herself.

He gave a wry laugh. "That's a no then."

"Gavin . . ."

"He's good, I'll give him that. Must be all that practice."

Her mouth worked for a moment. Words, none of them right, formed at the back of her throat. "I don't know what to say, Gavin. I made a terrible mistake."

"Look. As far as Cooper goes, I shouldn't be surprised. Women chase after him so he's used to getting what he wants. Maybe you were just a challenge."

Katie flinched. Was she an idiot for thinking she might be different?

"I'm just surprised you fell for him. I thought we had something special, and I never would've thought—Well, that's beside the point. You're not very experienced with romantic relationships, and I can see how he might've been able to take advantage of your naivete."

Katie blinked. Take advantage of her—

"He said it was the first and only time he kissed you. That true?"

Finally something she could get behind. "Yes, it's true. I promise."

"All right then. What's done is done, I guess. I mean, if I'm honest it sucks rotten eggs. But I'll deal. Relationships have hurdles, and I'm not incapable of understanding—and forgiving with time. Eventually I'll even forgive Cooper because he's my brother and I have no choice." The last was said through gritted teeth.

But she was too busy decoding the first part to lament his bitterness toward Cooper. Gavin still wanted to be with her.

The pull of hope was unreasonably irresistible. She could simply let Cooper take the lion's share of the blame. Take this life raft Gavin offered and make a future with him. Keep her surrogate family—the Robinsons would have to forgive her eventually. She could still have everything she'd been searching for. Almost everything.

There was only one problem: she didn't love Gavin.

In the past twelve hours her feelings for Cooper had become crystal clear. And Gavin deserved someone who loved him fully and completely. He deserved her honesty. Besides, how could she let Cooper take the fall when she was equally to blame?

But what if Gavin fell back into the despair he'd suffered before they'd gotten together? His family had been so grateful that she'd helped bring him out of that. But what if her rejection sent him spiraling again?

"Katie?" Gavin had taken a few steps closer in the quiet, closing the gap between them.

She couldn't lie and she couldn't make herself feel something she didn't. She would have to tell him the truth and trust God to get him through. She took a courageous breath and made herself say the words. "I'm so sorry, Gavin. But we can't be together anymore."

Furrows formed between his brows. "Why not?"

"I—I don't feel for you what I should."

Silence lengthened uncomfortably between them. "Since when? We have a great time together. Your kisses—you can't fake that, Katie."

Apparently she could. "I wasn't—" She fought for the right words but came up empty. How could she tell him his kisses felt platonic without insulting him? She couldn't.

"Don't let Cooper take this away from us." He took two steps closer. "I can forgive this. Give me some credit."

She let out a shaky breath and took his hand. "I give you all the credit in the world, Gavin. You are such a great guy, and you deserve someone who loves you. I just—I don't think I'm ever going to get there. I don't—I don't think of you that way."

His lips twisted and he pulled his hand from hers. "Boy, he's really gotten under your skin, hasn't he?"

"I can't let you blame Cooper for this. Not entirely. Regardless of any feelings I might have for him—"

"Feelings?"

"—this thing between you and me never could've gone anywhere. I kept waiting to feel more but it just—never happened. I'm sorry. I really am."

A shadow flickered in his eyes as his jaw knotted. "If that's true why didn't you just break up with me before now? It's been months."

"You're absolutely right. I'm so sorry. I should've said something weeks ago. That was selfish of me, but I just kept hoping—I didn't want to hurt you after everything you'd been through: the divorce and losing your so—" She bit her lip. Her gaze darted to his, hoping he didn't realize what she'd nearly said.

He narrowed his eyes. "My *son?* Is that what you were going to say?"

Katie wished she could reel the words back, but it was too late.

"How long have you known? And why didn't you say something?"

"I wanted you to be the one to tell me."

"Well, clearly I was too late. Who told you—some busybody in town? Avery?" Something shifted in his eyes. He gave a harsh laugh. *"Cooper."*

Katie looked away. She hadn't thought it was possible, but she'd just managed to make things even worse between the brothers.

"It was Cooper. Say it."

"It—it wasn't intentional. He thought you'd already told me. He felt terrible about—"

"Stop defending him." The words were clipped. "He's got you all messed up, and you don't even know it."

Katie pressed her lips together. Nothing she said right now would help.

"That was *my* story to tell, not his."

"I agree. I'm sorry. I kept hoping you'd—"

"What—tell you? I was planning to do that tomorrow night, actually. Remember our out-of-town date?"

"Right. I'm sorry, Gavin."

"You keep saying that, but you know what? It doesn't help. Doesn't change a thing." He shook his head. "You stayed with me out of pity."

"No." But wasn't that the truth? She was drowning in regret. She'd messed things up so badly. Her eyes filled again.

"So . . . what? You think you're going to be with *him* now? Good luck making it past date three."

He didn't give Cooper enough credit. But that was his anger talking. "I'm not going to date Cooper. I wouldn't do that to your family."

"No offense, but I'm finding that hard to believe just now." He palmed the back of his neck.

An awkward pause stretched between them. Katie longed to fill it with assurances, but he wouldn't believe her anyway. Words were cheap, especially now. She'd have to show him she meant what she'd said—and that would require time.

His laughter held an edge. "I feel like an absolute idiot. Right under my nose."

"Please don't feel that way. There was nothing going on. Nobody else even knew we—" She cut off when she realized that wasn't entirely true.

And Gavin was too astute to miss it. His eyes sharpened on her. "What? Did somebody else know about this?"

"There was nothing to know. We never did anything."

"But you had feelings." His nostrils flared. "And somebody else knew about them."

She held his stormy gaze for a long moment,

then released a resigned breath. "Avery walked in once during a . . . a moment."

"Avery. Great. Just great."

"Nothing happened and we told her that. She believed us."

"*We. Us.* Are you hearing yourself, Katie?" His eyes snapped with fire. "Wow. Great family I have. Really looking out for me."

Her stomach hardened at his words. "They *do* look out for you. You have no idea how lucky you are to have them."

Their gazes clashed. There was so much in his expression. His brows furrowed, his jaw clenched, but it was the despair in his eyes that crushed her. There was so much she wanted to say. She wanted to comfort him. Help put his family back together. But it was a little hard when she'd been the one who'd torn them apart.

"Know what? We really don't have anything else to say. I'm just going to leave now." He strode toward the door, his face a mask of anger.

Sensing his need for distance, she stood back as he let himself out. A minute later his tires squealed as he pulled from her driveway. Feeling like something a cat coughed up, she locked the door and turned off the light. Her chest was heavy with the crushing weight of Gavin's pain. The hollow ache of guilt.

She wiped her face as she made her way to the bedroom and crawled under the covers. She'd done this. She made this enormous mess. She'd been so desperate for love—anybody's love—that she'd broken an entire family. How selfish and pathetic was she?

Her eyes burned again, but with the resolve of a warrior she held back the flood of tears. She felt for her phone in the bed beside her. Once her hand closed around it she opened the photos again. In several quick motions she located the photos of Cooper and deleted every last one of them. Only then did she allow herself to give in to the raw grief.

37

Cooper hunched over his desk as he filled out paperwork on a fender bender. It was barely nine o'clock in the morning, and he'd rather be out on the streets. But they had a drunk guy in lockup, and it was his turn to babysit.

Then again, being shut away had its upside too. For one, he could escape the rumors still swirling about town—half of them true. For two weeks he'd endured the speculative stares and outright glares.

In other news, Megan had no doubt returned from vacation, but he hadn't made it back to Mars Hill to confront her. He had tried to call her at work twice but no luck. And in light of the new rumors, his hands were too full to worry about Megan and her false accusation.

Cooper touched the still-tender spot below his eye. The color had morphed to a sickly yellow, but the bruise was almost gone. His mortification was only outdone by his self-disgust. His family still hated him—not that he blamed them.

He hadn't seen Gavin since the fight.

At least Avery was finally talking to him again—though it was just barely and only about business. He'd wanted to put out a statement clarifying that Katelyn was not the pregnant woman who'd accused him of denying paternity. But apparently Kate didn't want that and Avery agreed. Such a statement would only bring more attention to the fated kiss and pregnancy rumor.

Cooper longed to check on Kate, but that would be a mistake for so many reasons. All the regret in the world hadn't taken away his feelings for her. No matter what he did, what he told himself, he couldn't stop thinking about her. Couldn't stop remembering the way her lips had felt against his. The way she'd felt so right in his arms.

At first he'd checked up on her through Avery. But his sister had finally put a stop to that. *"If you ask about her one more time, I'm going to slug you myself."*

"Hey, you . . . Officer."

The voice shook Cooper from his reverie.

The twentysomething guy in custody peered at him from across the hall through the bars, stringy black hair hanging in his eyes. "Dude, what happened? How'd I get here?"

"You were brought in early this morning. You passed out at the bar and fell off the stool." Cooper went back to the report.

"Am I under arrest?"

"No, I'll release you when you're sober."

"I'm sober now, man. Lemme outta here. I'm fine."

"Let's give it a couple more hours. You hungry? I got milk and donuts."

A moment later the sound of retching carried across the space. He hoped the guy had at least hit the receptacle. Cooper set down his pen and went to check on his guest—Jaron something. He found the man hunched over the stainless-steel commode, dry heaving. A sweat had broken out on his forehead.

Holding his breath against the stench, Cooper unlocked the cell door and handed the guy a water bottle.

Jaron moaned as he flushed the toilet and took the water.

"Small sips." Cooper felt a moment's pity for the guy. "Nothing's worth feeling like this, buddy. Remember that next time you're ordering shots by the dozen."

Cooper left Jaron huddled on the bench seat, eyes closed in misery, muttering something about his mama and daddy. He was almost finished with the forms when he heard the station door open down the hall.

A moment later his mom swept into the office in a light-blue top and jeans, her hair up in a messy do. Her eyes looked tired, and no amount of makeup could disguise the dark circles beneath them.

Cooper took that one on the chin. "Twice in one month. This is getting to be a habit, Ma."

Rodriguez strode into the room and caught sight of Cooper's mom. A dopey grin formed on his face as he grew two inches in stature. "Well, hello there, Mrs. Robinson. Aren't you a sight for sore eyes?"

"Déjà vu," Cooper muttered.

Mom patted Rodriguez on the arm. "Hi there, honey. How are you?"

"Better by the second." Rodriguez held out the box of donuts. "What's your pleasure, ma'am?"

"Thank you, but I already had breakfast."

"Suit yourself." The deputy snatched a sprinkled donut.

"I hope that's not your breakfast, Ricky. You need to start your day off with some protein."

"Aw, you do care about me."

Cooper gave the deputy a withering look. "You mind? We were about to have a discussion here."

Rodriguez winked at Cooper's mom. "I'll be in the break room if you need me."

"We won't," Cooper said.

"You shouldn't be rude," Mom said after the man slipped out of the office. "He's a nice boy."

A moan sounded from the jail cell.

Mom glanced that direction. "Is that man okay?"

"Just a hangover. What's up?"

The concern on her face shifted to something less sympathetic and infinitely more stubborn. "Jeff and I are calling a family meeting tomorrow night and you're coming."

He gave a slow shake of his head. "Listen, I'm really busy—"

"Well, get unbusy."

"I have an appointment with—"

"This is your family, Cooper Robinson. Nothing is more important than that."

"She's right, man," Jaron whined from his cell. "Family's all that really matters."

Cooper set down his pen, giving a hard sigh. "Look, Ma, I'm not sure this is a good idea. It's too soon. Gavin's still pretty upset and—"

"How would you know? You haven't seen him since your brawl."

"Hardly a brawl—I didn't even fight back."

"You want a trophy?"

He pressed his lips together. She had a sharp tongue, his mom.

"It's been two weeks, and I'm not letting you guys steep in this hogwash any longer. It's not healthy. It happened. We need to get it out on the table and deal with it."

"What else is there to say?"

"Well, gee, I don't know. You could apologize for starters."

"I did!"

"Maybe this comes as a shock, but you kissed your brother's girlfriend—it might take more than one apology."

"Dude . . ." Jaron muttered. "You poached your brother's girl?"

Cooper frowned at him. "Do you mind?"

Mom hitched her purse onto her shoulder. "I'm

312

not taking no for an answer. I'll see you tomorrow at six. Bring a dish."

From across the hall came a weak laugh. "And you were giving *me* advice?"

Cooper had intended to arrive early, but the stupid dish had taken longer to cook than he'd expected. When he rounded the corner of his parents' house, everyone else was already there. Jeff flipped burgers on the grill. Avery talked to Mom on the patio, and Gavin perched on the picnic table, looking like he'd rather be sitting atop an active volcano.

Cooper sucked in a breath of courage, his pulse thrumming in his ears. He'd missed his brother the past couple weeks and wanted nothing more than to put things right between them. He just didn't know what he could say or do to make that happen.

Gavin caught sight of him and his spine straightened. "Surprised you had the nerve to show up. Nice shiner."

Cooper held his tongue as he set his mac and cheese on the table with the other dishes.

"Thank you for coming, honey." Mom gave him a stiff hug, then shot Gavin a pointed look. "We're going to be adults about this. Aren't we?"

Gavin's gaze remained locked on Cooper. "Whatever you say, Mom."

From the grill Jeff greeted Cooper, and Avery

sidled over to the table, taking a precarious position between Gavin and him. "I, for one, am glad Dad and Lisa forced this meeting. Being the go-between is getting a little old."

"And Jeff and I are tired of hosting family suppers to have only Avery turn up. No offense, honey."

"None taken."

"We're family." Jeff appeared at Lisa's side. "No matter what goes down between us, we have to forgive and move on."

Gavin slowly stood, jerking a thumb in Cooper's direction. "And we just let him off the hook?"

Time to man up. "Listen, I'm really sorry, Gavin. I didn't mean to hurt you. I didn't mean to hurt anyone. I take full responsibility for what happened. It was all my fault."

Gavin smirked. "That's not the way Katie's telling it. Maybe you two should've gotten your stories straight."

Heat flushed through Cooper's neck. He had no idea what Kate was saying or thinking. "I haven't even seen or talked—"

"Sure, you haven't."

"—to Katie since . . . since that day."

"Since you kissed her, you mean?"

"All right, Gavin," Avery said. "Stop provoking him. That's not productive."

Gavin glared at her. "And keeping this from me

was? I haven't forgotten you betrayed me too."

"I did not betray—"

"You could've warned me!" He turned his glower on Cooper. "And you. You have a big mouth. You had no right to tell Katie about my son."

Jesse. Cooper grimaced. "I thought you'd already told her about—"

"Shut up! I don't want to hear your excuses."

Mom stepped closer. "All right, you guys, that's enough."

"Did you know about them too?" Gavin's tone was accusing. "You and Jeff? Was I the last one to find out?"

"Of course we didn't know, and I don't care for your tone."

"There was nothing to know. We hadn't even done anything."

"Until you made out at the Dairy Bar in broad daylight?"

Mom shelved her hands on her hips. "Can we please just have a calm—"

"Come on, sweetheart." Jeff eased Mom away. "Let them figure it out."

"What do you want from me?" Cooper asked Gavin. "I can't exactly turn back time and make a different decision. I said I'm sorry and I am."

"I was betrayed by my brother and the woman I was falling for. And my sister knew what was going on and didn't tell me. So excuse me if

315

forgiveness isn't the first thing that comes to mind."

"Then we're at a dead end because there's nothing else I can do at this point. And you can stop blaming Avery. I convinced her she had nothing to worry about."

"Aren't you a big man, taking all the blame. And you lied to her because obviously there *was* something to worry about."

"I thought I had it under control. I tried not to . . ."

"Kiss my girlfriend?"

Cooper threw his hands in the air. This was hopeless. There was nothing he could say right now to appease his brother. It was just like Cooper had told his mom. Two weeks hadn't been long enough. By all appearances Gavin needed more like two years.

"Do you actually have feelings for her, or were you just toying with her?" The words seemed grated from Gavin's throat. But they obviously came from someplace raw and real.

Cooper searched his brother's features for some hint of which answer would be the right one. His brother's eyes were tight at the corners, his breath heaving. But something less tangible flickered in his eyes. Desperation? A need to know. To understand.

And suddenly Cooper knew that the right answer was the truthful one. It would hurt his brother, but Cooper was done lying. Done trying to hide his feelings. Look where that had gotten him—gotten them all. "I have feelings for her."

Their gazes held for a long, uncomfortable moment. Tension thickened the air in the space between them. Cooper resisted the urge to take back his answer. To Gavin, the words must've felt like a knife piercing his heart.

Gavin's nostrils flared. "Terrific. I hope you guys will be very happy together." Then he stalked away.

"Gavin, wait," Lisa called.

Jeff whispered something in her ear, then took off after Gavin, leaving her behind.

Cooper stood helplessly, feet rooted to the ground. There was no point in chasing his brother. There was nothing he could say to fix this.

Avery crossed her arms. "Bravo, Brother. That went just great."

38

Katie awakened in a sweat. In the early morning light her heart pounded against her ribs, and she shoved away the suffocating covers. Her recurring dream was officially back. She'd had it three times in the past month.

As usual she'd been outside a house and was desperate for entry. The wind blew and wind chimes tinkled in the distance. Then it was pouring rain. She pounded frantically on the door. When nobody answered she peered through a window. Soft lighting brightened the interior. A large paper cup sat on the circular dining table. Suddenly it was raining inside now, too, and the cup was filling with water.

There was Cooper. She called to him through the torrential downpour and he turned her way. But as soon as their gazes connected, the window was gone. Somehow bricked over. *Cooper! Let me in. Please, let me in!* Rain poured down her face—or were they tears?

And then she awakened.

She rolled onto her back, letting her breath settle in her chest. Letting go of the last vestiges of the disturbing dream.

The month of October had been long and

grueling. She didn't hear from any of the Robinsons—except Avery, who couldn't possibly avoid her. She wrote a letter of apology to Lisa and Jeff, but there was no response. Not that she blamed them.

The rumor of Cooper and Katie had spread throughout Riverbend. She'd caused trouble between the beloved Robinsons and had been cast as the villain in the unfortunate drama. After being snubbed at the Grab 'n' Go Deli and shunned at Millie's Mug and Bean, Katie decided to stick closer to home.

But even at work things had changed. Her relationship with Avery was stilted at best. Katie couldn't blame her. She'd broken her friend's trust and wreaked havoc on her family. Avery must regret ever bringing her to Riverbend. Katie had never meant to heap more problems on her already-burdened friend.

She rubbed her eyes and sat up in bed. Today was the last day of Trail Days. She would go and support the event even though she was officially out of the loop. Technically that had been her choice.

The day after the photo of the kiss had materialized, Katie texted Beth Wallace. She sweated bullets over the wording.

Beth, I'm stepping out of the marketing for Trail Days. From now on please report directly to Lisa. Thank you for all your work on the event.

A while later Beth responded.

Will do. Happy to help.

Katie hadn't heard from her mother since—that pretty much said it all. She'd wanted Beth to be proud of her, but Katie only managed to humiliate and embarrass herself. She'd become the town pariah. Still, somehow, every day that passed without word from her mother felt like her childhood abandonment happening all over again. Insecurity festered inside like bacteria in an open wound.

She'd wanted to have her life together before she revealed her identity to Beth. She'd fought hard for her nursing degree, and she had a good job and a beautiful little house. But now the community, to which she was just starting to belong, had spurned her. And her mother's unresponsiveness had triggered all those feelings of unworthiness.

It was official: Katie had been rejected by everyone she cared about.

She'd walked around the past four weeks with a hollow ache inside. Her new home no longer felt like a sanctuary but a prison. Because nobody outside these walls wanted her.

For the first time she regretted spreading Spencer's ashes because there was no place she could go to remember him. To talk to him. And she desperately wanted to talk to him. She thought she'd known loneliness after her brother died. But it was so much worse now. Now that she'd been accepted into the Robinson family. For the first time she'd had a big family she was beginning to think of as hers. She was loved.

But obviously that love was conditional. Even her mother appeared to have ditched her. She pressed a palm to her tightened chest.

Beth and Lisa seemed to be getting on, however. Earlier this week Katie had caught Lisa's WPBR interview, promoting Trail Days. Everything was progressing just fine without Katie apparently. She should be used to being the odd man out, but strangely it hurt even worse this time around, when she'd been within arm's reach of what she longed for.

She closed her eyes against the sting, the image of Cooper forming behind her lids. Those deep-set brown eyes—the way they smiled just before his mouth did. The way they looked at her as if she was everything he'd ever wanted.

She allowed the memory of their kiss to wash over her like a warm rain shower. The mesmerizing ardor in his gaze as he leaned into her. The exquisite gentleness of his touch as he cupped her face. The bold desperation of his lips as they moved over hers. Her fingertips tingled as she remembered the silky softness of his hair.

She opened her eyes, breaking off the sweet memory, her pulse thrumming in her veins. What she'd give for one more kiss.

But there was no point in thoughts like that. Out of sight, out of mind was clearly not working. It was doing quite the opposite actually. Something had to give—but she had no idea what that was.

Resolved to making the best of things, she swung her feet over the edge of the bed. After weeks of being sequestered she was eager to get outside and be around people again. The town was filled with tourists, and it would be easy to get lost in the crowd.

Autumn had swept from the mountaintops down into the valley. The hills around town burst with autumnal colors, and the loamy aroma of earth scented the air.

Katie drew in a whiff of fall as she entered the throng of people on Main Street. A thrill of pride coursed through her. The streets were packed. Crowds gathered around the booths set up in the grassy town square. On the far side of the lawn, lines snaked from food trucks. People milled about, enjoying caramel apples, elephant ears, and turkey drumsticks as they listened to the band on the stage. The rousing country music and colorful flag banners created a celebratory backdrop while the tempting smell of fair food beckoned the hungry.

Along Main Street people wandered into the stores and restaurants. The event seemed to be a huge success. Hopefully the income stream for the weekend would be enough to make up for the loss of revenue from the temporarily rerouted trail. Hopefully the town would go on thriving.

After spending so much time at home, Kate welcomed the diversion of the festivities. She found a game booth, manned by a teenager she didn't recognize. She was no good at archery, apparently, as a boy of about ten thrashed her. She was better at rock painting and got to take her work of art with her.

On the other side of the square, Gavin was atop the dunking booth, shivering on the stand, having clearly been dunked already. It was the first time Katie had seen him since the breakup, and it warmed her heart to see him smiling.

Avery's high ponytail swung as she wound up and delivered a fast pitch. It just missed the target. Gavin laughed as she taunted him. It seemed the brother and sister had made up. Maybe Katie hadn't totally destroyed the family after all.

Avery delivered another pitch. This one hit the target, and Gavin dropped into the tank with a splash she couldn't hear from this distance. Avery gave a loud whoop.

A smile tugged at Katie's lips even as that familiar hollow feeling swelled in her chest. She turned the opposite direction, her breaths coming quickly. Okay. She'd seen them, and she lived through it. The family would be fine—that was all that mattered.

She needed a distraction. She stopped at a small stage that had been set up for guest speakers. A crowd had gathered and Katie soon saw why. The man with the red-tipped cane drew her in with his stories and inspiring attitude. He was the only blind man to have ever completed the Appalachian Trail. When he was finished the crowd offered thunderous applause.

By now Katie's stomach was rumbling, so she wandered over to the food trucks and bought an elephant ear. She walked the busy street, enjoying the sweet treat, working the bakery tissue down. She moved aside for a passing family. The couple's little girl struggled with her snow cone and a wooden walking stick she must've won at a game booth. The woman took the walking stick, then the dad swung the girl onto his shoulders, securing her legs with his strong arms.

Katie glanced around, suddenly conscious of families everywhere. A retired couple chatting at a booth. A family with three boys at the wheel-barrow races. A couple strolling down the street, a balloon tied to the baby stroller's handle.

Katie was only half finished with her elephant

ear, but the confection suddenly felt heavy in her stomach. She stopped by a trash can to throw the rest away, dabbing a napkin at the powdered sugar she probably had all over her mouth. As she tossed the napkins away a familiar laugh drew her attention.

Just across the way Lisa worked a booth, assisting an author with a book signing. Lisa opened a book and slid it toward the author as she chatted merrily with a customer. Beth flanked the author's other side, taking the money. The trio chuckled.

There they were: Katie's birth mom and the woman she'd begun to think of as her surrogate mother. They seemed to be having such a good time together.

And Katie was officially on the outside looking in, just like in her dream.

As if suddenly alerted to Katie's presence, Lisa's gaze darted in Katie's direction. She ducked behind the garbage can, her heart rate skyrocketing. Had Lisa seen her staring? Katie closed her eyes, wishing she could disappear. She never should've come today.

When she opened her eyes she focused on a pair of familiar black shoes, positioned only a few feet away in the grass.

39

The festivities were pretty tame so far. Cooper had taken extra hours to cover the event, wanting to stay busy. The starchy uniform was hot under the heat of the afternoon, but the distractions of familiar faces made time pass quickly.

He'd just finished chatting with a campaign donor when he spotted Katelyn on a curb near the craft booths. The sun glinted off her wavy blonde hair. She'd paired her white shorts—his personal favorite—with a pale-blue top that showed off her tan. She was a sight for sore eyes. Inexorably drawn to her, he headed that direction.

He hadn't seen her since the day he'd kissed her four weeks ago, but he'd thought of her a million times. Wondered how she was doing. If she ever thought of him. If she hated him. Because while the locals seemed to have exonerated him for betraying his brother, he wasn't sure they'd absolved Kate. He'd hoped that keeping his distance would rectify that, but he was beginning to wonder if it was enough.

As he neared she ducked behind the garbage can. He stopped, glancing the direction she'd been staring. Across the way his mom and Beth worked a booth together.

His gaze returned to Kate, still squatting—hiding, really—behind the garbage can. A vise tightened around his heart. She'd lost everyone she cared about and it was all his fault. If only he'd been able to control his feelings . . . If only he hadn't kissed her.

But he had and now his whole family had spurned her. Cooper had hardly spoken with Gavin since their argument at their parents' house, but according to Avery his brother hadn't spoken with Kate since the breakup. His mom and Jeff also seemed to be holding a grudge. Even Avery was still upset with her friend, though she claimed to be behaving at work.

But how bad must things be for Kate if she felt the need to hide?

Her head came up, her lashes lifting as she followed the line of his legs all the way up to his face. She shielded her eyes from the sun and rose slowly to her feet.

A pretty blush bloomed in her cheeks and she bit her lip. A wisp of hair blew across her face.

His fingers twitched with the need to tuck it back into place. When those blue eyes fixed on him, his heart flopped in his chest. "Hi, Kate."

"I was—I was just . . ." Her gaze fell to the ground, and she squatted to pick up a napkin. "I dropped this." She tossed the trash in the can.

"How've you been?" he asked.

"Fine. Great! I'm great. How are you?"

Pain unfurled in his chest at her forced enthusiasm. "I've been better."

Her smile faltered. "It's almost Election Day. How are the polls looking?"

His campaign had taken a hit from the rumors. "Not great, I'm afraid. But Avery scheduled me for the closing speech tomorrow since half the county's here. I guess she's hoping the last-ditch effort will be enough to save the campaign."

Her eyes filled with something more real. Sorrow. "I'm so sorry, Cooper."

"Come on, now. It's not your fault."

"Only it is—a little bit."

He shook his head. "I don't see it that way, Kate. Whatever's meant to happen will happen." Surprisingly, the sentiment rang true.

"Nobody deserves that position more than you."

Warmth flushed through him. He still wanted her. He wanted to pull her close right now and claim her as his own. Only thoughts of Gavin anchored his arms at his sides.

"Thank you." He'd have to satisfy himself with polite conversation. And in fact, he was hungry for the details of her life. "How are things progressing with your mother?"

Kate dug up a bright smile, glancing over her shoulder. "They're fine! Really good."

But if that were true, why had she ducked at the sight of his mom and Beth? He made a mental note to speak to his mom. Now that things had blown over a bit, there was no reason she couldn't reach out to Kate. Likewise, Avery needed to let the woman off the hook. If anyone deserved a little grace, it was Kate.

"And work?" he asked. "How's that going?"

His radio chirped and the dispatcher's voice came through. "Disturbance near the Trailhead Bar and Grill at the corner of Main and Walnut. Requesting immediate assistance."

"You're busy." Kate's smile wobbled as she backed away. "I should let you get back to it."

"Kate . . ." There were so many things he wanted to say. None of them wise. None of them appropriate.

"Have a good day, Cooper. Good luck on Tuesday." She gave one more dazzling smile, then turned and made her way between two booths. And then she was gone.

Cooper responded to the dispatcher, then headed toward the disturbance on foot as he was only a couple blocks away. While he walked he couldn't seem to get Kate out of his head. She was a poor liar. That overly bright smile wouldn't fool anyone, least of all him.

The crowded streets took a while to navigate, but soon he reached the corner, and it didn't take him long to see the problem. A fight had broken out right outside the restaurant. Cooper wove through the crowd that had gathered and when he broke through, his steps faltered at the familiar face.

His father had gained weight, adding to his stocky build. He now wore his gray hair in a crew cut, giving his face an intimidating bulldog look. His brown eyes, though, were like an older reflection of Cooper's.

His heart jackknifed in his chest. What was he doing back in town?

His father swung sloppily at another man, who easily dodged the fist. "I want my money!" his dad slurred, grabbing the man's shirt. "You owe me."

The man pushed him off with great effort. "I don't owe you nothing. Get away from me."

Cooper's father went after the guy.

Cooper shook himself from his stupor. "Deputy sheriff. That's enough!" He leaped forward and grabbed his dad by the back of the shirt.

His father fought for release.

"I said that's enough!" Cooper gripped his dad in a hold. "It's me, Dad. Settle it down."

Lonnie, the owner of Trailhead Bar and Grill, approached with a frown pulling his brows tight. "Your dad wrecked my bar. I'm pressing charges."

"I'm sorry. We'll get it sorted out."

The man looked less than impressed with his assurance. "You'd better. There's at least two thousand dollars' worth of damage in there."

"I said we'll sort it out."

With one last scowl at Cooper's dad, Lonnie stalked back into the restaurant.

His father struggled against him. "Let me go! I wanna go."

"Cool it," Cooper said firmly. "I mean it."

"He owes me money! I won that bet."

Cooper took in the crowd gathered around. "All right, folks, excitement's over. Move along now."

"I won that bet fair and square. He ripped me off!"

The crowd started to disperse. "We'll figure it out. Now, will you settle down, or do you want to do this the hard way?"

His father stopped struggling, his breaths heaving against Cooper's chest. He reeked of whiskey and desperation.

"Let's do this without cuffs, all right, Dad?" He slowly released his father, who wavered on his feet.

"Where are you taking me?" Dad yelled. "Am I under arrest?"

"We're just going to take a little breather. Let you sober up a little."

"I'm not drunk!"

"Don't lie to me!"

"It wasn't my fault. He wouldn't pay me—he owes me money!"

Cooper regretted not driving his cruiser because now he had to walk two blocks with his drunk, loudmouthed father. The judgmental stares took him right back to childhood. They were only tourists, but he recognized plenty of faces.

Cooper wasn't responsible for his father's actions. He was just a deputy doing his job. He loved this town—his town. But people could be fickle, their feelings and opinions manipulated by rumors and falsehoods. He didn't have anything to prove to them. He was square with God—if not with Gavin . . . or the county at large.

It was enough that he tried to do the right thing. He'd devoted his life to upholding the law, for crying out loud. How much more esteemed did he need to be? If being a deputy didn't mute the internal whisper telling him he was unworthy of respect, becoming a sheriff wouldn't either.

Cooper stopped at a crosswalk, a firm grip on his dad's arm. The man wavered, pointing. "I know that guy! Hey, I know that guy!"

Cooper glanced in the direction he pointed—a sea of faces, only one of them familiar. The light changed and Cooper tugged his father along. "Come on, we're almost there."

By the end of the day word would be all over Riverbend that Craig Burton was back in town. Maybe it would remind everyone exactly where sheriff-candidate Cooper Robinson had really come from.

But Cooper knew who he was now—and he was not his father.

• • •

"Is it true?" Gavin said as he entered the sheriff's office. He wore the same frown he'd sported last time Cooper had seen him.

"He's in lockup, sobering up."

Gavin's expression went a shade darker. "What's he doing back in town?"

"Who knows. Lonnie Purdy's going to press charges though. Dad caused a fight at the Trailhead and there are damages."

"Great."

Cooper pushed back from his desk. "Don't worry about it. You can go back to the festival. I'll handle Dad."

Gavin pinned Cooper with a long, unswerving look.

Cooper squirmed under his brother's perusal. He was almost afraid to ask. "What?"

"You've had quite the month."

Cooper gritted his teeth. He really didn't need this today. Gavin wasn't wrong though. How much bad luck could one guy have—and all of it leading right up to Election Day?

The thought gave him pause. *Was* it all just a coincidence? Megan coming to town, accusing him of impregnating her, only to disappear again? Someone catching him kissing Kate and posting the photo on his campaign site? His troublemaking dad turning up in town only days before the big vote?

Too many coincidences. And he couldn't see Megan instigating all this. But he could see someone else doing it. Someone who stood to gain plenty from trashing Cooper's reputation. And the very person who could help Cooper verify his suspicions was currently in the tank.

Cooper's whole body tensed. He pushed back the chair, strode out of his office, and crossed the hall. His dad was slumped on the bench, drifting off.

Cooper scowled at him. "Why did you come here?"

Dad squinted up at him. "You—you brought me here. Didn't you?"

"Not to jail. Back here, to Riverbend. You've been gone a long time. Why come back now?"

Cooper tried to bury the part of himself that hoped the answer might have something to do with missing his sons. But there it was, lingering just under the surface.

Gavin shuffled to a stop beside him. "What's going on?"

His father's eyes fluttered shut.

"Dad! Why did you come back?"

"I didn't wanna. But the man—the man gave me a hundred bucks."

Cooper's gaze connected with Gavin's, holding for a long beat.

"What man?" Gavin asked his father.

"I don't know. Don't remember."

Cooper tightened his jaw. His breaths felt stuffed in his chest. He strode back to the office, to his desk, and leaned over his computer. He pulled up a website, found what he was searching for, and hit Print.

"What's going on?" Gavin had followed him back to the office. "Who's he talking about?"

The printer went through its operation, then spit out the copy. Cooper snatched it up. As he passed his brother, he held up the photo. "This one."

"Sean Curtis? Why would he—?"

Cooper carried the photo to the cell where his father was drifting off again. "Dad, wake up. Look at this."

"What? What happened? Where am I?"

"I need you to look at this photo. Is this the guy who paid you to come back to town?"

His father blinked as if trying to focus on the picture.

"Is that him, Dad?" Gavin asked. "The man who paid you to come back to town?"

"Look closely. It's important."

Their father blinked his swollen eyes. "Don't remember. Hundred bucks. Same as that bet. Didn't get my money." His eyelids fluttered shut.

Cooper bit back an expletive. "He was probably too drunk to remember anything. But it was Sean. I know it was."

Gavin's scowl deepened. "That dirty dog. How low can you sink to win an election?"

"If he's low enough to pay off a drunk, he's low enough to bribe a pregnant woman to lie about the baby's father."

"And low enough to post a damaging picture to his opponent's social media page. He's been behind all of this."

Cooper grinded his teeth. His muscles quivered. They would probably never know who took and posted that picture—the profile had been gone the next day. But Sean was somehow responsible for it and all the rest—he was sure of it. He marched back into the office and swiped his keys off his desk.

"Where are you going?"

"To confront him."

"That won't get you anywhere."

"Well, it'll sure make me feel better."

"When he denies everything?"

"No, when I put my fist in his face."

Gavin blocked the doorway. "That isn't going to win you an election."

"I'm not letting him get away with this. Now, move out of my way." He shoved his brother.

Gavin shoved back. "I'm not suggesting you do. But you gotta slow down and make a plan or you'll end up as Dad's cellmate."

Cooper got up in Gavin's face. "He did a lot more than just hurt my reputation!"

"You think I don't know that? Huh? I'm collateral damage here, Coop, but we can't go off half-cocked. Come on now, we have to think this through."

Cooper's breaths came hard and his shoulders heaved. He was eye to eye with Gavin. Sean Curtis was guilty as sin, but he hadn't broken any laws. And short of finding Megan, what evidence did he have? Even if his dad remembered later, no one would take the word of a drunk man—Cooper's own father—over Sean. It was infuriating.

But the look in his brother's eyes calmed him. It said *We're in this together. I've got your back.* And Cooper needed to know that more now than ever before.

40

Evening had settled over Riverbend Gap, bringing a sense of calm over the festivities. But Katie's nerves still jangled as she stood near the back of the crowd gathered around the stage in the town square. In a few minutes Cooper would take the stage for the closing ceremony. Public speaking wasn't his favorite thing, even though he always presented himself well.

After running into him earlier, she'd hidden at home for the rest of the afternoon. Seeing him had been a punch in the heart. But she couldn't resist seeing him again, if only from a distance.

She crossed her arms against the cool fall breeze as Lisa took the stage. She looked every inch the organized planner with her smart dress and clipboard. Jeff and Avery, also dressed up for the event, met her on stage. They would stand behind Cooper tonight—literally.

Katie peered over the crowd, seeking Gavin's familiar face. It was go-time and he was nowhere to be seen. His absence would be conspicuous and would reflect badly on Cooper. Guilt compressed her chest.

From the side stage Cooper mounted the platform, and all Katie's thoughts turned to mush. Instead of his usual uniform, he wore a crisp gray suit. He was so handsome, that formfitting coat setting off his broad shoulders and trim waist.

Cooper took his place at the back of the stage while his mom approached the podium and got the closing ceremonies underway. She thanked a host of people, including Katie, and brought a few key volunteers onto the stage—Beth Wallace among them. After they exited the stage Lisa introduced her son to a smattering of polite applause.

As Cooper stepped up to the podium, Gavin mounted the stage. His gaze connected with his brother's.

She wished she were close enough to see their expressions. Surely Gavin wouldn't rebuff his brother in front of everyone. It would reignite the rumors. It might even cost Cooper the election.

But after a poignant pause Gavin gave Cooper a brief nod and joined his family.

Maybe all wasn't right between the brothers, but it would be eventually. Gavin's appearance, his support for Cooper, spoke volumes.

Cooper welcomed the crowd and thanked them for attending Trail Days. Katie's stomach was in knots, but as he settled in behind the podium she began to relax. He didn't read from a teleprompter or use a prepared speech. Instead he spoke from the heart on the importance of community. He talked about his love for the area and the people in it. The importance of maintaining law and order and his desire to keep Madison County a safe place to raise a family.

"This is a relocation community," he said. "People come to visit—they hike into Riverbend and love it so much they leave everything behind to come live here. I don't blame them.

"I'm not saying it's all sunshine and rainbows here. We have our good and bad, our ups and downs. Maybe I'm a little partial because this has always been my home. But this community is like a family in that it embraces you with open arms. I know a little about that."

He gave his family a sidelong look. "Sometimes family isn't the situation you're born into but the people who've chosen to love you along the way."

The words caught like a burr on Katie's heart, and as he wrapped up his speech, pride filled her chest. He was no politician. But he was authentic and sincere, and that rang through clearly tonight.

She joined in as the crowd applauded, whistled, and cheered. Cooper's family joined him at the podium and enveloped him in a group hug. Katie's eyes stung as she watched the poignant moment from afar. She was so happy for Cooper. Happy for his whole family. Despite everything they'd been through, they would be all right.

And win or lose, Cooper would be fine. He had a family who loved him. Gavin, too, would come through his heartache and move forward. His family would help him through. Avery, Jeff,

Lisa—they had each other. And no one knew better than Katie what a priceless treasure that was.

Her chest tightened with sorrow. She was once again alone. Once again on the outside looking in. That community Cooper talked about had accepted her . . . then rejected her, as had everyone she'd come to care about.

She slipped away from the crowd, her vision blurring more with each step. As she walked away she thought of her birth mother—the reason Katie had come here to begin with. Since she'd made a public fool of herself, the woman made no effort to reach out to her. Meanwhile, it seemed Beth had been absorbed into the Robinson family.

Once again her mother had soundly rejected her daughter. Once again Katie was not enough. The thought left her sucker punched. She hurried through the streets, barely seeing her surroundings. When she finally reached her house she was struggling to make her lungs function properly.

She pushed the door closed behind her and gulped back tears that had gathered at the back of her throat. Sometime during the walk back she'd reached a decision. She withdrew her phone and found the contact she sought. It rang only twice before the greeting came.

"Hi, Mama Jill. It's Katie. I'm just calling to let you know—I'm coming home."

41

Katie took the file before she entered the exam room, and Avery swept past, heading toward the front desk.

"Avery?" Katie's heart faltered as her boss turned with a placid smile. "I left something for you on your desk."

"Okay. Thank you." Avery continued down the hall, her ponytail swaying with each step.

Katie slipped into the patient's room, spoke with her briefly, and took her vitals. The twenty-something woman appeared to have a respiratory infection, but the diagnosis was Avery's call.

When she finished screening the patient Katie hooked the stethoscope around her neck. "All right, Miss Greenwood. The doctor should be in shortly."

When Katie exited the room Avery was waiting outside the door. "Can I speak with you in the office, please?"

"Of course." Katie's feet were heavy as she made the short walk. She gave Sharise a wan smile as she passed. The woman was a good nurse practitioner. She'd be a great asset for the clinic, a big help to Avery.

Katie stepped into the office, nerves making her hands tremble. The only thing that gave her courage was the knowledge that she was doing the right thing. With her out of the way Cooper and Gavin's relationship could heal completely.

And maybe, if she wasn't running into Cooper everywhere, she could finally get over him.

Avery closed the door, giving Katie a hangdog look. "I owe you an apology."

"No, you don't. That's not what this is—"

Avery held her hand up. "Let me finish. I've been a real jerk. Worse, I've been a terrible friend. You made a mistake—you acted on your feelings—and I've been treating you like you have a case of leprosy."

"No, you haven't. I don't blame you for being angry. I came between your brothers and made a mess of everything."

"Don't make excuses for me. This was every bit as much Cooper's fault, and I forgave him"—she gave a wry smile—"after I let him squirm awhile. You're important to me, Katie, and you're a good person. One mistake doesn't define you."

A little place inside healed up as Avery's words soaked in. "I appreciate you saying that. And I understand why you've been so upset. I dropped a bomb into the middle of your family, and I'm more sorry than I can say."

Avery wrapped her arms around Katie. "My family will be fine. And I forgive you."

Katie gave herself over to the embrace, tears prickling her eyes.

A moment later Avery pulled away. "Now please say I can tear up that resignation letter on my desk and we can go out tonight and celebrate."

Katie wilted. She was grateful for her friend's forgiveness, but she'd made up her mind: she had to move on.

"Oh, Katie. Please stay."

"You'll be fine. You have Sharise now, and you won't have to worry about having to let her go."

"I'm not just talking about the clinic. I don't want you to leave town. Even if I haven't been treating you like it, you're my best friend."

"I'm sorry, but I have to go—for my own well-being." She felt sick at the thought of never seeing Cooper again. Of never again peering into his warm eyes. Of never again feeling his tender touch. Her vision blurred.

A knowing smile turned up the corners of Avery's lips. "You're in love with him."

Despite Katie's best efforts, a tear spilled over. The catch in her throat prevented her from responding.

Avery drew her back into her arms, holding tight. "I'm sorry. What an impossible situation. I should've known how hard this was for you. And for what it's worth—"

Katie waited for her friend to finish the thought. When she didn't Katie drew away. "What?"

"I don't know if I should finish that sentence.

I don't know if it'll help or hurt, and I definitely don't want to hurt you any more."

Katie let out a dry laugh. "I don't think I could hurt any worse."

"Oh, Katie. This is so unfair—to all of you. At first when I caught you guys together, I thought Cooper was just . . . being Cooper. But I was wrong. You're different. He cares for you—really cares for you. He's been so sad this past month. He tries to hide it but I can tell."

Katie had been wrong about not hurting worse.

"Maybe if . . ."

"No. I won't come between your brothers again." That would be selfish. She of all people knew how important family was.

"Do you really have to leave though? I love having you here. Who's going to watch movies and eat brownies with me and tease me about my book boyfriends?"

"We can stay in touch. Asheville's only forty-five minutes away. And there's always texting and phone calls. We don't have to drift apart like we did after college." Remembering Avery's potential condition, she added, "And I'll always be here for you if you ever need to talk."

"Thank you." Avery gave her a pointed look. "And drifting apart is not an option. We're so much closer now."

Katie sniffled and dredged up a smile. "We are. And we'll stay that way. I promise."

"When are you leaving?"

"I can give you two weeks if you really want me to. But I'd like to leave as soon as possible—while I still have the nerve. We both know the clinic will be just fine without me."

Avery's face fell. "I guess I have to agree to your terms, seeing as how I've been such a rotten friend."

Katie took her hand. "I'd like today to be my last day."

"I hate this . . . But I understand. I really do."

Katie was relieved to have her friend back. It felt good, setting things to right before she left. If only she could figure out how to put her broken heart back together again.

42

Today had been the longest day of Cooper's life—not to mention the most unproductive. He shifted in his truck, eyes locked on Megan's apartment door. He'd taken the day off work, hoping to finally confront her about her false accusation. She'd apparently quit her job at the newspaper, so he'd spent the entire day staking out her place.

It was now the eve of Election Day, and he was running out of time. But at this point the campaign wasn't really the driving factor. He just wanted to set the record straight. Getting to the bottom of an injustice wasn't just part of his job. It was in his blood.

A flash of red snagged his attention. Across the parking lot Megan exited her car and strode toward her apartment building. Her long brown hair waved behind her like a flag in the autumn breeze.

Finally.

Cooper jumped from his truck and followed her into the building. She was unlocking her door when he caught up with her. He had to be careful not to scare her away. All she had to do was slip inside her apartment and refuse to answer the door.

"Megan . . ."

She whirled around. Her lips parted and her pallor went ashen. Her face was a little fuller than when he'd last seen her. His gaze dropped to the considerable bump of her belly.

"Go away." Megan scrambled with the lock.

"Megan, wait. I just want to talk."

"I don't want to talk. I'll call the—"

Panic flickered in her eyes as she no doubt remembered he *was* the law. Her fumbling finally paid off. She twisted the knob and pushed open the door.

"Please, Megan. I'm not angry. I just want to understand."

Her eyes locked with his and she hesitated.

He held up his hands, palms out. "You know me. You know I won't hurt you. I'm not that guy. Just give me five minutes. Please."

Her eyes teared up. "I'm sorry. I'm sorry I ever did it."

"Why did you then?"

Her attention dropped to the frayed carpet at the threshold. A moment later she stepped back and opened the door.

The apartment was warm from the heat of the day. She opened a window, and the breeze fluttered the thin curtains. "Might as well have a seat." She lowered her weight into an armchair. A gray-striped cat jumped into her lap.

He sat across from her on the sofa and

measured his words. "What happened? Why did you tell people the baby was mine?"

Her cheeks flushed as she stroked the cat. "I don't know where to start."

"Try the beginning."

She stared down at the cat, seemingly lost in the past. "Soon after we had that disagreement, I lost my job—the one I'd moved here for. I was feeling . . . pretty low. I went to a bar and ended up going home with some guy—I don't even remember his name. He was just visiting the area."

She gave him a wry look. "I guess you can see what happened after that. I got a job at the paper, but it was a severe pay cut. I wanted the baby but I didn't know how I'd take care of it."

"What about your family?"

She scowled at him. "I don't have any, remember?"

He really had been a jerk. "Sorry. I forgot."

"Back in September some man approached me when I was out with a friend. He said he'd pay me if I'd go into Riverbend Gap and spread the word that you'd fathered my baby and were denying it. He somehow knew we'd had a . . . dispute and that I was upset about it. He told me I could pay you back for being so awful to me. I said no at first. But then he told me how much he was willing to pay me, and I was still mad at you for calling me a liar."

349

Cooper clenched his jaw. She *was* a liar. "So you took the money."

"I was afraid I couldn't support my baby, and I've never had that much money!"

"You started a false rumor that ruined my reputation."

"I'm sorry! I know it was wrong, but I—"

"Who was it? Who gave you that money?"

Fear flashed in her eyes. "If I tell you, he'll make me give it back and I already spent some of it."

"By the time I'm finished with him, he won't be in any position to ask for it. I already know who it is—I just need you to confirm it."

Her face fell as his words sank in, and her eyes went glossy again. "It was Wayne Curtis."

Cooper rocked back in the seat. "You mean *Sean* Curtis."

She shook her head. "His father, the guy who owns that organic produce farm out on—"

"I know who he is." Cooper had spent an entire summer taking orders from him. He'd *liked* the man. Considered him a friend. He flinched from the sting of betrayal. That Wayne Curtis would trash Cooper's reputation over this election soured his stomach. "Did Sean know about all this?"

She lifted a shoulder. "I don't know. I don't think so."

Cooper wasn't so sure. "And the article in the *Herald*?"

She looked sheepish. "The journalist has family in Riverbend. He heard my name attached to the pregnancy rumor and starting asking me questions at work. He said he wouldn't use my name if I'd corroborate the rumor."

Cooper pressed his lips together so he wouldn't say something he'd regret.

Tears spilled down her flushed cheeks. "I know it was wrong. It was an impulsive decision, and then things just spiraled out of control. I'm sorry I ever agreed to take Wayne's money. I know you came here looking for me. A neighbor told me and I panicked. I used some of the money to skip town for a while. I was ashamed of what I'd done and afraid to face you. I'm sorry, Cooper. You didn't deserve that."

The honesty and raw regret in her pained expression soothed his anger. Now there was only one thing to decide . . . What would he do with this information?

Cooper felt lighter as he drove back to Riverbend. Maybe what he'd discovered wouldn't change the election, but the truth would soon be out. He wasn't guilty of what Megan had accused him of.

His phone buzzed. Avery. Probably calling about finalizing the speeches. He accepted the call on Bluetooth. "Don't worry. I got your email with the schedule and I'm free tonight to go over the speech wording."

"That's not why I'm calling. Have you talked to Katie?"

He paused at the tension in her tone. "I ran into her yesterday at Trail Days. Why? What's wrong?"

"She's leaving, Cooper. She resigned from the clinic today. She's leaving town tomorrow."

"What? Why?"

"Why wouldn't she? I've been a complete jerk at work this month, and she doesn't have any family here—or friends for that matter."

She had her birth mother, actually. But the woman apparently hadn't earned back her daughter's trust. He ached for Kate. And he ached for himself because he couldn't imagine his world without her sunny smile. Without the hope of running into her someplace—even if he couldn't act on his feelings.

This was all his fault. She belonged in Riverbend. If only he'd kept his lips to himself, the Robinsons would still welcome her.

"What are we going to do?" Avery asked. "I tried to talk her out of it, but she's determined to leave."

He thought of the relationship Kate had begun forging with his mom. After having been rejected by her own mother, it meant a lot to have a mother figure embrace her with such warmth. How much it must've hurt when his mom had also rejected her.

A fist tightened around his heart. "I'm calling a family meeting tonight."

"I shouldn't have—You should probably stay out of this, Coop. The family's just now starting to heal."

"This isn't fair to Kate. Why should she have to lose everything and everyone she cares about?"

"I get what you're saying. I feel that way too. It's just—"

"I'm doing this, Avery. You can show up or not."

She released a hard sigh. "I'll be there. But we have a million things to do before the polls open tomorrow."

"None of it is more important than this." He glanced at the time. "Seven o'clock at Mom and Jeff's. I'll call the rest of the family."

"See you then."

43

"What's this all about?" His mother's dimple was nowhere to be seen tonight.

Cooper couldn't blame her. He wasn't feeling very cheerful himself.

"Is this about the election?" Jeff asked.

Gavin shifted in the dining room chair. "This better be good. Barbara Jean's off sick so the campground office is closed."

"This won't take long." Cooper met Avery's gaze across the table. The smell of his mother's pot roast hung in the air, but she and Jeff had eaten before Cooper and his siblings' arrival. "The reason I asked you here has nothing to do with the election. But I do have news to share in regards to that. It's about Megan Taylor—I finally managed to track her down today."

He shared what he'd learned from Megan. His family's reaction went from outrage toward Wayne Curtis to reluctant sympathy for Megan as Cooper explained her situation and the woman's intentions to set things right.

"I'm glad you got to the bottom of it," Jeff said. "But it's the eve of the election, Cooper."

"It might be too late to turn it around," Gavin added.

"I know that. Whatever will be, will be. I want to be sheriff of Madison County. That hasn't changed. But I've also learned some things are more important than my career ambitions."

"I take it we're here because of one of those things," his mom said.

He met her gaze—she was key to this problem. Mom was the one who'd forged a close relationship with Katelyn. If his mother wouldn't accept Kate, then this was over before it even began. And there was a decent chance of that—Mom was fiercely loyal to her family. And it was her loyalty to Gavin that held her back.

Cooper stared at his brother for a long beat. "It's about Katelyn."

Gavin's lips flattened and his brows drew tight. "Here we go. I knew this was coming."

"It's not what you think," Avery said.

"Oh, really?" He speared Cooper with a look. "You don't want Katie for yourself?"

Mom set her hand on Gavin's arm. "Let's hear him out."

This wasn't starting off the way he'd hoped. "I'm not with Kate and I never will be. I may have made an impulsive mistake, but I would never ask that of you."

Gavin crossed his arms over his chest. "What, then? What's so important you called us here on the eve of election?"

"Kate resigned at the clinic," Cooper said.

"She's planning to move back to Asheville soon."

Mom's lips parted. "She's moving?"

Gavin's gaze fell to the table.

"I don't intend to be cruel," Jeff said, "but maybe that would be for the best."

Cooper's heart attempted to escape the prison of his ribs. "You don't understand. Kate's not like us. She doesn't have anyone."

"Doesn't her foster family live in Asheville?" Mom asked. "I assume that's why she's going back there."

"Sure, they do. And they have a houseful of foster kids and about forty who've come and gone through their house over the years." He shook his head. "I don't mean to dismiss what thcy do, what they've done. They sound like great people. But Kate's always been lost in the shuffle. It was bearable when she had her brother to cling to, but now he's gone and . . . she's all alone in the world."

Silence settled around the table. Cooper glanced from person to person, reading a mixture of pity and resistance.

He homed in on his mom. "When she was little her mom chose drugs over her and her brother. Kate's lived with that rejection, absorbed it into every cell of her being. But she came here all alone to Riverbend, and we welcomed her into this family. She felt a connection with us— with you especially, Mom. And now she's been rejected again, and I just don't—" The words died in his throat.

He couldn't bear the thought of what that rejection was doing to his bright, hopeful Kate. She loved her job, loved her little house, this town, and this family. How hopeless she must be feeling to give it all up.

Avery leaned forward, planting her elbows on the table. "I think we need to hear from you, Gavin. You're the one who's been hurt here."

All eyes swung his direction. He shifted under their attention. "I don't know what to say. Everything Cooper said is true—she's pretty much alone. And I regret how I've treated her the past few weeks. I've run into her a few times in town and I've . . . I've kinda snubbed her."

"Nobody can blame you for being angry," Jeff said.

"I'm pretty sure my actions have affected the way others in town feel about her. She made a mistake, but she doesn't deserve to be an outcast."

"I've been awful at the clinic," Avery said. "I haven't treated her like a friend should, and I have a lot of regrets. I don't want to lose her—at the clinic or as a friend."

Hope welled up in Cooper like an underground spring. "Did you tell her that?"

"I did. But it didn't change her mind about leaving."

"Who's to say anything will?" Gavin asked. "Maybe she's determined to leave."

"I don't believe that," Cooper said. "She loves you guys. Loves her life here in Riverbend. And if you accepted her, the rest of town would too. This family pulls a lot of weight around here—you know that's true." His mother had been uncharacteristically quiet. "Mom?"

Her gaze fell to the table. "A couple weeks ago she wrote us a letter, apologizing for her part in the whole mess. But I was still angry, and I told myself it would be disloyal to Gavin to respond. But I saw her yesterday at Trail Days. She was watching me from afar, and the regret and longing on her face was . . . palpable."

Mom blinked away tears as she gave Gavin a pained look. "I've felt just terrible ever since. I really do love that girl. I'm sorry, Gavin. I didn't mean to, but I do."

Warmth flooded Cooper. There was the Lisa Robinson he knew and loved. The tightness in his chest gave way, and he smiled at his mom.

Gavin put his hand over Mom's. "Do what you need to do, Mom. I'm not going to stand in your way."

Cooper joined Jeff at the kitchen sink where he scrubbed a dinner plate. Cooper grabbed a towel and began drying.

Gavin had returned to the campground, and his

mom and Avery went to the campaign office to make final corrections on the speeches—both acceptance and concession. Cooper would join them in a while to go over the final versions and do a few practice runs.

"Don't you have better things to do tonight?" Jeff asked.

"I'll get to it later. Mom hates dirty dishes in the sink."

"Don't I know it." They worked in silence for a minute before Jeff spoke again. "How are you doing with your father coming back to town?"

Cooper had already caught them up. "I'm fine. He was just a pawn in Wayne's game. But Lonnie dropped the charges, so I'm sure he already went back to wherever he came from and is doing whatever he does."

"I'm sorry." Compassion filled Jeff's expression. "Katie's not the only one who deserves better, you know."

"Thanks. But I've become acutely aware that I'm pretty darned fortunate in the family department. Maybe Dad abandoned us, but God turned it into a blessing. He brought you and Avery into our lives—and I can only be thankful for that."

Jeff gave him a sidelong smile. "The blessing goes both ways, Coop. Your mom is the love of my life. And you and Gavin? The sons I never had. I couldn't love you more."

"Love you, too, man." Cooper grabbed the dirty

Crock-Pot off the counter and handed it to Jeff. "You think Mom will go see Kate tomorrow?"

"If she doesn't, I don't know your mother. You think it'll change Katie's mind about leaving?"

"I don't know but I had to try. I couldn't just let her leave thinking . . . thinking nobody cared about her."

Jeff went to work on the Crock-Pot. "Know what I think is interesting? It's the eve of the election and instead of being out there pressing flesh, you're over here fighting for Katie."

Cooper took pains drying the plate. "I just want what's best for her. She deserves more than what she's gotten."

"No argument there."

Cooper tried for an offhand tone. "Besides, this thing between us . . . It'll pass. It always does." He almost choked on the cavalier words. Maybe if he told himself that enough he'd believe it. Or at least, maybe his family would.

Jeff thrust a wet hand into his pants pocket and withdrew two pennies. He set them on the counter.

Cooper put a dry plate in the cabinet. He could reach for the silverware and ignore the two cents. Jeff wouldn't say a word about it or hold it against him—Cooper had tested that theory enough during his teenage years to know that.

Or Cooper could pick them up.

He fastened his gaze on the shiny copper coins, sitting in a puddle of water. He slid them off the counter and tucked them into his pocket before he reached for the silverware.

Jeff waited only a moment before he spoke. "Where relationships are concerned, you tend to avoid commitment, Cooper. You only date women you could never come to care about. I think maybe you've intentionally kept things shallow and brief because you're afraid of love."

Cooper bristled. Pretty presumptive for a guy who was on his third marriage. "I think that was a little more than two-cents' worth."

"I'm not finished."

Cooper stopped drying and frowned at him.

"You picked up the coins."

Cooper didn't like what he'd heard so far. But maybe that was because the words had hit a painful target. "Fine. Have your say."

Jeff took his time finishing the crock and handed it to Cooper. "Your father was a bad example for you. He was a failure as a husband and father, and I think you're afraid you're just like him."

Something inside him cowered from Jeff's words. Cooper had already recognized his dad's impact on his career. But this was more personal. Cooper raised his defenses like a shield. He wanted to deny Jeff's words. He wanted to spit out that he was nothing like his father. *Nothing*. But the truth of Jeff's words penetrated deeper into that soft, aching target.

Jeff dried his hands and faced Cooper. "For the

record, you are *nothing* like your father. You're a good man, Coop. A loyal man. Someday when you figure out you're deserving of it, you're going to be a great husband and father."

Cooper clenched his jaw. "I'm not loyal. Look what I did to Gavin."

"And yet, out of concern for your brother, you've denied yourself the woman you've fallen in love with. If that's not loyalty, what is?"

"Not before I helped myself to her."

"You made a mistake. Happens to the best of us. You're a warm, caring person and you need to get this through your head—you are not your father, and you never will be."

Their gazes connected for a long, intense moment. Jeff was right about one thing. Cooper had been flittering like a moth around women because he was afraid he couldn't be the kind of man he longed to be.

"You deserve to be happy, and you deserve to be loved." Jeff squeezed Cooper's shoulder. "There. That's all the cents I have for you. Now, get down to the campaign office and get that acceptance speech nailed down."

Cooper gave a wry grin. "I should probably focus on the concession speech."

"Either way, it doesn't matter to your mom and me. We couldn't be prouder of you, Son."

44

ALLEGATIONS AGAINST SHERIFF CANDIDATE ROBINSON ARE FALSE

The article was on page 1 of the *Herald* just below the fold. Katie hunched over the table, reading every word, her heart pulsating in her chest. The article, written by the same journalist who'd posted the original accusation, contained contrite quotes from Megan Taylor. She claimed that the father of Cooper's opponent had bribed her to make the false accusation.

Wayne Curtis had refused to comment on the accusation, but Sean insisted he knew nothing about the things his father had allegedly done.

A weight fell from her shoulders. This was good news. Great news. She was elated for Cooper. Surely the article would earn Cooper the community's support. But even if it didn't, his reputation would surely be restored. And that would go a long way toward healing him. He needed to know he was a good man—and that the people around here esteemed him.

She whispered a quick prayer for him, for the outcome of the election. This morning she'd awakened jittery and nervous for him. But now that the truth was out, hope surged once again to the surface.

She gulped the last of her coffee and set the paper aside. She had a lot of cleaning and packing to do today—but first she had a very important vote to cast.

Katie's house had never been so immaculate. She stood, wet sponge in hand, and surveyed the sparkling kitchen floor. The clean scent of pine hung in the air, mingling with the lemony fragrance of furniture polish. The house looked like a model home, the colorful throw pillows placed just so, all evidence of her personal life packed into boxes.

She'd leave the furnishings for now—the house would show better staged. Once it sold she'd hire a moving company. And then someone else would move into her sweet little home.

Her gaze flittered around the house she'd made her own. The pretty blue walls and the curtains she'd painstakingly chosen. The light fixtures she'd hung and the faucet she'd replaced.

She thought of the leak that had sprouted and the way Cooper had rushed to her rescue. Remembered how he emerged from the cabinet wet and flustered. She tipped her lips in a wistful smile, and her chest gave a tight squeeze.

Oh, how she missed him.

She wrapped her arms around her middle, the thought of leaving him—of putting so many miles between them—almost unbearable.

A knock sounded on the door. *Cooper.*

She gave her head a hard shake at the wishful thinking. He was no doubt busy with his campaign today. Anyway, he had no reason to seek her out.

She headed for the door, wishing she wasn't wearing her grubbiest T-shirt and leggings. The mirror next to the door revealed a hairstyle that gave new meaning to the words *messy bun.* Oh well. Whoever was knocking would only be a distant memory soon. She pulled open the door and blinked at the sight of the woman on her stoop.

"Lisa . . . What are you doing here? I mean, I wasn't expecting you."

Lisa gave a contrite smile. "You once told me I was welcome here anytime. I was hoping you hadn't changed your mind."

"Of course not." Katie opened the door wider. "Come on in."

Lisa brushed past her, taking in the living room, her focus finally settling on the boxes stacked near the hall. "I see you've been cleaning—and packing."

"Avery probably told you I'm putting the house on the market. Would you like something to drink? Well, I guess I'm pretty much down to just water."

Lisa said nothing for a moment, and then her eyes filled with tears. "Oh, Katie. I am so sorry for the way I've treated you."

Apparently they were going to get straight down to business. "I understand, Lisa. Really. I hurt your sons and you're a good mother—a protective mother. I don't blame you one bit."

Lisa took Katie's hand. "Well, you should because I'm also your friend, and I've failed terribly at that. I've done nothing but avoid you for weeks. And if I were such a great mother, I would've been demonstrating forgiveness and mercy instead of holding one mistake over your head. No wonder you're leaving town."

"That's not why I'm leaving." She paused at the impulsive statement. It was actually true.

She strolled to the picture window, staring at her lovely little yard with its beautifully arranged flowers. At the hydrangeas Lisa had helped her plant—that she would never see bloom. Until this moment she'd thought the absence of family was driving her from Riverbend. But in the blink of an eye she'd realized that wasn't true.

She was leaving because of Cooper. He would never betray his brother by committing himself to her. Staying here would be a temptation neither of them could afford. And having him close by and still out of reach would be unbearable.

Furthermore, Cooper would eventually move on. How could she stomach seeing him with someone else? Someone he'd eventually fall in love with, get engaged and married to? How could she watch while she lost the only man she'd ever loved—the one she felt was meant to be hers alone? No, this town wasn't big enough for both of them.

The wind chimes on her porch tinkled as an autumn breeze swept by, reminding her of home. But she wasn't meant to belong in Riverbend. Maybe she wasn't meant to belong anywhere. Maybe the sound of that melodious chime was the closest she'd ever come to home.

"Honey, please don't leave." Lisa had come to stand near her, tears sparkling in her eyes. "I know I don't deserve another chance. But I speak for my whole family when I say—we want you to stay, Katie. You belong here. You've become part of the family. I know things are a little precarious with the feelings between you and Cooper, but we can work around that, can't we? I've missed you so much. I love you, and I can't stand the thought that I've caused you pain. That I've chased you away."

Katie embraced the woman, holding tightly to the mother figure who would always have a little piece of her heart. "You didn't chase me away, Lisa. I promise. And I love you too—but I do have to go."

Lisa pulled back, grasping Katie's forearms, eyes searching. "But why?"

Katie lifted her lips in a sad smile and said the only thing she could. "Because those feelings I have for Cooper? I can't work around them."

The corners of Lisa's pretty blue eyes drooped. "Oh, Katie."

"I'll be fine. I have family in Asheville, and I'm sure I'll find a great job doing what I love. Avery's already promised me a glowing recommendation." The optimistic tone she strove for fell short.

"Is there anything I can do to change your mind?"

"You've been great, Lisa. But no, my mind is made up."

Lisa held her gaze for a long moment, acceptance finally settling over her features. "When are you leaving then? The least we can do is help you finish packing up. Help you move."

"Tomorrow. And thank you, but I'm pretty much finished. I'm leaving the furniture and things for later." Katie squeezed her hand. "I'm so happy to have met you and your family. You and Jeff are the kind of parents I've always wished for."

A tear streaked down Lisa's face. She tenderly palmed Katie's cheek. "Just remember you're loved. Not only by us but by our heavenly Father. You'll always have a special place in His family and in ours."

Katie let the warmth of Lisa's words seep deeply into her heart. She breathed in that truth and exhaled the achy pain of rejection. The tightness in her chest loosened a bit. Sometimes she forgot she already had a Parent—one who'd chosen her from the very beginning. One who would never reject her.

Katie was leaving in the morning, but all she could think about were tonight's election results. The polls would be closing soon. She hoped Cooper didn't have to wait long—and that he would ultimately be declared the winner.

She'd heated up last night's pizza, but the slices sat on a paper plate, oil congealing on the surface. She couldn't eat a thing. So much had happened this week. And just now her mind spun with Lisa's words.

The reason Katie had come to town to begin with remained unresolved. Her mother's recent departure from her life stung. But being reminded she'd always have God had brought her a measure of comfort and solace. And a faith that one way or another . . . she wouldn't be alone. She would be okay.

But in the hours since Lisa's departure, an idea had come sharply into focus. A decision had been made. Katie had to face her fears. She couldn't leave Riverbend without telling her birth mother who she was.

Beth might reject her. But Katie owed it to herself to lay it all on the line and find out for sure. If the woman didn't want Katie in her life, that was *her* loss. No doubt it would sting. But

Katie was stronger than she'd given herself credit for. God had gotten her through so many things; He would get her through this too. Cooper had helped her see that.

The thought was freeing. She got up from the table and tossed the cold pizza into the trash. *Ready or not, Mom, here I come.*

Beth Wallace lived in a pretty little Craftsman in a neighborhood just outside of town. The house squatted on a grassy knoll, which sported several big oak trees. Crispy leaves cluttered the green grass and scuttled across the walk as Katie approached the porch.

She'd been here only once to drop off flyers. Beth invited her inside for coffee, but Katie was due at work.

She took the porch steps on trembling legs. Twilight crept across the valley, making the interior lights obvious. Even if not for Beth's Camry parked out front, the woman clearly was home.

Uncertainty sprang into Katie's mind, stopping her a few feet shy of her goal. Her heart thrashed in her chest. Was she making a terrible mistake? If she knocked on that door, would she regret it ten minutes from now?

The thought gave her pause. She imagined driving away from town tomorrow morning with all of this left unresolved. She couldn't let that happen. The thought of not knowing bothered her far more.

She approached the door and gave a firm knock. Fear sucked the moisture from her mouth. She wiped sweaty palms down the sides of her jeans.

The door swept open and Beth's pretty face lit in a smile. "Katie! What a nice surprise. Come on in."

The pleasant reception buoyed Katie's spirits. After all that had happened she wasn't sure how the woman would receive her. She brushed past Beth, taking in the warm colors and comfy feel of the space. The living room boasted a brick fireplace, and a thick area rug hugged the wood floor. The scent of something savory filled the house. As the kitchen came into view, Katie spied a plate of food, half eaten, on the island.

"I'm sorry. I've interrupted your supper. I should've called."

"Don't be silly. Have you eaten yet? There's plenty enough for two."

"No, I—maybe I should just come back later."

"Please don't leave." Beth's gaze sharpened on Katie. "You seem like you have something on your mind. Have a seat. Would you like something to drink?"

No going back now. Katie perched on the leather sofa. "No, thank you."

"What can I do for you?" Beth sank into

the armchair across the way, the concern on her features reminding Katie of the way she'd reentered Beth's life—the AA meeting.

"I'm not an alcoholic," Katie blurted.

Beth blinked at the sudden declaration. Then her lips softened into a smile. "You have no idea how relieved I am to hear that."

Katie waited for more but the woman remained silent. "Aren't you upset with me for coming to those meetings? Aren't you wondering why I was even there?"

"If you want me to know, you'll tell me."

Resolve swelled inside Katie. For better or worse she did want Beth to know. She opened her mouth and the words spilled out. "I'm your daughter."

Beth blinked. Tension stretched between them like a long electric line. An interminable moment later Beth's eyes grew glassy. The woman opened her mouth, but nothing came out.

Katie's breath seemed locked in her lungs. She wanted to fill the awful silence, but she had no idea what to say.

Beth swallowed. A tear trickled down her cheek.

"Say something," Katie begged. She desperately needed the truth, whatever it was. "What are you thinking?"

"That I don't deserve this." The words were as broken as the woman they spilled out of. "That I don't deserve *you*."

Katie gulped in a breath. Her own eyes stung. They stared at each other, the moment drawing out between them.

"I knew who you were, Katie. I knew why you came to that meeting."

Katie reared back.

"And I'm sorry for the deception. But I didn't want to rush you into something you weren't ready for. And yet I couldn't resist getting to know you—and I really was afraid you'd inherited my genetic tendency for addiction."

"How did you know?" Katie squeezed out.

"After I got sober I found you on Facebook. You'd changed your last name, of course, but I took one look at your face, and I saw myself twenty years ago—before I'd made a terrible mess of my life. So when you showed up at the meeting, I knew who you were."

Katie thought back to those first words they'd exchanged. "You must have the best poker face on the planet."

"I was so afraid I'd scare you away. So hopeful that you'd come to Riverbend searching for me. That you were somehow willing to give me another chance."

Might as well lay it all on the line. "That's exactly why I came."

A fresh batch of tears appeared in Beth's eyes. "Katie, I'm so terribly sorry for the hurt I've caused you. I chose drugs over my children, and

373

as a result you lost your mother. Your childhood was filled with uncertainty because of me, and I regret that with all my heart. I wouldn't blame you for keeping your distance. I would respect that, if that's what you want."

Katie's eyes stung with tears. "Thank you. But I forgave you a long time ago and I'd like to get to know you better . . . If that's something you'd be interested in."

"I want that more than anything in the world. But how can you not hate me for what I did? How can you even want to know me now?"

"I was angry with you for a long time. And when Spencer died—" She bit her lip. Did her mother even know she'd lost her son?

"It's okay. I learned about Spencer on Facebook. When he passed I was devastated, and I wanted so badly to contact you. I knew you were hurting, too, but I was afraid my appearance would only make things harder for you."

Katie thought back to that time. She'd been neck-deep in grief. Her mother might be right.

Katie gave her head a shake. She couldn't absorb all of this. Beth had known whom she was communicating with all along. Katie thought of all their time together since she'd come to town. The coffee shop, the Trail Days meetings, the numerous texts.

But then that rumor about Cooper and her had spread through town. And when Katie dropped out of Trail Days, Beth abruptly fell out of her life. "Why haven't you contacted me since the rumor spread through town? Are you ashamed of me?"

"Ashamed? Of course not. Why would I be ashamed?"

"Those rumors didn't exactly cast me in the best light—and they were partially true."

"Katie, after what I did to you and Spencer, that was nothing. All you did was follow your heart."

"I came between brothers—two men I cared deeply about. There's nothing admirable about that. I thought when you saw what kind of person I'd turned out to be, you didn't want anything to do with me."

"Oh, Katie. I could never feel that way about you. If anyone understands the need for grace, it's someone who's been on the receiving end of it more times than she can count. I didn't contact you because of that last text you sent. I thought you were breaking ties with me. I thought you'd decided you didn't want a relationship with me. That grieved me terribly, but I didn't feel I had the right to push."

Katie's vision went blurry again, and she expelled a puff of laughter. She'd been so hurt at what she thought was a dismissal. She regarded her mother with a solemn expression. "I have a lot of questions about what happened when I was a kid."

"I'll tell you anything you want to know. But let's start with this, Katelyn Elizabeth Loveland: I love you more than I can possibly express. And I want nothing more than an opportunity to prove that to you."

45

Despite the hubbub in the campaign office, Cooper couldn't take his eyes off the large TV screen as the local election results trickled in. It was going on ten o'clock, and he and Sean were neck and neck with 82 percent of the precincts reporting.

Fifty or so volunteers, financial supporters, and fellow deputies surrounded him. More people stopped by long enough to wish him luck. Even Amber Clarke had stopped to offer support—and to apologize for believing the pregnancy rumor. He got the feeling she was willing to pick up where they'd left off, but that ship had sailed. At this point he couldn't imagine loving anyone but Katelyn.

The crowd cheered loudly—he'd pulled ahead by a point. The presence of his supporters only increased the pressure, and his jaw ached from the plastic smile he'd worn all night. His stomach twisted at the savory smell of the catered food.

He suddenly longed for Kate. For her small hand in his, comforting. Her sweet voice in his ear, encouraging. He wouldn't have to fake a smile for her. She'd know how nervous he was and tell him it would be okay. That win or lose, he'd be just fine. But according to his mom, she was leaving tomorrow. His hopes of changing her mind had been dashed, and he hated that she was losing so much.

Stop it, Robinson.

He glanced at the clock, forcing Kate from his mind. How long would this go on? Cooper wiped sweaty palms down the front of his suit pants. Reporters from two local television stations waited in the wings. The podium was set up, both speeches prepared and rehearsed. Which one would he be giving tonight?

Avery lowered herself into the chair beside him. She seemed calm and collected in her blue dress, her hair up in a professional knot. "How's it going, Brother? Hanging in there?"

"Between you and me? This is more nerve-wracking than a carnival Tilt-A-Whirl. Why'd I let you talk me into an election-night party?"

"Because you knew you'd win this thing and want to be surrounded by all your supporters when the final results came in."

"This thing could go either way, you know."

"Well, regardless, the people who helped along the way will be here to support you." She nudged his shoulder with her own. "But you're going to win."

Jeff and Mom took a seat across from them. His mother squeezed his hand. "How you holding up, honey?"

"I'm fine. One way or another, this will be over soon."

"After that article in the paper," Jeff said, "I don't see how anyone could vote for Sean Curtis."

"Some people won't blame him for what his father did." Gavin appeared, his gaze drifting around the room. "Who did the decorations? It looks like an American flag factory exploded in here."

Avery frowned at him. "It's patriotic. And back to the topic at hand, I agree with Dad. The article was a game changer whether Sean knew or not."

But Gavin was right too. Though Avery had done her best to spread the word today via social media and local TV interviews.

"It might be a case of too little, too late," Cooper said.

"Stop being a Debbie Downer," Avery said.

"You might have a case for his dismissal if it turns out he knew what his father was up to," Jeff said.

"It's not easy getting a sheriff fired once he's elected," Cooper said. "Anyway, I'm not going to be that guy. I'll abide by the will of the—"

"Shhh!" Avery said. "It's coming up."

A hush fell over the crowd. A moment later the numbers for the sheriff's race appeared on the screen: Robinson: 51 percent; Curtis 49 percent, with 100 percent of precincts reporting.

A cheer rose from the group.

Cooper blinked as the words *Final Results* splayed across the screen.

Avery grabbed his arm. "You did it! You won!"

And then everyone was there, shaking his hand and congratulating him. A load of heavy bricks fell from his shoulders. He'd be in the position to protect this little town he loved so much.

The next hour flew by in a rush of interviews. In between he shook hands and thanked each person for their support.

Cooper was running on adrenaline. Even though it was a work night, everyone hung around the office, waiting for Curtis's concession. Only then could Cooper give his acceptance speech. But Sean hadn't even called to concede yet. After his father had dragged Cooper's name through the mud, he wasn't looking forward to that awkward call.

Avery wove her way through the crowd and extricated him from a group of reporters. "I just got word from a friend at Sean's headquarters. He's bitter and isn't planning to call you."

"What does that mean? Is he going to demand a recount or something?"

"He'd be crazy to do that at this point."

"Well, what do I do about the acceptance speech?"

"It would be bad form to make it before he publicly concedes."

"But it's getting late, and the party's starting to fizzle."

"And we only have one television network still hanging around. I think you should hold off till morning. Give Sean a chance to concede. I'll make some calls to the networks and let them know to be here."

"If you think that's best."

"I do. And Cooper"—she squeezed his arm—"congratulations. You deserve this."

He drew her into an embrace. "Thanks, Sis. I couldn't have done it without you."

One by one Cooper's supporters drifted away. It was well after midnight, and the place was all cleaned up by the time Mom and Jeff left for home. They'd be back at seven in the morning for the acceptance speech. Only Avery and Gavin remained.

Cooper's adrenaline had drained away, leaving him happy but wilted. Clusters of helium-filled balloons still floated from colorful ribbons, and the smell of grilled burgers hung in the air.

Loosening his tie Cooper strolled over to the buffet where a dozen burgers still sat in a foil pan over a flame.

Cooper poked at a burger. "You think these are still good?"

"I was just getting ready to pitch them," Avery said.

"Well, I'm starving," Gavin said. "And I'm out of groceries at home, so . . ."

"I was too nervous to eat, but I'm ravenous now."

"Well, you two help yourselves. I need to get some beauty sleep." She addressed Cooper. "Meet you here at six thirty?"

"I'll be here." He gave Avery another hug. "Thanks again, Sis. You're the best—I don't care what everyone else says."

After she left he and Gavin filled their plates with food and sat at one of the circular tables, now devoid of tablecloths and centerpieces.

"Glad to have all of that over?" Gavin asked a while later when he came up for air.

"Definitely. But the real work is still ahead. I'm eager to dive in to my new position." His predecessor had done a bang-up job for twelve years, and many before him had worked hard to build a solid department. But Cooper had a few things he wanted to do differently—all in good time.

"You'll make a good sheriff," Gavin grated out.

Cooper took in the compliment that had probably not been easy to say, everything considered. "I really appreciate you being here for me this week. I haven't been much of a brother lately and still, when it counted, you showed up. So thanks."

Gavin chewed his last bite of burger, then gave Cooper a long look. "You've been a better brother than I've given you credit for."

Cooper's gaze fell to his plate. He didn't see himself winning a best-brother award anytime soon.

"I can tell you love her."

Cooper's stomach gave a hard twist, his appetite suddenly gone. He set down the remainder of his burger. "You don't have anything to worry about. According to Mom, Kate's leaving tomorrow. And even if she wasn't, I wouldn't make the same the mistake twice—I give you my word."

"You didn't deny it."

Cooper opened his mouth to reply.

"And don't try and make it sound like she's just another one of your fans. We both know better. The way you rallied our family so she wouldn't leave? So she wouldn't feel rejected?"

Cooper swallowed hard and gave a slow nod. "All right. I'm not going to lie. I care about her. But you're my brother."

"You love her."

Gavin just wouldn't let this go. He clenched his jaw. "Fine, I love her. But my promise still stands. You're my *brother*."

"And what kind of brother would *I* be if I let you give up the only woman you've ever loved for me?"

Cooper had no words. He stared at Gavin, speechless.

"Katie's an incredible woman, I'll give you that. She's strong and resilient, and she dragged me out of a funk I'd been in for a long time. We had fun together. She made me laugh. And it felt great to feel good again. For a few months there I thought I might be falling in love with her. But now . . . I don't know. I think maybe I was just in love with the idea of feeling like myself again. Feeling something other than grief and guilt."

"You deserve to be happy, Brother."

Gavin gave him a pointed look. "And so do you."

Cooper couldn't believe what he was hearing. Why was Gavin telling him all this? "What are you trying to say?"

Gavin rolled his eyes. "You're an idiot. Katie wasn't the one for me. That's what I'm trying to say. And it's become pretty clear she's your . . . soul mate or whatever. I'm not going to stand in your way, doofus. Now stop making me say things that make me sound like a girl."

Cooper huffed a soft laugh, his thoughts spinning. "Are you sure, man?"

"Keep it up and I'll take it all back."

A light feeling bubbled up inside Cooper, like he was filled with helium. "You're a good brother—better than I deserve."

He embraced Gavin, his throat aching with emotion. Despite the way Cooper had hurt him, Gavin still wanted what was best for him. If that wasn't what family was all about, he didn't know what was.

46

The sitting sheriff was a class act. Cooper shook Roy Gilmore's beefy hand. "Thanks for coming, Roy. I appreciate your support."

The man's bushy gray mustache lifted with his smile. "My pleasure. Let me know if I can help in any way."

"Will do." Cooper turned to find another reporter waiting and tried to patiently answer the woman's questions. He'd been hanging around campaign headquarters long after his acceptance speech. It seemed the rumors—and the article that had outed Sean's father—made Cooper's election big news.

Sean never had called him or publicly conceded—but early this morning he had resigned from the Madison County Sheriff's Office. That would save Cooper the trouble of firing him.

He answered a question about the county jail, then checked his watch. He wasn't sure what time Kate was leaving town today, and he needed to talk to her before she left. His conversation with Gavin last night had changed everything. He'd wanted nothing more than to show up on her doorstep and declare his love, beg her to stay. But it had been almost one o'clock in the morning.

The headquarters' door opened, and Gavin whooshed in, along with a gust of wind and a few dried leaves. His gaze sharpened on Cooper's face.

Cooper gave the reporter a parting smile. "Sorry to cut this short, Miss Beaman, but there's someone else I need to speak with. Thank you for stopping by."

He met Gavin in the middle of the room. "What's wrong?"

"Have you seen Katie yet? I mean, I assume you want to talk to her."

"Of course I want to talk to her, but I've been tied up here since six thirty." He checked his watch again. Eight fifteen.

"Are you trying to blow this? I just passed her on my way here—she was headed out of town."

"What? How long ago?"

"Ten minutes."

Cooper pulled out his phone and called her. He frowned when it went straight to voice mail. "She's not answering."

"You'd better go." Gavin gave him a little shove. "Hurry. I'll wrap things up here."

"Thanks," Cooper called over his shoulder. She was ten minutes ahead of him, and he'd have to do some serious driving to catch up with her.

Katie's heart actually clenched as she left Riverbend proper. For a while the place had truly felt like home. She prayed she'd find that feeling elsewhere someday.

After the bittersweet reunion with her mother last night, she really hated to leave. They'd talked long into the night, and Beth had answered all her questions. When Katie had been young, the drug addiction had a terrible hold on her mother. It blinded her to her obligation and love for her children.

It was a story repeated too many times, in too many families. Katie hoped this one at least would have a happy ending. Beth asked her to reconsider leaving. But if her mother was serious about their relationship, a forty-five-minute drive wouldn't stand in her way.

As Katie drove through the county, she passed sign after sign bearing Cooper's name. She smiled as she thought back to the moment late last night when the final election results had come in. All evening Beth kept the news muted in the background, and when Cooper officially won, they toasted him with their water bottles.

Katie was so happy for him. Knowing he was here, living his best life, would go a long way toward soothing the ache of separation.

As she passed each campaign sign along US-70, she wondered if it would be the last one she'd see. Eventually she'd exit Madison County altogether and leave Cooper and his family behind. She'd done what she could to cut the ties that bound them. She'd even gone as far as to block Cooper's number—not that she expected him to call. But at least now she wouldn't be hoping for it. She had, however, rescued one photo of him from her deleted file. It was all she had left of him.

She glanced at her speedometer. She was actually going under the speed limit. It revealed her reluctance to leave, she supposed. But the sooner she got on with her life, the better. Resolved, she pressed the accelerator harder.

It would be good to see Jill and James again, as well as her host of foster siblings. Thanksgiving was coming up. That was always fun, if totally chaotic, at the Clemson household. And soon after that, Christmas. There was a lot to look forward to.

But she thought of the Robinsons. What did the holidays look like at their house? What kinds of traditions did they keep? Would the mood be quiet and reverent or loud and fun? Did they open gifts one at a time or in a flurry of papers and ribbons?

Stop it, Katie. You have to move on.

Something blue and flashing caught her attention in the rearview mirror. She frowned at the black cruiser, lights strobing and siren wailing as it closed the distance between them. She glanced at her speedometer again. She was only going five over. Must be on his way to an emergency.

She slowed her vehicle, steering onto the shoulder to allow the cruiser to pass. The boxes in the back jostled and rattled as she ran over the rumble strip.

But the cruiser didn't pass; it slowed down.

He was coming after *her?* For going a measly five miles over? Just her luck. Not only was she having to leave her job and home, but they were giving her a parting gift on her way out of town.

Sorry, you lost. Thanks for playing though.

She pulled well off the road, coming to a full stop, and lowered her window. Then she leaned over and began rooting through her messy glove compartment. Where was that registration? She knew she'd put it in here. Why had she kept all these receipts? Could she get a ticket for not having her registration?

Outside her window, feet shuffled to a stop in the gravel.

"Just a minute, Officer." Her eyes homed in on the white registration, covered by several packets of ketchup and a napkin. She snatched the paper. "I know I was going five over but—"

Her tongue froze in her mouth. Her thoughts turned to slush. The sight of him in uniform had always taken her breath away. But just now he looked especially handsome—mostly because she'd never thought to see him again.

"Cooper." His name whooshed out on a breath.

Expression enigmatic, he handed her a slip of paper.

"What—what's this?"

"A warning for having a headlight out."

"But . . . I didn't even have my lights on."

"Have you replaced it?"

She was so confused. "Um, no, but—"

Before she could complete the sentence, he ripped off another slip of paper and handed it to her. "Also, you should slow down. The deer like to jump out around here."

"You don't say." She narrowed her eyes at him. "Was this the only reason you pulled me over?"

He slowly lowered the pad. His shoulders fell as if weighted by gravity, and his features softened.

As their gazes locked, awareness crackled between them. She searched his eyes and was mesmerized by everything she saw there. All the feelings she had for him were reflected back to her. Was it possible he cared as deeply as she did?

"Katelyn . . . Don't you know?" He regarded her with a helpless expression, the corner of his lip finally turning up. "You stole my heart."

Oh. She pressed her palm to her heart. His words were a balm to her soul.

"You had me from the moment we met. You had me in a way no one else has, before or since. You get me. You see me for who I am—the real me. And I see you too. I see the warm, loving woman you are, and I can't imagine not having you in my life—I don't want to. I love you, Kate."

Her breath hitched. Her heart grew two sizes. It was everything she'd wanted to hear him say, and she couldn't resist the urge to respond in kind. The words bubbled out. "Oh, Cooper. I love you too."

His features eased into a smile, and the look in his eyes held her captive.

"But . . . what about Gavin? I couldn't come between the two of you again. I won't."

"Gavin knows how I feel about you—I was helpless to hide it. He's the one who sent me after you."

Hope bucked in her chest. "He—he's okay with this? With us being together?"

"Turns out you're not the love of his life after all." His gaze drifted over her face like the softest whisper. "Man must be stark raving mad."

He planted his hands on her door and leaned down. "We've been fighting this long enough, don't you think? I'm done fighting. Please don't leave. I want you to stay—my whole family wants you to stay. You belong in Riverbend. You belong with me."

Katie blinked back tears. Oh, those words. "I don't want to leave."

"Then don't."

This was crazy. Joy welled up in her. "But I just put my house on the market."

"Take it down."

"I don't even have a job."

"Avery will hire you back."

"My car is packed down with all my belongings . . ."

"I'll help you unload."

She laughed. "Do you have an answer for everything?"

"Yes, I do." He leaned in closer and did the one thing she could never refuse. He settled his lips on hers.

Oh.

The man could kiss. Could make her forget everything else. She yielded to his soft exploration—what else could she do? She drew in a whiff of his familiar scent, savoring it, and lost herself in the kiss. Her whole world closed down to just the two of them. She flushed with heat from the fire he kindled inside her. She could get used to this.

He opened the car door, parting only long enough to draw her out. Then he was kissing her again. She leaned back against the car, savoring the taste of him. She couldn't believe he was here in her arms. That he loved her. That he wanted her to stay.

A car passed in a rush of wind, and the driver tooted his horn in approval.

Cooper drew away, his hungry eyes settled on hers. He cupped her cheek. "Come home with me, Kate," he said on a soft breath.

Those words might've been her favorite of all. Her lips lifted of their own volition. "Lead the way."

He smiled broadly and leaned in, pressing a kiss to her forehead. "I'll see you at home, honey." He headed back for his cruiser.

Katie glanced down at the scraps of paper in her hand. She gave her head a shake. What had just happened? "Hey, Sheriff Robinson!" she called, amusement lacing her voice. "What am I supposed to do with these warnings?"

"Save them." He turned, walking backward, and flashed a smile. "Someday we'll show them to our children."

EPILOGUE

It turned out Katie had been right—and wrong—about Christmas with the Robinsons. Their annual traditions began on December twenty-fourth when the Robinson family met at the church to box up food for those in need. At least fifty townspeople pitched in, forming a massive assembly line in the fellowship hall.

Once the boxes were full, the drivers, including Katie and Cooper, delivered the food to neighbors in need. It was Katie's first time meeting most of the families, many of whom lived out in the hills, away from the valley. It did her heart good to know that those families would have what they needed for a nice Christmas supper.

It was dark by the time she and Cooper had unloaded the last box from the bed of his truck. They had just enough time to shower and change before the Christmas Eve candlelight service. At the church Katie took her candle and filed into the packed pew with the Robinson family.

A string quartet played Christmas music, and children dressed as shepherds and angels acted out the Christmas story in a way that was both adorable and reverent. In the manger lay an infant, a symbol of the Christ child who would later make the ultimate sacrifice for all humankind.

As the story unfolded before her, she reflected on this, the greatest Gift of Christmas, and whispered a prayer of gratitude. Because of that miraculous gift, she'd one day see her brother again.

Last Christmas Spencer had just passed away. Grief swallowed her whole, and she only wanted to survive the holidays. Her life had changed so much in a year. Her brother was gone, but she'd been reunited with her mother. She'd found a place to call home, and she'd found true love.

In the quiet glow of the sanctuary, peace settled over her soul. She reached over and took Cooper's hand in hers. She loved the rugged feel of his hands, so big and warm around hers.

His gaze connected with hers, growing more intense as the moment drew out.

The past seven weeks with him had been wonderful. They hiked and talked and got to know each other better. On mild days they went on long motorcycle rides in the mountains. When they'd passed the spot where her car hung on the edge of the cliff, he pulled over and gave her a memorable kiss. Then he whispered, "I knew that day you were the one for me."

A shiver passed over her as the music swelled, and love for him filled her to overflowing. All her life she'd been searching, and she'd finally found her home. As hard as she'd fought it, she'd also known from the very first meeting that Cooper was the one for her.

As if he could read her mind, his lips lifted at the corners. He squeezed her hand and she squeezed his right back.

After the service Cooper took her to his place to exchange gifts. A week after Thanksgiving she'd bought a small artificial Christmas tree for his apartment, and they'd decorated it together. The red and silver glass bulbs made for a somewhat generic-looking tree, but the colorful lights gave the room a beautiful glow.

They settled in front of the fireplace, and Cooper unwrapped his gift: a pair of work boots he'd been wanting. His hours as sheriff were long, and though he rarely complained, his feet sometimes ached at the end of the day.

"Kate . . ." He removed a boot from the box. "These are so expensive."

"You're worth every penny." She would empty her bank account to see his eyes light up like that.

His gaze practically caressed the weatherproof leather exterior, the dense rubber sole, the lace-up front and the side zipper that would get him out the door quickly in an emergency.

"I saw you eyeing them online."

"I decided they were too expensive."

"And I decided they weren't."

His hand glided over the leather, then he turned

and brushed her lips with his. "I love them. Thank you. My *feet* thank you."

After taking a few minutes to appreciate the boots' workmanship, he stood. "Your turn. You have to close your eyes."

"Okay . . ." She did as he asked and listened to his footsteps retreat. Sounds came from down the hall. She was so tempted to peek, but she kept her eyes closed. A moment later footsteps sounded again, growing nearer.

"Don't open them yet," he said from someplace close by. "I hope you like it."

"I'm sure I will. You have exquisite taste."

"I do, don't I? Okay, you can open your eyes."

Cooper stood in the middle of the living room. And standing right next to him was a bike. A mint-green bike with a white seat and a white basket.

Oh. It was just like the one she'd coveted as a child. Katie's breath caught and tears stung her eyes. She pressed a hand to her chest. "It even has a bell."

"Do you like it?"

She couldn't respond; there was a catch in her throat. A tear escaped and trickled down her cheek.

"Hey . . . It's not supposed to make you cry."

She jumped from the sofa and was in his arms in two seconds flat. "They're happy tears. It's so beautiful. I can't believe you did this. I can't believe you remembered."

He drew back, his gaze piercing hers. "I want to give you everything you've always wanted."

Her heart squeezed tight. "Oh, Cooper. You already have."

At ten o'clock on Christmas morning the Robinsons gathered in Lisa and Jeff's living room for a gift exchange. Delicious smells emanated from the kitchen, making Katie's stomach growl.

Christmas decorations littered the room: a Santa doorstop, a mantel garland, a nativity, three stuffed snowmen, and candles galore. The live Fraser fir stretched toward the ceiling, topped with a glowing angel. Its limbs were adorned with homemade ornaments, most of them made once upon a time by the Robinson children.

"Mom was supposed to pass our ornaments to us when we struck out on our own," Cooper explained as Katie perused the dozens of baubles. "But as you can see, mine are still hanging on her tree."

"So are mine," Avery said. "She can't bear to give them up."

"Oh, that's not true." Lisa smacked Avery's shoulder. "I'm waiting for you to get married is all."

"Really?" Gavin said. "Because I got married and you never gave me mine."

"Oh, hush, you guys."

Jeff wrapped his arms around his wife. "It's

Christmas. She's allowed to be sentimental."

Coming around the family—around Gavin—had been a little awkward at first. But Katie and Gavin soon settled into a comfortable friendship. When they had nice weather they sometimes teamed up to beat Avery and Cooper at cornhole.

He'd also begun dating again, though there was no one serious yet.

As the family exchanged gifts, laughter and inside jokes abounded, all of which Cooper patiently explained. By the time the wrapping paper lay in shreds on the floor, Katie was richer by one sweater, a pair of leather gloves, cordless earbuds, and a gift certificate to a spa in Asheville.

Over the past couple months, things had gotten back to normal between she and Avery. Avery had been thrilled to take Katie back at the clinic. And so far, even with the bridge out, business was enough—just barely—to keep them all employed.

The other businesses, including Jeff's store, were surviving too. Even better, Trail Days had been such a boon for the town that the council had agreed to make it an annual event.

The doorbell rang and Katie's mother arrived, bearing two freshly baked pies, just in time to join the Robinsons for Christmas dinner. Her relationship with her mom had found solid footing in the past weeks. They met for coffee nearly every Saturday morning, and the more Katie learned about Beth, the more she respected all the woman had overcome.

In late November she and Beth had driven up to Max Patch, where Katie had spread Spencer's ashes. There, Katie had borne witness to the remorse of a woman who'd been too late. It broke Katie's heart. But the time on the mountain had been healing for Beth. Sadly, some regrets could never be fixed. They just had to be endured.

After clearing the living room the family gathered around the table, ready to dig into the feast spread before them: baked ham, mashed potatoes and gravy, green beans, sweet potato casserole, and yeast rolls. As good as the food smelled and would no doubt taste, the people surrounding Katie outshone it by a thousand kilowatts.

Katie's gaze drifted around the table at the people who'd become her family, and Cooper's words from Trail Days played back in her mind. *"Sometimes family isn't the situation you're born into but the people who've chosen to love you along the way."* The truth of those words settled over her like a warm blanket. And when they bowed their heads to say grace, Katie said an extra prayer of thanks for the unexpected blessing of family.

ACKNOWLEDGMENTS

Bringing a book to market takes a lot of effort from many different people. I'm so incredibly blessed to partner with the fabulous team at HarperCollins Christian Fiction, led by publisher Amanda Bostic: Kimberly Carlton, Jodi Hughes, Margaret Kercher, Becky Monds, Kerri Potts, Savannah Summers, Laura Wheeler, Nekasha Pratt, and LaChelle Washington.

Not to mention all the wonderful sales reps and amazing people in the rights department—special shout-out to Robert Downs!

Thanks especially to my editor Kimberly Carlton. Your incredible insight and inspiration help me take the story deeper, and for that I am so grateful! Thanks also to my line editor, Julee Schwarzburg, whose attention to detail makes me look like a better writer than I really am.

Author Colleen Coble is my first reader and sister of my heart. Thank you, friend! This writing journey has been ever so much more fun because of you.

I'm grateful to my agent, Karen Solem, who's able to somehow make sense of the legal garble of contracts and, even more amazing, help me understand it.

To my husband, Kevin, who has supported my

dreams in every way possible—I'm so grateful! To all our kiddos: Chad, Trevor and Babette, and Justin and Hannah, who have favored us with two beautiful granddaughters. Every stage of parenthood has been a grand adventure, and I look forward to all the wonderful memories we have yet to make!

A hearty thank you to all the booksellers who make room on their shelves for my books—I'm deeply indebted! And to all the book bloggers and reviewers, whose passion for fiction is contagious—thank you!

Lastly, thank you, friends, for letting me share this story with you! I wouldn't be doing this without you. Your notes, posts, and reviews keep me going on the days when writing doesn't flow so easily. I appreciate your support more than you know.

I enjoy connecting with friends on my Facebook page, www.facebook.com/authordenisehunter. Please pop over and say hello. Visit my website at www.DeniseHunterBooks.com, or just drop me a note at Deniseahunter@comcast.net. I'd love to hear from you!

DISCUSSION QUESTIONS

1. Who was your favorite character in *Riverbend Gap*? Why?
2. What was your favorite scene, and why did it speak to you?
3. Come up with a trail name for yourself and explain why you chose it.
4. Katie was taken from her home as a child, losing all sense of stability and belonging. How did her need for a place to belong cause her to make poor decisions?
5. Through shared crises, Katie and Cooper bonded quickly, despite their wishes not to hurt Gavin. How did this make you feel? Were you rooting for them, or did you feel more for Gavin, who'd already lost so much?
6. Because of her childhood Katie's worst fear was rejection. Describe how the events following her kiss with Cooper triggered that fear.
7. Discuss how Cooper's alcoholic father might have played a part in his decision to become a deputy and then a sheriff.
8. As Jeff pointed out in the story, Cooper avoided relationships because he was afraid of acting like his father. Have you ever

avoided something out of fear of becoming like a parent?

9. When the rumors about Katie swirled through town, she was afraid her mother had rejected her again. Has deep-rooted insecurity ever dredged up fear in you? How did you handle it?

10. Avery revealed a significant secret to Katie regarding her health. What do you think might be in store for Avery?

ABOUT THE AUTHOR

Denise Hunter is the internationally published bestselling author of more than thirty books, three of which have been adapted into original Hallmark Channel movies. She has won the Holt Medallion Award, the Reader's Choice Award, the Carol Award, and the Foreword Book of the Year Award and is a RITA finalist. When Denise isn't orchestrating love lives on the written page, she enjoys traveling with her family, drinking good coffee, and playing drums. Denise makes her home in Indiana, where she and her husband are currently enjoying an empty nest.

DeniseHunterBooks.com
Instagram: @deniseahunter
Facebook: @authordenisehunter
Twitter: @DeniseAHunter

Books are
produced in the
United States
using U.S.-based
materials

Books are printed
using a revolutionary
new process called
THINKtech™ that
lowers energy usage
by 70% and increases
overall quality

Books are
durable and
flexible
because of
Smyth-sewing

Paper is
sourced using
environmentally
responsible
foresting methods
and the
paper is acid-free

Center Point Large Print
600 Brooks Road / PO Box 1
Thorndike, ME 04986-0001 USA

(207) 568-3717

US & Canada:
1 800 929-9108
www.centerpointlargeprint.com